ID0984226

"'Anne-Droid of Green Gables' just blew me away. 'Benchwarmer' and 'Soulmates' were also particularly good. I also enjoyed both 'The Close Shave' and 'Making the Cut,' especially the joint setting of these two stories in a paranormal barbershop. Not surprisingly, the rest of the stories in *Soulmates* were up to snuff, too (nary a bad story in the bunch)."

—*Goodreads Reviewer*

"The themes that pervade the story carry weight. It's not just loneliness, but also a feeling of being loved and being needed. It helps that the story's straightforward prose whisks the story along. All of this conspires to give 'Benchwarmer' an emotional strength that, while reminiscent of the *Toy Story* films, stands quite well on its own merits."

—*SFSignal*

"'The Close Shave' and 'Making the Cut,' both set at a barbershop that specializes in after-hours service to the supernatural crowd, aim for a light, harmless sort of humor and feature a henpecked vampire, a pacifist medusa with bad-tempered snakes for hair, and a world-weary Wandering Jew, among others. 'Shame' and 'Soulmates' are much more thought-provoking, philosophical works, exploring free will, friendship, euthanasia, and taking responsibility for one's mistakes.... This is a satisfying sampler of solid stories from a team that rarely disappoints."

—*Publishers Weekly*

"A collection of short stories, one by each of the authors and seven collaborations, two of which gained awards. The standard is high— and while the two winners deserve their award, there is not a duff story in there. The two solo efforts are, oddly, both based on classic works—'Anne-Droid of Green Gables' on the LM Montgomery book which I have recently read, luckily, so I was well able to gauge how cleverly the 'junior' author had used that original; 'Hunting the Snark' on the Lewis Carroll poem and there are many references to it, including most of the characters as well as the name of the alien planet: several stanzas are quoted in full at appropriate times in the narrative."

—Amazon Reviewer

"'Benchwarmer' by Mike Resnick & Lezli Robyn: There's no TZ twist here, but a touching story about where imaginary friends go after we've left them behind. Along the lines of the famous 'Kick the Can' episode of TZ, 'Benchwarmer' is more about whimsy than terror."

—SfRevu

"Other standouts include...Mike Resnick and Lezli Robyn's beautifully sad 'Benchwarmer,' which takes us into the world of imaginary friends, and introduces us to one friend who simply can't let go of the boy who created him."

—io9

"The tough topic of euthanasia is explored in 'Soulmates' by Mike Resnick and Lezli Robyn. A night watchman named Gary has trouble living with the guilt of pulling the plug on his wife Kathy, left brain dead after an auto accident. He's on the verge of losing his job due to heavy drinking when he becomes acquainted with a troubleshooting robot he dubs Mose. This tale centers on those two characters' conversations concerning Gary's decision and Mose's job of repairing or terminating broken robots. Resnick and Robyn utilize these discussions for both character development and plot advancement for maximum effect. The man's raw emotions contrasting with the robot's logic add poignancy and credibility to the novelette."

—Tangent

"Mike Resnick has—according to the story's introduction—won more awards than any other writer of short fiction. In 'Soulmates,' written in collaboration with Lezli Robyn, an alcoholic widower close to losing his job as a night watchman encounters a troubleshooting robot. Resnick and his collaborator provide an unfussy, deceptively simple story that provokes thought with almost every question the robot asks. It will probably feature on the 2010 *Hugo* ballot, and that wouldn't be an injustice. Highly Recommended."

—*Suite 101*

"Mike Resnick is the all-time short fiction award winner and here he is paired with newcomer, Lezli Robyn, for the novelette 'Soulmates'. One thing I always find in Resnick's stories is Heart and this one has plenty of it. Gary is a man racked with guilt. His wife, Kathy, had been badly injured in a car accident and was brain-dead. On the advice of doctors, he had turned off the machines keeping her breathing. He feels that he killed her. He has begun to drink, heavily, and is in danger of losing his job as a night watchman where he keeps an eye on sixty pre-programmed robots. He starts drinking early in his shift one night and falls down. He is helped by a robot called MOZ-512 and leans on it to complete his shift. He starts talking to the robot and calls him Moze. They have an effect on each other and therein lies a wonderful tale. That's the second story that will be considered by me for next year's *Hugos*; this one in the Novelette category."

—*SFRevu*

"The authors weave themes of loss and friendship together well in this poignant tale ['Soulmates'] about a man who has lost his wife and finds himself spending time discussing serious issues with a maintenance robot. The story uses dialogue very effectively to advance both plot and characterisation."

—*Aurealis Award 2009 Judges*

"'Report from the Field' by Mike Resnick & Lezli Robyn. This is a very funny story. If you have ever wondered what our society looks like from an objective third party, this is your answer. Maybe this is why no one visits? Seeing our sports, entertainment, figures we admire (twiggy-like models), sexual habits, and integrating our movies figures as cultural icons; you can see by the end of the story why anyone might be a little hesitant to come by and say hello!"

—*Scifi Geeks*

"'Report from the Field' by Mike Resnick & Lezli Robyn is a series of observations made by aliens who are contemplating asking mankind to join the galactic civilized races. In a classic example of cognitive estrangement, we learn the absurdity of our own cultural norms as seen by those on the outside…effectively played to humorous effect."

—*SFSignal*

"Mike Resnick & Lezli Robyn's 'Report from the Field' is a very quirky tale done in field report style from an alien determining if Earth is ready for inclusion in [the] Galactic Community. This story had me chortling left and right like few other writers can do and the only funny story in the bunch. In many ways humor is more difficult to relay in written form than something dramatic or action oriented. Resnick and Robyn excel at the funny asides as well as the satirical while this particular alien sees us at a skewed angle from viewing our television, movies, and documentaries, trying to make sense of what they selected. These are perfect examples of humanity's absurd and violent side, which make me question our place in the cosmos and the fact that if there is life out there we'd probably just screw up first contact."

—*Booktionary*

SOULMATES

SOULMATES

by

MIKE RESNICK
&
LEZLI ROBYN

CAEZIK
SF & FANTASY
ARC MANOR
ROCKVILLE, MARYLAND

❋

SHAHID MAHMUD
PUBLISHER

www.CaezikSF.com

Entire contents copyright © 2016 by Mike Resnick and Lezli Robyn

"Hunting the Snark," copyright © 1999 by Mike Resnick, originally appeared in the December 1999, *Asimov's*

"Idle Roomer," copyright © 2008 by Mike Resnick and Lezli Robyn, originally appeared in the November 2008, *Clarkesworld*

"Soulmates," copyright © 2009 by Mike Resnick and Lezli Robyn, originally appeared in the September 2009, *Asimov's*

"Benchwarmer," copyright © 2009 by Mike Resnick and Lezli Robyn, originally appeared in *Twilight Zone: 19 Original stories on the 50th Anniversary*, Tor

"Shame," copyright © 2010 by Mike Resnick and Lezli Robyn, originally appeared in the January-February 2010, *Analog*

"Report from the Field," copyright © 2010 by Mike Resnick and Lezli Robyn, originally appeared in *Is Anybody Out There?*, DAW Books

"Anne-droid of Green Gables," copyright © 2010 by Lezli Robyn, originally appeared in *Classics Mutilated*, IDW Publishing

"The Close Shave," copyright © 2010 by Mike Resnick and Lezli Robyn, originally appeared in *Blood Lite II: Overbite*, Simon & Schuster

"Making the Cut," copyright © 2011 by Mike Resnick and Lezli Robyn, originally appeared in *Blood Lite III: Aftertaste*, Simon & Schuster

Cover art copyright © by Juanmi Aguilera

ISBN: 978-1-64710-010-0

First CAEZIK Edition. 1st Printing. October 2021.
1 2 3 4 5 6 7 8 9 10

An imprint of Arc Manor LLC

www.CaezikSF.com

To Shahid Mahmud, of course
—Mike & Lezli

··◆··

To Carol, as always
—Mike

To Robert and Sylvia Glover,
for being amazing parents, friends,
and—above all—Soulmates
—Lezli

Contents

Introduction

It began, curiously enough, not at a convention, but rather on eBay. I live in Cincinnati, and I put an autographed, limited-edition novella by Anne McCaffrey up for sale, and Lezli, who at the time was living in Australia, bought it.

We got to corresponding, and Lezli remarked that my books were difficult to find in her neck of the woods, so I sent her a few. We corresponded further, and finally I suggested that she pushed nouns up against verbs with enough grace that she should consider doing a little writing.

She replied that she had always wanted to write science fiction, had even written McCaffrey as a teen asking how to go about it. I suggested that we collaborate on a story, Lezli replied that she was very interested but didn't want to commit until after she met me, just in case I was science fiction's version of a fire-breathing monster...so in the summer of 2008 Lezli flew nine thousand miles from Australia to Denver to attend the Worldcon, her very first convention.

We hit it off, and we wrote and sold our first collaboration within a month. And I, after more than fifty collaborators on short stories, found that I enjoyed it so much that I invited her to write six more pieces in the next year and a half, with two of them winning awards.

When the dust had cleared we'd sold all seven stories that we had written together, Lezli took some time to move to the United States, and a few years after that is now solidly entrenched in the science fiction scene after being hired as Editor and Assistant Publisher for Arc

Manor, the company that publishes—among other things—*Galaxy's Edge* magazine and the Stellar Guild line of books, both of which I edit.

And while we haven't collaborated on another story, we remain good friends, and as these words are being written we are also collaborating on a new book for Stellar Guild.

—MIKE

And I'm still loving every minute of it.

—LEZLI

We were invited to contribute to the Tor 50th Anniversary Twilight Zone anthology that was being edited by Carol Serling, Rod's widow, and we came up with what we both feel is our strongest story, "Benchwarmer." It also sold to Spain and Italy, and won us our second Ictineu Award for Best Story Translated into Catalan.

—MIKE

Benchwarmer

BY MIKE RESNICK & LEZLI ROBYN

H e'd been sitting on the sidelines, warming the bench, waiting, for almost seventy years. The winds of Time chilled him to the bone, and all he had to keep him warm were his memories, which got a little older and a little colder each day.

He wasn't an imposing figure. There were days he looked like Humpty Dumpty before the fall, and days he looked more like a teddy bear. It didn't make any difference to him. He had never seen a mirror, nor did he care to.

He could have chosen any name he wanted, but he stuck with Mr. Paloobi, for reasons only one other person would understand. It didn't have much dignity to it, but then, dignity was not his stock in trade.

He envied his companions. Not their grace, their easy athletic ability, or their infectious laughter, because those traits were unimportant to him. No, what he envied was the fact that sooner or later they were all called back into action, they all returned to what he thought of as The Game. He wanted desperately to leave the bench, but he didn't know the ground rules. He couldn't even discern that there were any.

He'd been given two brief chances, but he didn't last any longer than a sore-armed pitcher on the mound, a lame thoroughbred in the Derby, or a tennis player with no racket. He had tried his best, had given it his all, but he hadn't been up to the job, and indeed had to face that fact that there was only one job that he was truly suited for—and that job had ended sixty-eight years, four months, and seventeen days ago.

It happened on the last day that he was called forth from the limbo where he was born, where he existed now until he was needed again. It was a day filled with the same promise as the day before, the same exciting horizon to be approached, the same challenges, and the same goals. But there was one thing that was not the same.

On that day the Boy outgrew him, and nothing was ever the same again.

Even after all of those years, he was still unable to remember that day without feeling a keen sense of loss, and the thought that he'd never be complete again. Day after day, year after year, he sat on the sidelines and watched as his companions came and went. And while he kept the bench warm for the others, he waited for his chance to do what he was born to do.

All he wanted was to be needed again.

Mr. Paloobi could hear the contented rumble of Lionel's purr long before he ambled out of the mist and made his way to the bench.

Looking more like a four-hundred-pound tabby cat than a true lion, Lionel nevertheless appeared quite impressive as he bounded onto the bench, the seat automatically changing shape to accommodate the gentle beast that now lay curled up on its surface.

Mr. Paloobi turned to look at him expectantly as the big cat nestled his head in amongst his forepaws and curled his tail around his body, softly purring a lullaby to himself.

Sensing his gaze, Lionel opened one lazy eye. "My boy is sleeping after our safari in Darkest Africa."

"Africa?" said Mr. Paloobi. "I thought he lived just outside of Wichita."

"He does," confirmed Lionel. "But his imagination doesn't. We tracked zebras down Maple Street, made a kill at the corner of 3rd and Main, and barely avoided a stampede of mad elephants on wheels over on Elm Street. There were spear-carrying natives, whose witch doctors had made their spears appear like briefcases (though we knew better), and as we passed a brick hut with a huge screen we saw hundreds of disguised hyenas laughing as they came out. Oh, yes, it was quite a safari. You have no idea how many scrapes we got into, how many hairsbreadth escapes."

"And you enjoyed every minute of it."

Lionel's eyes softened perceptively, glowing amber. "And I enjoyed every minute of our time together. I'll miss him—until my next charge comes along." He sighed contentedly, settling his head back down onto his forepaws again. "I could sleep for a couple of months. That boy wore me out!"

"Try sitting on the same hardwood bench for decades and then complain to me," replied Mr. Paloobi bitterly.

"Try wearing this goddamned costume day in and day out," retorted a fairy princess who suddenly appeared before them in a burst of pink glitter. "Then you'd have something to really complain about. This corset is *killing* me." Her golden curls bounced, as if to emphasize her point. "A pox on the girl who designed me! Who in their right mind decides that princesses should wear such constrictive dresses?"

"So take it off, Sugarblossom," said Mr. Paloobi.

"It doesn't *come* off," said Sugarblossom. "You know that. And the worst part is the smell."

"The smell?"

"She heard they used whalebone stays, so it smells exactly like a dead fish."

Mr. Paloobi chuckled. "I'm sorry. But welcome back anyway. You were with your current charge longer than usual."

"Oh, yes, I was! And what a charming young lady she'll grow up to be," she said proudly, beaming at him, her smile more brilliant than the sequined dress, crystal tiara, and glitter-covered shoes combined. "It turned out my girl needed a substitute mother even more than she needed someone to play make-believe with." Her smile became wistful, her eyes getting a faraway look to them as she continued. "She lost her mother recently, and she was grieving. Her mother always used to let her dress up in her old fancy clothes, and so did I. I also took over the role as her confidant until she could adjust to the changes in her life." She, paused, twirling her skirt around softly, absentmindedly, with her hands. "Every child is a wonder, but this one was something special. She won't remember me when she's older, of course, but I truly believe I was able to help her."

"I don't help 'em," said Lionel. "I just play with 'em." He opened his mouth to roar; it came out as a squeak.

The bench adjusted to accommodate Sugarblossom as she sat down.

"Why does it supply *you* with pillows?" Mr. Paloobi asked, trying unsuccessfully to hide his exasperation.

"Because a princess needs her comfort," she replied with a smile. "Besides, *this* princess needs her rest. There is always a little girl somewhere in the world, with a teacup set or a fairy costume, that wants to play make-believe." She smoothed out the sumptuous velvet pillows with delicate little hands. "I think I deserve a little luxury in my down time."

He didn't reply. Only the soft rumble of the slumbering cat broke the silence.

After awhile Sugarblossom looked at him, the sparkles in her eyes softening. "I'm sorry. That was inconsiderate of me. How can I complain, when…?" She let the words hang in the air.

"There's nothing to be sorry about," answered Mr. Paloobi. "If I'm to have my innings in the Game only once, at least I cherish every second I spent with the Boy who called me forth."

"But it was so long ago," she said sympathetically.

Mr. Paloobi's hand reached up to his shirt pocket and felt the little object it contained, and his mind raced back across the decades to the day he was born.

As the Boy painstakingly placed the pewter pieces on the ornate chessboard his father had bought back from his last trip abroad, he wished that *someone* would teach him how to play the game. But his parents always seemed to be absent, even when they were there, and it was obvious that he was going to have to teach himself—and he had no idea how to go about it. It wasn't chess itself that appealed to him anyway. The satisfying thing was to sit across the board from a parent, a sibling, a friend, even a stranger, and not feel so terribly, achingly *lonely*.

When he'd finally finished setting it up on the rickety little card table he had dragged from the spare room, he placed a chair on either side of it and sat down.

And then it hit him: he had no idea if he'd put the pieces on the right squares, and he *still* had no one to play it with. He closed his eyes as tears of frustration began to form. *I'm a big boy now,* he told himself, as little balled-up hands angrily dashed across his eyes, scattering his tears. *Big boys aren't supposed to cry.*

But he couldn't help it. He just wished for someone, *anyone,* to acknowledge he was there.

"It's just a game," said a friendly voice. "It can't be *that* hard to play."

The Boy stopped crying, startled. He gingerly opened one eye, then both. He couldn't see anyone, blurry eyes or not. He sighed and closed them again.

"Surely if we put our heads together we can figure this thing out," the voice continued.

The Boy started again. This time the voice had sounded as if it came from the other side of the table. Someone else *was* in the room! He opened his eyes just in time to see a figure coalescing across the table from him.

It wasn't his father, he was certain of that, but he looked kind of tall and burly—just like his Dad. And yet, he had sounded so affectionate. *The man must look cuddly,* the Boy reasoned. He rubbed his eyes again to clear them, and sure enough, he was right: a nondescript, but definitely cuddly, teddy bear of a man sat across from him, a gentle smile on his face. He was dressed like Dad, but that was where the resemblance stopped. He had fuzzy ears, warm brown hair and even warmer eyes, the least threatening adult the Boy had ever seen.

Speechless, but remembering his manners, the Boy extended his tiny hand across the table, trustingly, to greet his new guest. A huge furry paw of a hand encompassed his before pulling back to pick up one of the chess pieces. The stranger studied it for a minute, clearly curious, then looked up at the Boy. "So, shall we learn how to play chess together?" he asked.

"But you're a grown-up," the Boy replied somewhat petulantly. "Grown-ups *know* how to play chess."

"Well, then, of course I do, too," replied the gentle giant. Without preamble, he started moving all the pieces into their proper positions on the board while the Boy watched him, marveling at how such a huge man found it possible to balance on such a small chair.

All of a sudden, the chair collapsed beneath the man, sending him sprawling. The Boy broke into a fit of giggles. When he finally got control of himself, he looked up, somewhat sheepishly, to see that the man was looking sheepish himself.

"Obviously the chair didn't like me," stated the man.

"Nope," the Boy agreed, and they shared a smile.

Suddenly the Boy's aunt walked in, carrying a tray laden with food and depositing it on the toy chest beside the table. "Your parents have gone out for dinner," she said. "I'll be in again at eight, to make sure that you've put yourself to bed." She walked toward the door, and then paused in the doorway, turning to glance quickly at the chess set, and then down at the Boy again. "There's an extra dessert on the tray," she added with what she thought was a kindly smile. Then she was gone.

The Boy immediately looked across to the table to see a bear of a man leaning over to look at the contents of the tray with evident curiosity.

"She didn't even say hello to you!" the Boy exclaimed, indignant.

The man shrugged unconcernedly. "What difference does it make? *You're* talking to me, and that's all that matters."

The Boy looked at him for a long time before responding. "Well, as long as you're my friend, I'll never ignore you," he said with conviction. "I know what it's like to be invisible to other people."

Again they shared an understanding smile, and feeling happier than he had in a long time, the Boy hopped off his chair and scooted across to the toy chest to see what extra sweet had been put on his tray. He uncovered the first plate to discover meatloaf and veggies. Screwing up his face in distaste at all the green confronting him, he uncovered the second plate to reveal chocolate pudding and a slice of hot apple pie.

He was about to dig in when a slight movement caught his eye. He looked over at his new friend, who was delicately sniffing the chocolate pudding with interest, and he realized that the gentle giant didn't have a meal of his own. The Boy was torn. He *wanted* to share his meal—he'd never had anyone he could share with before—but he was rarely given chocolate pudding as dessert, and it was his favorite.

And then it dawned on him. Bears, even ones that were half man, wouldn't like chocolate; they'd like sweet foods like honey—or apple pie. "If you are going to be my friend," he stated with youthful certainty, "then friends share *everything*—even meals." And he handed over the apple pie, feeling quite pleased with himself.

They ate in companionable silence for a few minutes as the Boy mulled over what they were going to do after dinner. He'd never had a friend before; he didn't know quite where to start.

"Do friends play chess together?" came the muffled question from across the table, as the bear-man attempted to talk and eat at the same time.

"Yes, they do. Friends play *lots* of games. And they share food— except for chocolate—and they tell magical stories to each other and pretend to be warriors." He used his knife to mimic a swordfight, fatally spearing the meatloaf. "They also talk about *everything*, and...." He paused, not knowing how to say it.

"And they are always there when you need them."

"*Yes!*" the Boy exclaimed. He understood!

The huge man smiled. "Well, now that that's settled, why don't we play a game of chess?"

"That sounds like a great idea, Mr...." The Boy halted, realizing he didn't know the man's name. He considered the man's bear-like features with interest. "You know, you're kind of roly-poly, and you kind of look like Winnie the Pooh..." his voice trailed off, and he bit his bottom lip in concentration. Suddenly he clapped his hands together enthusiastically. "I know! I'll call you Mr. Paloobi!"

Mr. Paloobi looked *chuffed*—there was no other word for it. His chest puffed out proudly as he repeated the name to himself, and then he beamed at the Boy. "Thank you," he replied. "I always *wanted* a name."

Mr. Paloobi was prodded back to the here and now—well, the here and *somewhere*—by a huge paw landing heavily on his arm. He turned his head to find himself looking directly into Lionel's eyes.

"I don't appreciate being awakened between safaris," the cat stated with a silky purr.

"Why tell *me*?"

"Your sighs are too loud."

"My sighs?"

"Like this," said Lionel, giving him an overblown demonstration. "It's been seventy years. Get over it."

Mr. Paloobi looked back down the timestream. "You don't get over something like that," he said wistfully.

He spent half an hour explaining the rudiments of chess to the Boy. But when the Boy started getting frustrated at being unable to remember all the different types of moves and suggested they give up, Mr. Paloobi changed his approach and performed a pantomime with the chess pieces instead.

As he moved the pieces across the board with gentle furry hands, Mr. Paloobi told a tale of twin sisters married to kings who were at war with each other. "Both queens, each in love with her husband, devise a plan to infiltrate the enemy castle in order to get close enough to kill the enemy king," he stated in a conspiratorial tone. "It is a journey fraught with danger for them both, but their identical appearance gives them great range of movement in the enemy camp." He demonstrated by moving a queen around in all directions on the board. "Along the way there are male pawns to fight," he continued, picking up one pawn and pouncing it diagonally across one square onto an enemy pawn, eliciting a giggle from the Boy when the defeated pawn went flying. "Female pawns also try to sneak across enemy lines and supplant them as queen." He made a show of another pawn creeping forward one square, all the while whistling innocently. "And even if the queen or her supporters get past the enemy watchtowers undetected," he continued, show-ing those pieces performing horizontal and vertical sweeps of the board, "what kingdom doesn't have a nosy clergyman or two trying to edge their way into the thick of things?" And he demonstrated by diagonally sliding a bishop into a position of power on the board.

Mr. Paloobi paused, making sure he still had the Boy's rapt atten-tion. "Now, even when the enemy draws closer, the king tries to stay one step ahead of them at all times. But he's so heavily protected that he can only move so far," he continued, a furry hand demonstrating that a king could only move one square in any direction at any time. "If all his defenses fail, he has to rely on his knights and their valiant steeds to protect him, for they are well versed in tactics." He picked up a knight, making him prance one square over and then gallop two more in another direction, until he was in a better position to protect the king. "But will the queen get to the king before he flees to safety—or will she die in the attempt?"

The Boy waited for an answer, and when none was forthcoming he lifted his eyes from the chess board for the first time since the story started. "Don't stop now," he pleaded. "How does the story end?"

Mr. Paloobi grinned at him. "Well, to find out, you're going to have to play the game, aren't you?"

"Bright kid," said Lionel.

"A special kid," agreed the October Hare. He'd been christened the March Hare by his creator, but since he couldn't hold the calendar back, he had become the April Hare and then the May Hare, and now, in his eighth month of existence, he was the October Hare.

"Welcome back," said Sugarblossom.

"Thank you," said the October Hare. "But I can't stay long." He glanced at his wrist. "I'm late."

"You don't even have a watch," said Lionel in bored tones.

"It doesn't matter," said the October Hare. "I'm always late. It's part of my nature." He made as much of a face as a white rabbit *can* make. "One of the things I'm always late for is dinner, and it's always gone. I wish my little girl read something, anything, besides *Alice in Wonderland* when she created me." He turned to Mr. Paloobi. "I wish, oh, I don't know, that she played chess like yours did."

"He was more than a chess player," replied Mr. Paloobi. "He had the most inquisitive mind. He was reading when he was three, you know. I remember once when he was five, he had just seen a Sherlock Holmes movie on television, one of the old ones with Basil Rathbone, and I mentioned that according to Watson, Sherlock Holmes had neither any knowledge of nor interest in the Copernican system. Just that, nothing more. But within three days, this five-year-old boy had read the complete works of Copernicus!" A smile of pride crossed his face. "*My* Boy did that!"

"Good thing it was Sherlock Holmes," said Lionel sardonically. "If you'd quoted Johnny Unitas or Joe DiMaggio, he'd probably be the only boy who wouldn't have known who you were talking about."

"Then he'd have learned!" said Mr. Paloobi heatedly.

"Come on," said the October Hare. "We all admit he was bright, but when all is said and done he was just a little kid."

"And you're just a bunny in a topcoat with a wristwatch," said Mr. Paloobi, still angry.

"I don't *have* a watch," complained the October Hare, getting up from the bench. "I'm heading off to find a carrot before they're all gone. No one can talk to you when you're like this. Lionel's right: it's time for you to wake up and smell the coffee."

"I *am* awake, and I don't drink coffee."

"That was just an expression," said the October Hare. "How can you be so literal-minded, especially when your mind is just a product of *his* mind?"

"You'll never understand," said Mr. Paloobi moodily.

"Enlighten me," replied the October Hare. "Pretend I'm the kid and explain it to me."

"You're not as smart as he was," said Mr. Paloobi. He looked up and down the bench. "None of you are."

His companions knew enough not to argue with him when he was like this. In fact, there was only one person who *could* argue with him, and they hadn't spoken in seven decades....

"Doesn't it bother you that your parents don't seem to notice that you are a part of their life?" Mr. Paloobi asked, so annoyed on the Boy's behalf that he looked more like a grizzly bear than Winnie the Pooh.

The Boy simply shrugged. "I'm pretty used to it now."

"It's not something you *should* get used to."

The Boy looked up from assembling his toy train. "They ignore you, too."

"Yes, but I'm not their son or their friend," Mr. Paloobi replied, exasperated. He sighed deeply as he watched the Boy go back to working on the intricate circuitry on his train.

After a long spell, the Boy spoke up. "Yesterday, when I asked Dad if I could buy a train track with my pocket money, he told me I should save it. And I told him I *had* to have the track, because playing with the train wouldn't be the same without it." He started screwing the last panel onto the side of the train. "And then Dad told me that a person can't miss what he's never had." He put the almost-finished train on the ground gently, and then looked up at Mr. Paloobi, his eyes sad. "Well, I've never really had parents."

Mr. Paloobi couldn't think of a response, so he remained uncharacteristically silent.

Then the Boy smiled, a youthful sparkle returning to his eyes. "You should be *happy* they're never here, because if they were, they'd never let you visit on a school night—even if you are my only friend."

And, as always, whenever the Boy mentioned their friendship, Mr. Paloobi found that he could not argue with him. So they played a game of chess, and when the Boy's aunt, who was filling in for his absent parents yet again, delivered his dinner, they divided it between them as they'd been doing for almost two years now, and ate in companionable silence.

When the Boy uncovered his desert tray to discover a generous helping of chocolate mousse, he looked at it as if it had suddenly grown antlers and tried to walk off the plate. He toyed with it for a few minutes. "Girls are so annoying," he suddenly blurted out.

"Oh?" Mr. Paloobi turned to him in surprise. "And why is that?"

"Because I got the last bowl of chocolate mousse in the cafeteria last week and Colleen wanted me to share it with her."

"You don't share chocolate with anyone," noted Mr. Paloobi. "I'm assuming you said no."

He nodded emphatically. "But then she kissed me on the cheek, real quick like, and then she said I *had* to share it with her now." He frowned, remembering the moment. "I told her that I never wanted her to kiss me, so why do I have to share my mousse with her?" He paused, fidgeting uncomfortably. "And then she cried." A puzzled frown. "She cried a *lot*."

"Why?" asked Mr. Paloobi, just as confused as the Boy.

"She said that if I liked her, I would have shared it with her after she kissed me," the Boy said. "Well, I told her I liked her just fine— for a girl—but I don't share my chocolate with *anyone*."

"And what was her response?"

"She asked me if I would share some chocolate with her when we're older."

"And you said?"

"I said maybe, because I didn't want her to cry again." He continued to push the mousse around the bowl with his spoon. "Now she smiles at me whenever I see her at recess and lunch."

"What's wrong with that?" asked Mr. Paloobi. "It's good to know that you didn't permanently hurt her feelings."

"But every time she smiles at me now my stomach goes all funny inside, and I can't get any words out." He looked up at his friend. "Why?"

For the first time in their association, Mr. Paloobi was stumped for an answer. "Maybe you're worried that she'll kiss you again?" he asked finally.

The Boy shrugged. "It wasn't so bad."

"Well, then, remind me never to ask you to share your chocolate with me if you're still this upset a week later," he said, forcing a very insincere laugh and trying to cheer the Boy up.

"It's not about the chocolate," he replied with certainty.

"Then maybe you're nervous about having a new friend," said Mr. Paloobi, grasping at straws. "You've skipped a year in school and you're still brighter than all the kids in your class. I know how hard it is for you to make friends—to feel as if you fit in."

This time the Boy shook his head even more emphatically. "We're not even friends. She hangs around with other girls, and I sit near the other boys." He paused, screwing up his nose in distaste. "Girls play with dolls and pretend they are fairy princesses. I don't even think I *want* to be her friend…." His voice trailed off. "But I *do* kind of like her, so why does she annoy me so much? And why does it feel like an elephant is sitting on top of me every time she smiles?"

Mr. Paloobi walked down the bench to where Sugarblossom and Hawkmistress sat, the former shifting uncomfortably in her corset, the latter petting her hawk, which perched on her left shoulder.

"You look troubled," said Hawkmistress.

"Tell me about girls," said Mr. Paloobi.

"We're sweet and beautiful and delicate and we smell wonderful," said Sugarblossom. "At least, we'd smell wonderful if"—she raised her voice—*"someone would read a book and learn what whalebone does and doesn't smell like!"*

"I think you're very nice," offered Mr. Paloobi.

"Thank you."

"But I don't get all fidgety and nervous when you smile at me," he continued. "I don't spend endless hours thinking about you."

"Ah!" said Hawkmistress. "Your Boy is growing up."

"What does that have to do with anything?" asked Mr. Paloobi. "I'm grown up and I just told you that I don't feel like that."

"You're two years old," said Hawkmistress, "and no matter what you look like, you are *not* a man."

"Certainly I am."

"You were created by a four-year-old who probably thought the only difference between sexes was that men shave," she said.

"Nonsense!" said Mr. Paloobi. "I'm every inch a man. A little bear-like, perhaps, and my eye color keeps changing to suit his moods, but I'm a man, all right."

"You think so, do you?" said Hawkmistress.

"Absolutely."

"Do you have...?" she began. "Lean over. I'll whisper it to you."

He leaned. She whispered. He straightened up with a shocked expression on his round face.

"You're kidding, right?" he said at last.

"I am not."

"Sugarblossom, can she possibly be telling the truth?"

"I don't know what she said," replied Sugarblossom.

He placed his lips next to her ear and whispered.

"Oh, absolutely," she assured him. Then she slapped his face.

"What was *that* for?" demanded Mr. Paloobi.

"That's for talking about such things to a fairy princess."

"Well, what am I to tell the Boy about girls?" asked Mr. Paloobi, thoroughly confused.

"Tell him all will become clear in the fullness of time."

"That isn't the kind of answer that a six-year-old wants to hear," he said.

"The world—the *real* world—is full of problems," said Hawkmistress. "This, at least, is one that will solve itself."

"And in the meantime," added the hawk, speaking up for the first time, "watching a boy adjust to it is always good for a laugh."

"There is nothing funny about my friend being distressed," said Mr. Paloobi heatedly.

"There's nothing unique about it either," Hawkmistress assured him.

"Are you sure you're not putting me on?" asked Mr. Paloobi.

"Why do you think Prince Charming faces death in a thousand forms just for my kiss?" said Sugarblossom.

Mr. Paloobi was still thinking about that when both women were summoned back onto the playing field by their young charges.

This time it wasn't Lionel's insistent prodding that brought Mr. Paloobi back to the present, but a peculiar feeling that, despite nearly 70 years of absence, he recognized immediately. For a moment, the briefest and most blissful of moments, the Boy had somehow connected to him again. Before he knew what was happening, he was watching the Old Man that the Boy had become gently leaf through the pages of a leather-bound *Sherlock Holmes* book, and then slowly wrap it up and put it in one of the several cardboard boxes that littered the floor of his personal library.

"You know you can't take everything with you, Grandpa," a kindly young voice pointed out. "There's simply not enough room where you're going."

"I know that," he replied, as he started painstakingly wrapping up one of the chess pieces on the table beside his recliner chair. "But I'd like to take as many keepsakes with me as I can."

"Well, surely you don't need to take that chess set with you," said his granddaughter. "I've never seen you play even a single game with it."

"I think I played once, maybe when I was a boy," said the Old Man.

"But not anymore," she noted.

"No, not anymore," he agreed. "Not in a long, long time."

"Then why take it? Besides, one of the pieces is missing."

He paused, looking at the bishop he held in his hand for a long moment. "I've taken it with me every place I've ever lived."

"But *why?*" she persisted.

He shrugged. "I don't know," he admitted. "And until I *do* know, I suppose I'd better keep taking it along."

"Maybe I'll ask Miss Juniper why you keep it," said the girl. "She knows *everything.*"

"Who is Miss Juniper?" asked the Old Man.

"My playmate."

"Funny name for a playmate. Have I met her?"

"Only I can see her." She looked at him thoughtfully. "Didn't you ever have a playmate like that?"

The Old Man shrugged. "I suppose I must have."

"What was his name?"

"Damned if I know," he said as he began wrapping again.

With that comment Mr. Paloobi felt the newfound tie between them start to dissipate. The Old Man's thoughts of the distant past began to vanish, his mind moved onto other things, and Mr. Paloobi felt the solidity of the bench starting to form beneath him again, as the coldness of the mist surrounded him once more.

He missed the Boy that had become the Old Man, missed him desperately, and painful as it was, he let his mind drift back to their last day together.

The Boy's interests were expanding apace with his intellect. He had less time for games of make-believe, even for chess. There were entire days when Mr. Paloobi was never summoned to the here and now. He didn't know what he had done wrong, but the Boy seemed content, indeed happier than ever, so he uttered no complaints. Besides, he knew somehow that they would do no good.

The Boy sat before his tray. His parents were out for the evening (some things never changed), and he separated the meal from force of habit, placing the greens and the non-chocolate dessert on a plastic plate, then pushing it to the other side of the empty table before rearranging his own plate.

"Could you please pass a spoon?"

The Boy looked up to see Mr. Paloobi on the other side of the chess set, sitting on the little rickety chair that had broken countless times under the gentle giant's weight over the years, yet was always undamaged when the Boy woke up the next morning.

Smiling, Mr. Paloobi reached out a furry paw, squeezing the Boy's hand gently when he accepted the spoon. Then, instead of eating in quiet companionship as they usually did, the Boy spoke excitedly about his forthcoming excursion to the planetarium the next morning.

After dinner the Boy pulled out an astronomy book he'd been given for his birthday, and they lay together on the floor, holding the book over their heads as they pointed out all the star constellations they remembered.

Then, just before bedtime, they played their first game of chess in a month, the Boy successfully protecting his king from the evil queen with one of his bold knights, their movements mirroring the story Mr. Paloobi had told when they first met. When the Boy hopped into bed that night, the knight was still clasped tightly in his hand.

Rather than listen to a bedtime story, he told Mr. Paloobi about his day at school. His teacher had started to give him some extra work, so he was no longer bored in class, and he could now boast that he had four friends, not counting Mr. Paloobi. He had just started discussing the possibility of a camping trip with his friends when he noticed the sad smile on the Mr. Paloobi's face.

"You know I can't come, don't you?" said Mr. Paloobi gently.

"I know," said the Boy, quietly.

"Perhaps we had better talk about it."

There was no response.

"Are you all right?" asked Mr. Paloobi.

Still no response.

He waved a huge hand in front of the Boy's open eyes. They didn't blink.

30

He spent another few minutes trying to get the Boy to react, to acknowledge that he was there. He was still trying when he was pulled inexorably back to the bench.

When the Boy woke up in the morning, he was no longer holding the knight in his hand.

Mr. Paloobi sighed, uncomfortably shifting his weight so he wouldn't wake Lionel, who had rolled over sometime during his ruminations of the past and now lay curled up against his side. The benchwarmer smiled wryly to himself. If anyone could see them, they'd probably do quite a double take: an impeccably dressed man who looked like a bear, and a 400-pound lion who looked like an oversized tabby cat.

He found Lionel's nearness comforting, his remarks amusing. But even after 70 years, Lionel's friendship couldn't fill the void the Boy's absence had made in his life. His two brief excursions with new charges seemed like failed job interviews. He felt lonely and incomplete.

And suddenly he knew that someone else felt the same.

He just had time to rub Lionel's head apologetically before he was called forth from the bench once more, hearing the discontented rumble of his feline friend as he left the limbo in which he had lived for so long.

The Old Man was having a difficult time of it. Yesterday he had forgotten his granddaughter's name—just for a moment, mind you; just once. And when the nurse walked in, young and pretty, immaculate in her white outfit, he momentarily thought it was his wife, remarked that he didn't remember the white dress, and asked when she had bought it.

But he knew who the nurse was when she came by with his dinner. She asked if she could turn the television on for him, and he thanked her and asked if it was time for *Maverick* yet. She explained gently that *Maverick* wasn't on this week, and had left the set tuned to some mindless comedy with a bunch of actors he couldn't recognize.

The Old Man knew that these were just momentary glitches, but he also knew that the very best way to keep an aging mind sharp was to give it puzzles and problems to solve. He looked around the room for something to occupy him. It would have to be quiet; his wife was three months pregnant with their first child and he didn't want to wake her.

He got up and walked to a dresser, pulling open the top drawer. There was the first letter he'd ever earned, for making the baseball team. He ran his hand over it proudly. If he worked hard enough, maybe next year he could be a starter.

He heard a feminine laugh from somewhere beyond his door. He shook his head. Colleen was getting to be such a pretty girl these days. He still felt awkward and tongue-tied from time to time, but at least now he knew why.

He rummaged further, and then he came to the chess set. It had been awhile since he'd played—maybe a week, maybe even a little longer.

He sat down at the same table he took his meals at, opened the board, and began painstakingly placing ivory and ebony pieces on it.

It took him a long time, because he had trouble remembering the specific placement of the pieces, but he was determined to get it right. When it was finally set up, he sat back with a satisfied smile on his wrinkled, grizzled face.

Then, suddenly, something on the board caught his attention. Or, rather, the *lack* of something. He leaned forward, frowning, as he realized there was a piece missing. He stared intently at the chess board, knowing that it was significant for some reason, but not quite certain *why*.

A furry hand reached across the table, gently placing a knight on the empty square where it belonged.

The Old Man looked up to see a man with warm, friendly eyes sitting across the table from him. He might have trouble recalling faces and names now, but he could never forget those bearlike features.

"So are we going to play a game?" asked Mr. Paloobi.

The Old Man smiled happily. "Welcome back." He reached into his pocket, then stretched his hand across the table. "Have a piece of chocolate before my queen conquers your kingdom."

And they spent the night playing chess, nibbling on chocolate, and talking about things that were of great import to very young boys and very old men.

This was our first collaboration. After we met for the first time at the Denver Worldcon in 2008, and decided we could stand each other, we came up with "Idle Roomer" for Clarkesworld *a month later. It has since sold to Italy and Greece.*

—MIKE

Idle Roomer

BY MIKE RESNICK & LEZLI ROBYN

The room was on the second floor of the dilapidated old building, overlooking what had once been a garden and now was a concrete parking slab filled with cracks and potholes. It had a narrow bed next to a small nightstand with a cheap lamp and an old, battered desk by the single window. A rickety wooden chair, a phone, an ancient dresser, a tarnished floor lamp, and a small closet completed its uninspired furnishings.

And, thought Maria, *Mr. Valapoli has lived here for sixteen months.* How could anyone live in this cheerless place for sixteen days, let alone months?

Maria surveyed the room from the door. She'd been cleaning this room five days a week for sixteen months, and she'd still never laid eyes on him. His bed was always made, the top of his desk always barren. The only way she knew he actually existed was the nightstand, which had a different library book almost every morning, and the

33

bathroom, which held a dozen bottles of pills that were replaced with new bottles from time to time.

Oh—and the statuette on the top of the dresser. She didn't quite understand what it was. Sometimes she thought it might be a woman, holding her arms out to the viewer. Other times she wondered how she could have been so mistaken, for clearly it was a small animal with large trusting eyes, possibly something from the deepest jungles of Africa. Once she even thought it was a twisted tree. Maria shook her head; she would never understand modern art.

She would never understand Mr. Valapoli either. Every day she plugged the phone into the jack, and yet the next morning the end of the cord always lay on the floor. She checked the dial tone; it was functioning. Why did the man pay for a phone if he had no use for it?

She'd never liked Sherlock Holmes much, but she thought it might be interesting to work at being the Miss Marple of housemaids and see what she could deduce about the mysterious roomer. He had to have a beard, because there was no shaving equipment, manual or electric, in the bathroom. Yet she never found any hairs, from his head or his chin, on the bed or the floor. He was probably color-blind, for there was nothing blue, or purple, or violet in the drawers, no shirts of those tones in his closet. When she thought of it, she couldn't even remember a blue cover on any of his books.

She swept the floor, which hadn't seen a carpet or even a rug in perhaps half a century, went through the motions of dusting the desk and dresser and nightstand though as always they were as clean as if they'd been on display in a store.

Every other tenant was a transient. Even those who were down on their luck never stayed more than a week. And here was this poor man spending sixteen months of his life here. No matter what misfortune had befallen him, he didn't deserve *this*. No one did.

Her heart went out to him, and on an impulse, she took a piece of paper out of her pocket and left a note on his desk:

Don't give up hope, Mr. Valapoli. People do care. I care.
            Maria

She thought about the poor man all day. It was only when she was on her way home that she realized that he would have no idea who she was.

Maria's hand hovered just above the doorknob, hesitant and expectant. Last night she agonized over whether she should have left the note. Surely it wasn't wrong to let another person know that she felt for the predicament she saw him in? But then again, he could be a proud man who might see her sympathy as pity.

She shook her head, dispelling uneasy thoughts as she coaxed the creaking door to open. No, the note was well-meant and surely Mr. Valapoli would understand that.

At first glance the room appeared the same as always. As she absentmindedly plugged the phone cord into the jack again, the statuette caught her eye. Now it seemed to mildly resemble a curious owl, the eyes tracking her everywhere she went in the room.

You're being ridiculous, Maria Saviari, she reprimanded herself. *Next you'll be jumping at shadows.*

She continued cleaning the room, pausing only to pick up her daily tip from atop the immaculately made bed. As she placed the dollar bill in the pocket of her apron, her keen eyes noticed something different on the nightstand. This time there were two books upon it instead of the usual lone library book. Curious, she moved around to the nightstand, automatically smoothing the bedspread as she went.

Wondering fingers traced the cover of the second book, resplendent with its rich burgundy leather and gold foil embossed title: *A Meeting of Minds.* Gingerly she picked it up—ostensibly to dust underneath it, but actually to look more closely at the cover—when she noticed a piece of paper lying beneath the book.

"For Maria" appeared in a childlike scrawl—it was as if the writer had trouble forming the letters into legible shapes. Suddenly she realized that the book she now held in her hands was actually for her. It was his reply to her note.

Curious, she carefully opened it, the musty smell reaching her nostrils as she leafed through the first few pages. She stopped at the title page to discover more words written by the same hand as the note, but other than her name and a touchingly clear "Thank you" at the bottom of the inscription, the rest of the words were composed in a language she didn't recognize. She stared at it. Somehow the words looked neither awkward nor badly scrawled; rather, they seemed to possess some indefinable cogency and even beauty.

How do I reply without knowing what the inscription in the book means? The phone started ringing, breaking her train of thought. She jumped, startled, and for the briefest instant it seemed to her that the statuette jumped as well. *Get ahold of yourself, Maria,* she thought; *it's only a gift. No need to be so jumpy, or to feel guilty because you're looking through it, After all, he wants you to.*

Aware that she still had six rooms to clean before the end of her shift, she reluctantly placed the book in her apron pocket and continued working, the feather duster making short work of an already clean dresser and desk.

On an impulse she went back to the bed and replaced the tip there before she left. It felt wrong to take it now that they'd exchanged communication and she'd accepted his gift, and she hoped he'd see it as the small gesture of friendship it was.

As she finally closed the door behind her, the phone began ringing once again, as if impatient to be answered. *Maybe Mr. Valapoli had some friends after all,* she thought as she pushed her cleaning cart into the next cheerless hotel room, one hand unconsciously checking to make sure that the book was still safe in her pocket.

Maria watched tenderly as her grandmother leafed through the book, smiling when she saw her bring it close to her face, shut her eyes and breathe in the scent of the leather binding. Golden light filtered in through the window, dancing on the last auburn strands to be found in almost snow-white hair, the years of hard work and laughter defined on her face by the late afternoon sun.

"Smells expensive" was her first comment as she glanced up to look squarely at her granddaughter.

"I very much doubt that." Maria smiled. "It's a gift from someone staying at the boarding house." She reached over and turned the pages until she came to the inscription. "This is what I came here to ask you about. What language do you suppose this is?"

"My dear," said her grandmother, "this wilted English Rose might have married a Sicilian but that does not make me an expert in other people's languages. However," she continued, as one finger traced the letters softly, "it's definitely not a romance language, and I don't think it looks Oriental. In fact, it doesn't look similar to anything I've encountered before. Those elegant pictographs are quite distinctive." She looked up sharply. "*Who* did you say gave this to you?"

"I didn't say. This book is from a man I've told you about previously Grandma; Mr. Valapoli, the one that's had the misfortune to stay in the boarding house for the last 16 months."

"Is it normal practice for guests to give you inscribed gifts?"

Maria sighed. "No, it's not, but…"

"Let me guess. You want to help him." She closed the book quietly, setting it down on the table in front of her. "You can't help every lost soul you come across, Maria—no, don't interrupt me." She reached out and placed a hand on her granddaughter's cheek, gently brushing an errant ebony lock back as she did so. "You have too generous a heart; it makes it all that much easier for someone to break it." Abruptly she stood up, her hand shaking as it moved to pick up her walking stick. "And if you don't leave now it will be dark by the time you get home. Besides, you can't keep a frail old lady up past her bedtime," she intoned, the twinkle in her eyes still bright despite darkness falling outside.

Replacing the book in her uniform pocket, Maria laughed softly, and arose to kiss her grandmother on the forehead. "You are eighty-eight years young and definitely not frail of mind. Thank you for your advice, Grandma."

"If it's my advice you want, I'd take that gift of yours to the university tomorrow before you work. There's bound to be someone there with enough degrees to translate it."

Seemingly endless rows of books towered over Maria as she made her way to the back of the university library, feeling more insignificant with every step she made. As her fingertips ran featherlight along the spines of the books, she looked up at the ornately carved bookshelves in awe. Every dust-filmed tome seemed to hold a wealth of knowledge, representing privilege to her uneducated eyes.

An officious library clerk had told her that she'd find the man she was looking for with his class at the back of the library. She suddenly spotted him at a circular table already surrounded by students, one of whom was draped nonchalantly over a huge padded chair at the side of the table. He appeared exactly the way she thought a professor should look: peppered black hair, a neatly trimmed silver beard, and glasses perched low on a nose that he buried deeper into a book the closer she got to him.

"Professor Albright, may I have a moment of your time?" she asked politely, her eyes focused on the top of his head.

"Certainly," came the aloof yet slightly amused reply from the direction of the armchair. "In fact, you can have several."

She started in surprise, turning to stare at the man now confidently vacating the chair. *This young man is a Professor of Linguistics?* She knew appearances could be deceptive and she'd seen all types come and go at the boarding house, but this man with his surf-blond hair and cornflower blue eyes was *not* what she was prepared to meet.

Professor Albright addressed the older man firmly. "Mr. Tripoldi, the class, if you please." Without waiting for a response he strode over to the partially secluded corner of the library, Maria scurrying in his wake.

"How can I be of service to you?" he inquired, eyebrows raised as he turned to look at her. "I really only do have a few minutes to spare you, so please be concise."

"I've come across a language I cannot identify," she said. "It's an inscription in a book I've been given." She began rummaging through her work bag, wishing now that she'd thought to put the book on top of her change of clothes.

"Why don't you simply ask the person who gave you this inscribed gift?" he asked, staring at her with mild annoyance.

"I could. Or"—Maria matched his stare—"I can politely ask a leading academic on dead languages his expert opinion rather than hurt a considerate friend's feelings by asking what it means."

Surprise and a hint of respect flickered briefly across Albright's face before he once again adopted a mask of detached boredom. "You could indeed."

She held out the book to him, feeling suddenly more comfortable when his eyes left hers and refocused on the leather binding of her gift. "The inscription is on the third page," she explained, "and it's…"

The book was all but snatched out of her grasp, the Professor unable to hide his excitement over what now lay in his hands. "It couldn't be…could it?" The Professor opened the book to the copyright page, and began reading intently, then turned the page again. Suddenly there was a sharp intake of breath. "Do you realize what you have here?" he exclaimed, not waiting for an answer. "This is a numbered first edition! Do you know how rare it is? It must have cost a fortune!"

Maria was confused. "What does that mean?" *Surely Mr. Valapoli didn't have the money to buy her a rare and valuable book—not if he had to live in a boarding house.*

The Professor sighed suddenly, calming himself by sheer force of will. "It means that *before* this book was desecrated by an inscription, it was one damned expensive book for your friend to buy. It's worth a lot less now though—it's no longer in its original condition."

While she tried to assimilate all this startling information, Albright leafed through the pages to find the inscription. Suddenly he looked as surprised as Maria felt.

He started pacing up and down with the book, an intent look in his eyes, his brow furrowed, his veneer of smug superiority completely vanished. Suddenly he looked up. "This is not any spoken language—and I can tell you that this is not a dead language either." He paused, squinting excitedly at the page again. "In fact, this appears to be an *extinct* language. It's certainly alien to anything I've ever encountered. The structure is…let me put it this way: I'll bet a week's pay that not one word of this can be translated into English, and if it was a dead language I'd be able to do so, or at least see how to attack it." The book snapped shut as if to emphasize his point. "I'm afraid I can't help you."

Maria was dumbfounded. She gave Albright permission to photocopy the inscription before leaving for work, filled with more questions than before. Money was clearly not a problem if Mr. Valapoli could buy and inscribe this book regardless of its worth, simply because it made the gift more personal.

So why was the man living in that rundown boarding house if he could afford better? She didn't know then, and she still had no idea when she finally went back to work.

Just as she was about to reconnect his phone line yet again, Maria paused and decided instead to roll the cord up neatly into a bundle and place it beside the handset on the desk. She might not understand what Mr. Valapoli had against receiving calls, but after receiving such a present it was time that she started heeding his wishes.

Having finished dusting the desk and nightstand, she moved over to clean the dresser, and her gaze fell upon the statuette. It looked different again today. The change was subtle as always, but she thought she could almost discern the vague shape of an elephant, the trunk curving gently around the base, serene and contemplative. Even the color had subtly changed to match that of a pachyderm.

Mr. Valapoli was such a tidy tenant that she rarely had to use more than a feather duster to keep any surfaces clean. However, she couldn't remember the last time she had actually picked up the statuette to clean it properly, or indeed if she ever had. Possibly the greyish tone was simply the result of accumulated dirt.

Maria reached out to pick it up. The instant her fingers came in contact with it she felt some kind of *joining*, something she had never experienced before. She blinked very rapidly as she was suddenly overwhelmed by a sensation of *otherness*.

Suddenly a montage of images appeared, not before her eyes, but inside her mind—but they were like no images she had ever seen, or even imagined before. She saw three moons racing across a coal-black sky, their trajectory reflected in the murky waters of a silent ocean, and a sense of tranquility swept over her. Pastoral pictures followed, also not of anything she had ever seen, but lovely nonetheless.

And then she felt an air of foreboding, of dread, and the images, blurred beyond recognition, turned blue, became larger and bolder without taking any discernable shapes, and seemed to be converging on her.

She screamed, just once, and pulled her hand back—and the instant she did so, all the images, all the emotions, vanished, and she was alone in the room, her forgotten feather duster still clutched in her left hand. She held up her right hand and studied it, as if it was no longer part of her, as if it had somehow betrayed her. There were no marks on it, no burns or bruises, and she knew instinctively that it wasn't the hand that had taken her out of the here and now, it was the *contact*.

And now she turned her attention to the object that she had been in contact with. The statuette looked harmless enough, a peaceful, tranquil, not-quite-elephant, not-quite-anything. Had she imagined it? And if so, what exactly *had* she imagined?

She extended a forefinger and reached out to touch it lightly, then drew back before she made contact. Four more times she tried to work up the courage, and then, finally, her finger gingerly touched the statuette.

An image appeared in her mind, not of too many moons or flowers that didn't exist or oppressive blue *somethings*, but rather of a bookstore. A not-quite-human hand was thumbing through the pages of a book. *Her* book.

This time statuette didn't hold her against her will. She withdrew her hand, stood back, stared at it once again, and waited for her heart to stop pounding so hard against her chest.

If I'm not imagining this, what does it mean? And what have I stumbled into?

Evening and midnight came and went, and she still didn't know. She barely slept, and made up her mind to finally confront Mr. Valapoli and get some answers. She knew he was always gone when she arrived at nine o'clock, so she showed up at six thirty, just as dawn was breaking.

Probably he's asleep, she thought, staring at his door. *I'll just wait for some sound of movement.*

She learned against the wall for five uneasy minutes, then stood erect. This was too important to wait. She had to get some answers *now*.

She knocked at the door. No response. She turned the knob and gingerly tried to open it. It was locked. She knew that using her master key was against regulations, probably against the law, but she didn't hesitate. A moment later she was inside the room.

Mr. Valapoli wasn't there. The bed hadn't been slept in. She looked in the closet to see if he'd packed and left. It was filled with his clothes.

41

Was it all a hallucination? There was only one way to find out. She walked over to the statuette, summoning her courage to touch it again. It had changed again, no longer vaguely elephantine, no shape that she could identify...but she could identify an emotion, its every line seemed to project: *fear*.

It couldn't be afraid of *her*. All she wanted were answers. What could be scaring it?

And suddenly, instinctively, she *knew*. It was the blue, shapeless things she had sensed yesterday. They were not part of her life, or even her world—and that meant that the fear was Mr. Valapoli's.

She laid her hand on the statuette without hesitation now. Images, blue and garbled, flooded her mind, and she seemed to hear voices inside her head, not human voices, not speaking any language she had ever heard, but somehow she understood what they were saying.

A voice that sounded blue (*how was that possible?*) was saying, "You hid well. But now you must come back with us."

And a gentle voice, a voice she instinctively knew was Mr. Valapoli's, a very tired, very weary voice said, "It's a big galaxy, and this is such a small world. How did you find me?"

"We have our methods," said the blue voice. "Will you come peacefully or must we use force?"

"These are decent beings, these people. They are without malice. Do them no harm, and I'll come back with you," said the tired voice.

"I do not envy you when we get home," said the blue voice.

Maria withdrew her hand. They were going to take him away, back to something awful! She raced to the window to see if they were in the yard. There was a hint of something large and blue beneath a tree, but she couldn't make it out.

"No!" she yelled, turning and preparing to run to the door.

And the statuette, suddenly more human—or at least humanoid in shape—raised a hand as if to tell her to stop.

She froze, shocked, and the gentle voice spoke inside her head.

"It's all right, Maria."

She stared at the statuette, and its expression seemed to soften. Finally, after another minute, it lowered its hand.

"Thank you for caring."

She walked to the window, and the blue shape was gone, and somehow she knew Mr. Valapoli was gone too. Forever.

Sunlight streamed in through the single window of the bedroom, bathing the statuette in warm golden light as it sat on the dresser, the focal point of the small, uncluttered room.

Still half asleep, Maria stretched languorously, thinking of all she had experienced over past few weeks. Ever since Mr. Valapoli left and she had brought the statuette home, it felt like it truly *belonged* with her, and she liked to imagine that the statuette itself felt comfortable on her dresser.

Its shape had continued to change. Each morning she would wake up to see the magic that had been wrought overnight, and each day it became somehow less alien in its form and more distinct in its features, softening into the image of a man, with eyes as kind as Mr. Valapoli's voice had been gentle.

She no longer questioned how the statuette could change. She *knew*. Every time she touched it she could sense him. The connection was very faint, and growing fainter with each passing day, but she took comfort in the fact that it was *there*.

Until the morning she touched it and *didn't* feel anything but the cold contours of the statuette itself. Not sure of what was happening, she reached out to make contact with it again, but before she could, her eyes widened in wonder as she realized she was witnessing its very last change, her unseen friend's final parting gift to her, the one that let her know he also cherished their strange connection.

There upon the statuette's face was a smile, and in her mind she clearly heard the echo of Mr. Valapoli's voice for the last time.

"Thank you for caring, Maria."

We were invited to submit a story to DAW's Is Anyone Out There? *and decided to go against the grain and came up with a humorous answer to Fermi's Paradox, "Report from the Field."*

—MIKE

Report from the Field

BY MIKE RESNICK & LEZLI ROBYN

TO GALACTIC COORDINATOR RYLLF:

Day 1, Year 403,772,109 of Project Earth

I can't begin to tell you how thrilled I am to receive this assignment. We have been observing the planet the inhabitants call "Earth" for almost four hundred million years now. At first we couldn't understand why they would not respond to our signals, which was the reason for the First Expedition, but what we discovered was that evolution seemed to be occurring at a much slower rate here than in neighboring systems. We came back sporadically, and although a race known as Man had finally developed sentience, it did not have the technological wherewithal to receive our signals or send any of its own, so we passed to word to our member worlds not to bother trying to contact Earth until we informed them that the inhabitants were capable of capturing and interpreting our signals.

It was less than a century ago that our observation post in the Spiral Arm observed a marked increase in Earth's level of neutrino activity, and we have given them these few extra years to develop before telling the Galactic Community at large that it was acceptable to make contact with them. We never want to be guilty of rushing things; I'm sure we're all painfully aware of the unfortunate situation on Blarnigog IV. (Well, on what used to be Blarnigog IV, anyway.)

I will be using our standard procedures to monitor their transmissions and get a better idea concerning how best to approach them and alert them to the fact that there is a vast and long-established Galactic Community that has been observing them for almost half a billion years, just waiting to welcome them into the fold.

I am both proud and honored that you have chosen me to be the one to make the initial contact.

Day 2, Year 403,772,109 of Project Earth

I am truly impressed by this gritty little race. Most of them live in cities, all concrete and steel and glass, and some of these cities hold ten million or more inhabitants. All right, that's insignificant compared to some of *our* megalopolises, but a million years ago, on our last visit here, their progenitors were living in trees.

They are centuries, perhaps a millennium, away from fast and inexpensive forms of transportation such as teleportation, but they have developed mass travel on land, on sea, and in the air. They have created written languages, eliminated most disease, have invented a remedial (but functional) form of computer based on, of all things, the silicon chip, and have even managed to construct an orbiting space station.

I am sure I will report that they are ready for membership in the Galactic Community—and oh, the things we can teach them! I hate it when we offer to initiate a race such as the Breff, and they arrogantly claim to need none of the myriad benefits we can bring them. The people of Earth still die of old age, they haven't yet discovered even the simplest means of exceeding the speed of light, their medical science hasn't yet mastered the brain transplant, and their agriculture is so backward that there are actually hungry people on the planet. In a week's time we can show them how to feed everyone on a continent with the food that is produced on only six square *pryllches*, and with a simple injection at maturity no one will ever show the effects, visual or internal, of age.

This world has been isolated long enough. I will monitor its transmissions for a few more days, making notes on all the areas in which we can bring our expertise to bear, but there is no question in my mind that it is time to invite Earth into our community and give it the full range of benefits that accrue to all our members.

Day 4, Year 403,772,109 of Project Earth

I may have spoken a bit too soon.

I saw some disturbing transmissions today. I am not sure that I fully understand them, but they have convinced me that the situation bears further study before we make too hasty a decision.

There seems to be a small round creature, relatively helpless, without any discernable means of locomotion. It is spherical in shape, white, clearly defenseless, resembling in almost every way the adorable *quiblit* of Altair IV. You might remember that more than a million *quiblit* were slaughtered on their home world when one race from the Galactic Community first colonized their planet an eon ago, not realizing that they were sentient—or even alive. I have not as yet been able to determine the genus or species of *this* white sphere, but I feel I must do with some degree of haste, for clearly its existence on Earth is otherwise of limited duration.

I was subjected the appalling spectacle of Men taking turns beating these poor creatures with elongated clubs in the most sadistic possible displays. Not only that, but literally tens of thousands more Men cheered lustily every time one of these creatures was struck with a club.

The worst part? Many of the creatures somehow survived, and their reward was to be pummeled by the club-wielding Men again and again.

Such public displays of brutality are not readily discerned except in select locations, but that they exist at all gives me a very uneasy feeling about this race.

Clearly a certain degree of sadism exists just beneath the surface. When I could no longer force myself to watch the endless torture of the round creatures I sought other transmissions to see if this was an aberration I had uncovered, or if I had not previously been looking deeply enough into the race's motivations.

And what I found was a transmission labeled "Late Night Entertainment," depicting a confrontation between a male and a female of the species. The lighting was poor, even after I internally adjusted my optical lenses, but I was able to make out most of their actions. At first I thought they were simply practicing a new means of sharing their food supply, because they kept pressing their mouths together— but then (and I am not fabricating this, bizarre as it seems) the larger of the two began peeling layers of skin from the smaller! A moment later the instigator was running his manipulators and mouth all over what was left of the smaller one's body; she was clearly too terrified to contemplate escaping, and her moans and screams were so horrifying that I fear I shall hear them to my dying day.

"Entertainment?" What kind of race can possibly find this entertaining?

Day 8, Year 403,772,109 of Project Earth

It may be noted that it has been some time since my last report. It took longer than expected for me to be able to purge the negative emotions I experienced when watching the last transmissions I reported on; and this was necessary for me to objectively consider the latest revelations of this complicated race. I was determined to discover some more positive aspects of Man, and I did indeed do so—at least initially.

Man has a rather remarkable ability to empathize with creatures of limited intelligence, which I find puzzling when I consider how I've just seen him treat his own kind. They even call one species that often cohabits with them "Man's best friend," and can be heard cooing to it in high-pitched tones, thereby causing the creature's nethermost appendage to spasm uncontrollably. For reasons unbeknownst to me this seems to be a desirable response. So is allowing these four-footed creatures to drag their owners around the city, usually before the sun has arisen, just so they can defecate on the very objects Man seemed to take such pride in building. And here is the most puzzling part of all: the creatures—their most common identifications seen to be Pookey, Cuddles or Fluffy—are often being overfed to death in the name of love.

Is this another example of cruelty (albeit a passive version) on the part of Man? I was not sure, so I decided to investigate how they treated their own young. The transmissions I found on the subject were, in a word, astonishing.

First I saw something termed a "documentary" on water births, which is apparently a modern way of helping the females expel their offspring. However, I couldn't see how it could possibly help the female, who alternated between screaming incoherently and yelling "I will never let you touch me again!" to her mate during the final stages of the process.

It should also be noted that once the offspring is born it is immediately turned upside down and pelted sharply on its waste conductor—an unnecessary torture that caused the offspring to cry in agony and begin gasping for air.

And this barbaric ritual is not just confined to water births. Indeed, many human medics (the ones I had previously praised for eradicating many diseases) seem to take great pleasure in pelting a newborn infant immediately after it is born in a hospital, just to hear it scream in pain, before returning it to the mother so they can move on to pelt the next one.

I am at a loss to discover the purpose of this ritual, other than to introduce the offspring to violence at an early age, and I am starting to strongly suspect that this sentient race is not as evolved as I initially thought. In fact, I am beginning to have considerable doubt as to Man's ability to interact and work with the civilized races of the Galactic Community. How could this race have made such huge scientific advancements in such a short time, and still exhibit such obvious signs of barbarism? Clearly I will have to study them further.

Day 9, Year 403,772,109 of Project Earth

For today's research I decided I needed to determine how Man instinctively perceives himself before I can fully understand how *we* should perceive them as a race. So I looked for transmissions that focused on the race's artistic development, to see what I could glean from their use of creative mediums.

Again, I was surprised. For a sentient race, they seem to have very primitive means of expressing themselves. While I discovered some simply beautiful art pieces, such as the statue of David, generally Man seems to have an inclination to revere the more flawed pieces of creation, perhaps as a metaphor for how he sees himself. The armless Venus de Milo and the headless Winged Victory are held in no less esteem than the complete David.

There is a museum in Amsterdam that showcases the art of one Vincent Van Gogh, who by all accounts was a mentally disturbed being, mutilating one of his own auditory appendages before self-terminating more than a century ago. For reasons that elude me, members of his own species *still* revere the paintings he created, calling them "cutting edge." (I haven't been able to adequately translate that term, though I suspect it may refer in some obscure way to the removal of his auditory appendage with a sharp object.) The proportions of the various structures depicted in his "paintings" are clearly mathematically inaccurate, and yet it is that very inaccuracy that seems to inspire the most admiration. So I decided to look at the work of more-recent artists on the assumption that Man's creative ability must surely have evolved in the intervening century. After determining only to research artists whose work is respected by a large percentage of the population (thus ensuring I would have a more complete understanding of Man's perceptions in general), I discovered the paintings of Pablo Diego José Francisco de Paula Juan Nepomuceno María de los Remedios Cipriano de la Santísima Trinidad Ruiz y Picasso—an impressive name, to be sure—and was shocked to discover that this man, probably the most revered artist of the past millennium, had such a distorted vision of humanity. He often painted faces in which both optical lenses were on the same side of the olfactory appendage, or that the skin—which comes in various shades of black, brown, tan, red, yellow, and pink among Man's sub-races—was *blue*. In fact, he frequently painted contorted images of both the male and female members of his species, their forms brutally mutilated and twisted almost beyond recognition.

I must conclude that if this is what is praised above all other artwork, Man is still a barbarian at heart—even his depictions of himself are violent. However, just to be certain, I examined the works of one other highly respected artist, Salvador Dali, but words are inadequate to describe the endless aberrations I encountered in painting after painting.

At this moment, based on these observations, I am leaning toward the conclusion that Man is not ready to be offered membership at this time. However, before I make my final decision and formally submit my findings, I feel I must determine if there is a *potential* in Man that outweighs what I have seen to date.

Day 12, Year 403,772,109 of Project Earth

It occurred to me, as I again consigned myself to watching more of Earth's transmissions, that the two genders of this race—so different as to almost be considered separate species—do not appear to have equal status on their world. It is clear to me that the female gender of the race is weaker in physical proportions, so I sought out transmissions that focused on the limitations of female form—and what I unearthed appalled me. I discovered that, as small as they already are, it is an accepted notion in their society for females to deny themselves the necessary nutrients to be physically healthy, because apparently starving their form makes them more attractive to their potential mates.

Yes, I know this sounds absurd, but the evidence is overwhelming, In fact, females who obtain the truest form of man's desire are designated by the term "Models." So using that word I intercepted a transmission depicting "catwalk Models," to see what represents perfection in Man's eyes. To say that I was shocked is actually understating the case. The transmission displayed females whose skeletal structures often showed through various points of their skin, their fragile frames encased in uncomfortable-looking coverings that appeared to limit their movement.

And they did not look like happy specimens of their race. All of the females exhibited unresponsive—one might even say lifeless—facial conformations, clearly to mask their pain as they strode down the "catwalk" wearing long-spiked torture devices on the bottoms of their locomotive appendages.

They would not even react when the spectators surrounding them started banging their manipulators together (to keep them submissive with the threat of violence, perhaps?) as they reached the end of the "catwalk." Instead each Model would turn this way and that with that soulless look to her face, pause as if stunned to realize she was trapped, and then turn around and retreat the way she had come— only to repeat the torture encased in another more uncomfortable contraption not five minutes later.

Not only this, but in transmission after transmission I find that females, and to some extent males as well, mutilate their flesh, piercing auditory and olfactory appendages and even more personal body parts with everything from metal to superhardened carbon, evidently on the assumption that such displays of courage in the face of senseless pain finds favor in the eyes of the opposite sex.

I was utterly confounded. I had to discover if the threat of violence was the underlying reason females mutilated various body parts and deprived themselves of life-sustaining nutrients in order to attract a mate, or whether there was a deeper psychological reason that could explain such unnatural acts. So I began to research what females desired in a mate to better understand their mentality, and quickly discovered there were many mating manuals on the subject, all helpfully categorized (and thus easily researchable) as "Romance Novels."

To make sure I was getting an accurate perception of the female mind in general, I only read the manuals that were considered the most popular of their kind—and there I made the most horrifying discovery. It appears that there is a subspecies of Man that Earth females are unable to resist. This object of lust is always "tall, dark, and handsome," exhibiting "bedroom eyes" (which I assume are carried in with them and donned only within the confines of the sleeping quarters) and a "silken touch" (incomprehensible) that can immediately mesmerize the female when employed—and once mesmerized, *he actually drinks their blood!*

Yes, you read correctly. This subspecies of Man practices a form of barbaric cannibalism that either kills the victim to unnaturally sustain his own violent existence, or infects them so they devolve to also live the "tortured life of the undead." And for some baffling reason, the females of Earth find it wildly pleasing when a Vampire (the designation of this violent subspecies) tells them that their blood is so desirable to him that he has to fight not to "drain her dry," which I have since discovered is a euphemism for killing them.

How could *any* sentient creature find the threat of death attractive? That they willingly put themselves in violent life-threatening situations, declaring their (ironically) undying love for these dangerous and dominating Vampires, leads me to the conclusion that this race is instinctively drawn to violence on nearly all levels of their collective psyche.

And if Man's propensity for violence could possibly deny him a position in the Galactic Community, I believe the presence of Vampires (even if they are just a minority) requires that First Contact to be made by a member of our Interplanetary Relations Division that is from a race without a bloodstream. We don't want to risk spreading such an insidious disease throughout the galaxy until a vaccine can be successfully created and tested, and/or the Vampires are completely exterminated.

My last chance to determine if Man has any potential to evolve past his current self-destructive tendency lies with his spiritual beliefs—but that is a task for tomorrow. I have spent several days pouring over these mating manuals, and desperately need to purge the violent images before I can begin to continue this report with any degree of impartiality.

Day 13, Year 403,772,109 of Project Earth

I never thought I would be the one who could potentially deny a sentient race's entrance into the Galactic Community, but it is becoming more and more likely.

Today I endeavored to discover this race's spiritual underpinnings. I elected to study only the most popular and well-known beliefs to get the clearest picture of the race as a whole. What I discovered was nothing short of appalling.

Man is a race of Death Worshippers!

53

There can be no mistake about it. At least a third of Earth's population, a staggering two billion beings, practice a religion that is based on the death of one man some two millennia ago. Although there appears to be some discrepancy between the texts of the various sects practicing this religion, the violent nature of the man's death is beyond disrepute. There are literally tens of thousands of graphic representations in museums around the world, depictions of how his manipulators and motor appendages were "nailed to the cross" preceding his death, a procedure whereby spiky objects were inserted *through* the flesh of the victim to forcibly affix him to an artificial structure.

Coming from an enlightened race that believes all sentient life is sacred (well, all that they know about, anyway), I was shocked to discover that instead of *saving* this man from such a violent death, his friends stood by and *watched* him die, then created a religion that postulates the theory that it is acceptable for an innocent being to die in order to atone for someone else's crimes—someone he did not even know.

Followers of this religion wear replicas of the instrument of his death—the cross—around their necks, and more than half of them practice symbolic cannibalism in their designated buildings of worship, drinking his blood and eating his flesh (well, artificial substitutes thereof) as a way of spiritually connecting to his violent murder. They even go so far as adorning their own burial sites with representations of this instrument, a clear statement that they admired a brutal and violent death, even if their own leave-taking was peaceful.

I would veto Earth's membership right now, except for this one fact: the object of their worship seems to have been imbued with an inexplicable power to heal all pain and cure all suffering—true acts of kindness. If that is so, it may well be that he was an early mutation, that Man is still capable of evolving as a race, and this endless violence I have catalogued is merely an adolescent stage through which the race is passing. It is with that single hope that I will put off my decision for another day, while I scour the planet to see if there are any other heretofore overlooked forms of benevolent mutation.

Day 14, Year 403,772,109 0of Project Earth

Yesterday I was appalled. I mean, here was a race, clearly in its adolescence, a race that hadn't yet outgrown sadism, brutality, ignorance, even death worship.

But that was yesterday. Today I am terrified.

I began my search for the advanced members of the race, the possible mutations, those who demonstrated those qualities and abilities that would reassure the Council that Man indeed deserved to be invited into our vast community of civilized worlds.

Where does one look for such beings? In the most popular transmissions, of course. And so I did.

And yes, they exist.

Very few of them represent themselves as they truly are to the rest of their race. At first I thought it was because they are *so* advanced it would generate feelings of inferiority in those who interact with them. It turns out that the truth was much more diabolical.

For you see, Man's mutations are not mental, not spiritual, but physical. They hide behind what they call "secret identities," though the reasons for this are vague, since they are clearly impervious to permanent injury. Most of them wear colorful, formfitting costumes. Many wear capes, which seem to hinder movement and I suspect serve the same purpose as brightly colored feathers in avian species: to attract the opposite sex for procreative activities.

They have not all evolved in the same ways. One has blinding (and I mean that literally) speed. One morphs into a muscular giant of a color not seen on any other member of the species. One stretches almost to infinity. One female is equipped with phenomenal strength and a set of artificial implements that are little short of magic. One climbs walls. One's manipulatory appendages actually become sharp-edged metal weapons, his every injury healing instantaneously. And the most revered of them all has every physical asset of the others: invulnerability, unlimited strength, the ability to levitate at phenomenal speeds, and even the ability to see through solid objects.

And what do they do with these attributes?

They fight.

Who do they fight?

Another class of costumed mutants, clearly for dominance in the power structures of Earth.

I have observed only a few such encounters in public transmissions, but the collateral damage must be almost unimaginable.

I am forced to face the following conclusions:

1. There *are* physical mutations in the race of Man, and there is no reason to think they will not continue to increase in numbers, as clearly these particular mutations are survival traits.

2. Based on my observations, the fact of the mutation does not cause a diminution of aggressive behavior.

3. We in the Galactic Community have no defenses and no weaponry capable of dealing with the most powerful of these mutants.

4. Based on everything I have learned about Man during the past fourteen days, it would be foolhardy, indeed suicidal, to assume they will be content to be a small cog in the galactic machine, or that they will not look farther afield for additional conquests once they have pacified their enemies on their home world.

Therefore, it is my recommendation to the Galactic Coordinator that Earth be isolated for another hundred millennia. There must be no contact, no radio or microwave transmissions, no attempt at communication of any kind. I further recommend that the entire Sol system be placed off-limits for that same duration.

It's a pity. It seemed such a promising little planet when we discovered it four hundred million years ago. Perhaps if the Neanderthals had won that first great war....

Just before moving to the United States, Lezli was invited into IDW's Classics Mutilated *anthology. Since a child, her favorite series was the Lucy Maud Montgomery's Avonlea books, and the anthology called for her to rewrite a classic from the viewpoint of another genre, giving birth to the utterly charming "Anne-droid of Green Gables." The novelette has since been republished in the Czech Republic, in the annual* Year's Best Australian Fantasy and Horror *anthology, and is going to be expanded into the novella forthcoming from Hadley Rille Books.*

—MIKE

Anne-Droid of Green Gables

BY LEZLI ROBYN

(with a little help from L. M. Montgomery)

The Station Master whistled to himself while the steam engine puffed into the small Bright River station, rocking back and forth on the balls of his feet as he checked his brass pocket watch to verify the arrival time for his logbook. He had been told to expect an important delivery today, and so he was personally going to oversee the unloading of the cargo carriage. There wasn't much excitement to be had on Prince Edward Island, so he was very curious as to what the package contained; he'd been told to unpack the box with care upon arrival.

The train chugged slowly to a stop, and the Station Master scanned the carriages to see if all was in order before pressing an ornate but bulky button on his lapel pocket. It whirred perceptively and then emitted a piercing whistle to alert the passengers that the train was safe to disembark.

He tilted his hat in greeting to the first young lady to step onto the platform, but she didn't have eyes for him. She was gazing about her with a soft smile on her face, smoothing out her skirts. So he made his way to the back of the train, signaling for Oswald to keep watch on the platform while he began to search for the precious cargo, and wondering why the owner hadn't arrived yet.

On the way he detoured to pull a brass lever on the side of a machine fixed to the platform near the last carriage door. The device wheezed to life, numerous brass and wooden cogs beginning to whirl around, steam pumping out of several exhaust valves as the leather conveyer belt sluggishly sprung into action. He then walked into the carriage and lit the gas lamp hanging just inside the doorway, automatically picking up and placing all the small packages and bags onto the conveyer belt so they would be transferred to the station office for sorting.

He paused when he came across a large trunk in the dark recesses of the carriage, the layer of dust that shrouded it a testament to its long journey on more trains than this one. He grabbed the lantern and held it over the trunk, wiping the corner clean to expose the sender's stamp.

"LUMIERE'S REFURBISHED MACHINES-TO-GO"

Satisfied, the Station Master pulled out his Universal Postal Service key, and inserted the etched brass device into the leather buckle locks that were holding the lid of the trunk down. He heard a perceptible whir as the key activated in each lock, and they sprung open. He paused, his hand hovering just above the lid, wondering what he would find in the trunk. It was not often that city machines, even refurbished ones, made their way to the tiny coastal towns.

His curiosity got the better of him. The stamp told him that the trunk would be too heavy to carry off the carriage without extra help, so he knelt down, checked that all of the buckles had completely disengaged, and lifted the lid slowly.

Only to find himself looking into a pair of brilliant green eyes.

They blinked, and then focused on him.

His blinked too, very rapidly, his mind a jumble of uncoordinated thoughts.

A small hand reached out of the trunk and took the lid from the Station Master's frozen grasp, pushing it completely open.

The man's mouth fell agape in response, as he stared anew at the trunk in wonder. Matthew Cuthbert had always been a man of few words, but his reticence in this case was a little extreme. A machine indeed!

There, pulling itself into sitting position, was an *android*. The Station Master had never seen one of these sophisticated machines before, and he didn't know how go about interacting with them.

"Are you my new Father?" the android asked.

He shook his head somewhat absently, gathered his wits together, and rediscovered his voice. "Your new owner will be here soon," he offered gruffly. He gestured towards the carriage doorway. "Shall we go wait for him?"

The android looked towards the doorway, and then back to him. "I can go *outside?*"

Again, he was taken aback. "Of course. If you want to meet your new owner you *have* to."

He stood up and hesitated, looking down at the android sitting in the battered travel trunk, and then reached down. A dainty hand rose to meet his, and he was startled by its warmth. For some reason he had expected android skin to be cold. Lifeless.

Like a machine.

But, instead, the hand he clasped in his own felt like that of a child. Somehow that thought put his mind at ease. He helped the android out of the trunk and then stepped out of the carriage, turning back to see what such a sophisticated machine would make of their humble station.

The android moved tentatively into the light and the Station Master gasped. It was female in form! He had previously thought all androids were made to appear androgynous.

He watched her look up in wonder at the sun when she felt its rays fall upon her face. In the full sunlight her skin shimmered with a slightly golden hue, but that was not her most distinguishing feature. It was her hair—or more the point, her two braids of very thick, decidedly red, woven copper filaments that fell down her back. The worn sailor hat didn't disguise the brilliance of the fine metallic strands, nor did the yellowed threadbare dress detract from the elegance of her form. While too slender to be considered very feminine, and her face too angular to ever be considered classically beautiful, she was a striking figure with her huge expressive eyes and the delicate brass nails that graced her little fingers.

In one hand the android held a carpetbag that had clearly seen better days, but she was holding it with such care that the Station Master couldn't help but be intrigued. He'd never considered the fact that an android could have luggage; it must have been stowed in the trunk with her.

She moved forward, turning around slowly as if to soak everything in, but when she spotted the conveyer belt she walked up to it, curious, and without preamble started fiddling with the various levers and cogs on the side with her free hand, only flinching—but not pulling back—when the steam from one valve hit her.

She had clearly done this before. Her tiny hand fit into the tight spaces to tweak this or that with such precision that within minutes the machine was running smoother, much to the Station Master's astonishment. She kept working until the chugging sound of the machine had turned into a soft purr, and then she turned back to the Station Master, who stammered his thanks.

"Oh, no need to thank me," she replied. "This machine is a primitive version of the sorting machines I used to operate at my previous home every day. It's such a pleasure to be able to work out how things operate, don't you think?" The android didn't give him the time to answer. "I've always thought so. There is something beautiful about seeing a machine work to the optimum of its capacity."

The Station Master couldn't agree more. He couldn't take his eyes off the android in front of him. She was an absolute marvel. He wondered where her new owner was.

He turned slightly and gestured towards the station building. "Would you like to wait in the Ladies Sitting Room until Mr. Cuthbert arrives?"

She tilted her head, considering both him and his offer. "No thank you," she replied. "I'll wait outside. There's more scope for the imagination."

The Station Master smiled. What a charming girl.

Matthew Cuthbert looked at the android from the far end of the platform and hesitated. He had never been much of a conversationalist, and had always found talking to girls to be one of the most awkward experiences in the world, so it was daunting for him to discover his most recent purchase was female in form. He had been told that he was buying a prototype whose model had never been put on the production line, but he hadn't thought to ask about gender.

He couldn't help but be intrigued however, despite his anxiety. Androids had first been created to replace the child workforce in the factories that were expanding throughout the major cities. For many years children had often been the cheapest and most practical workers because their tiny hands and slight forms meant that they were able to manipulate delicate machinery, and so naturally the androids were modelled after them. But their creators soon discovered that their clientele did not want their new workforce looking like children—innocents. Nor did they like that the prototypes were created with advanced problem-solving skills, because some people believed it gave the androids individuality as they adapted to what they learnt, leading them to want to try new things outside the factory walls. As a consequence, the androids that eventually populated the factories all over Canada were created to be completely unremarkable in their subservience and androgynous appearance.

Matthew couldn't fathom how they could be considered superior in design to the original prototypes, but he wasn't going to complain. It meant he could afford to buy the "flawed" machine sitting on the platform in front of him.

He took a deep breath and walked towards the android—and then right on past. He realized at the last moment that he had no idea what to say to her. *How exactly does one greet an android?*

He reached the end of the platform, and stood there for a minute before turning around to see the android now eying him with evident curiosity. Matthew wondered what such a sophisticated machine would make of him, for he was very unassuming in appearance. Tall, with lank shoulder-length hair that was now more steel-colored than the black of his youth, he had a stooped frame, as if his very posture reflected his wish to not stand out in a crowd. But the shy smile he gave the android when he finally walked up to her was welcoming, and his eyes were kind. Before he even had time to consider how to greet her, the android had stood up and reached out her hand.

"You must be my new father, Matthew Cuthbert of Green Gables." She shook his hand in greeting, still clutching the carpet bag to her side. "I'm Anne—Anne with an 'e.' Most people believe that Anne is short for android, and so often they leave off the 'e' when they write it down. However the 'e' is the letter that completes the name. If I met someone else called Anne, but spelled without the 'e,' I just couldn't help but feel they were somehow lacking. What do you think, Mr. Cuthbert?"

He blinked, surprised. "Well now, I dunno." He had a simple intelligence, but he wondered if the android was expressing her insecurities about being accepted. And more importantly, did she *know* she was doing that? "Can I take your bag?"

"No thank you, Mr. Cuthbert. I can manage. I have to make sure I hold the handle with a forty-three degree tilt at all times or it's prone to falling off. An extra degree either way and the bag has an eighty-two percent chance of losing its structural integrity. It's a very old, very dear carpetbag."

Matthew smiled at the unexpected mix of technical evaluation and human sentiment in Anne's statement, seemingly fitting for a machine made in Man's image. He gestured for the android to follow him, and they made their way to his horse and buggy in silence, Matthew looking at the ground, and Anne looking at everything else.

She appeared captivated by the most commonplace things. Even while one of the very rare and expensive steam-operated carriages rolled on by with the girl from the train gracing its leather seat, protecting her fair skin with her lace parasol, Anne's attention stayed focused on the old draft horse hitched to Matthew's buggy.

"I'm at a loss to see how you power this locomotive," she replied after a moment.

The corner of Matthew's mouth twitched, and he ducked his head to hide a smile, realizing that the android had never seen a horse before, and that this particular one was close to comatose.

He walked up to the horse, rubbing the gelding's neck gently, prompting him to shake out his mane and seemingly coming to life. "There are no steam-generated levers needed to operate this buggy. I just tell Samuel here to pull it for me."

The android blinked. "Samuel isn't a machine?"

"No," he said simply.

"But this creature's purpose is to serve humans?" she asked, her head tilting to the side.

Matthew's hand paused mid-stroke. "Well, yes, I suppose in a way that's true."

"Does it have free will?"

This time it was Matthew who blinked. "He lives and works on my farm."

She didn't miss a beat. "Because he has no other choice."

"Yes."

She nodded to herself. "I understand."

Matthew was struck by how definitive her answer was. "How so?"

"That existence was not unlike my life at the factory." She reached out her hand and gingerly mimicked Matthew's actions a minute earlier, her brass nails glinting in the filtered sunlight as she rubbed the horse's neck.

Matthew watched her for a long moment, then: "Did that bother you? Being told what to do all the time, I mean."

"No. Why would it?"

Matthew didn't know how to reply.

Anne continued on, almost absently. "I like to learn, and to keep busy. I also like to discover how things work. The Supervisor told me that that was a flaw in my makeup, and that I had to be terminated. I didn't know why I was going to lose my job when I had just surprised him by halting production of the main sorting machine in the factory to improve its performance by 6.3 percent, but he wouldn't listen to me anymore." Her hand stilled, and the horse head-butted her to resume. "It was Father who intervened. He told the Supervisor that termination was too final a punishment, and that I could still be of some use. However, I don't understand what he meant by that comment, because I no longer work for the company."

Matthew's depleted bank balance told him exactly how Anne had still been of use to the company, but it was her naivety that fascinated him the most, not the reason why she had been sold.

The journey home was filled with more discoveries for them both; the android talking nonstop, and the man appreciating the fact that she didn't expect him to talk too.

"You and I are going to get along just fine, Mr. Cuthbert."

"Call me Matthew."

"I'm not sure why I know this, or why I know I belong at Green Gables, but I've always thought there was more…"

The android stopped mid-sentence, her crystal green eyes going wide as her eyes fixed on the sky in front of her. For a moment Matthew couldn't take his eyes away from Anne's face, struck by how the sense of wonder really brought her features to life. But her attention didn't waver, so he drew his gaze away from her striking features to look up and see an airship sailing gently through the sky, the golden light of the setting sun lapping against the hull as it gently surfed the clouds.

It was barely perceptible to Matthew, but he was sure that Anne could hear the whir of the enormous steam engine at work, pumping hot air into the enormous canvas balloon that the old seafaring ship was now suspended from.

"What a wondrous invention!" the android breathed in amazement.

Matthew looked back at her in surprise. "How so?"

She turned to him with bright eyes. "This machine gives you the ability to fly, which would be one of the most incredible experiences. Imagine being able to look down at the world! It would create such a sense of freedom, don't you think?"

He nodded. He'd never thought of it that way before.

"Have you ever considered flying in one of those machines?"

"No, I can't say as I have," he replied, intrigued by her child-like curiosity.

"Oh, Matthew, how much you miss out on!" They both looked back up at the airship in shared silence for a long minute.

Matthew glanced at Anne out of the corner of his eye, amazed that such a sophisticated machine could be in such awe of an old sea-faring ship that had clearly seen better days. It had been hobbled to a simple canvas balloon and operated by the most cumbersome steam engine he had ever encountered, simply so its owner could maximize his resources and try to keep at the cutting edge of the transport industry. He supposed the idea was ingenious, but the execution didn't strike him as being very safe or too elegant.

"I have worked with many machines," the android said quietly, her gaze still on the airship as it disappeared slowly over the horizon, "but I have never seen one that was so beautiful."

"I have," Matthew responded in his quiet, shy manner. "*You.*"

She turned to him, her eyes now wide. "But I'm just a girl."

The innocence in her statement went straight to his heart. Matthew had never been one to talk much, but now he was literally speechless.

She didn't see herself as a machine!

Although he didn't realize it at the time, that was the moment *he* stopped seeing her as one too.

Anne discovered that being accepted by her classmates at school wasn't something she could learn from an instruction manual. When she queried Matthew about how to secure a Bosom Friend, he simply told her to "Be yourself," which puzzled her as she couldn't physically be anyone other than herself anyway. When she asked his wife the same question however, her curt response was to "Forget that non-sense! If you prove your worth, friendships will seek you out. Be kind, considerate, and above all, bite that tongue and mind your manners!"

"Biting my tongue will help facilitate friendships?" Anne asked, perplexed.

"You do beat all, girl! Of course not," Marilla replied, frustrated. "It's an expression—a human expression. But then, I suppose you shouldn't be expected to know that."

The old lady sighed, looking at the android. Ever since Matthew had bought Anne home, the peace and order at Green Gables had been thrown in disarray.

"We have to send her back," she had told him the very first hour he'd returned home with the android.

"But she's such a sweet little thing," he had replied softly as he watched Anne walk around the house for the first time, reaching out her hand to touch the most random of things in fascination: the intricate embroidery on the tablecloth, the leaves of a plant, or the polished wood of the rocking chair. She had never seen such diverse textures before.

"Matthew Cuthbert, the entire reason for buying an android in the first place was so you can have help on the farm. It's unseemly to put a girl to work in the fields, even if she is android in form. And we're both too old to be nursemaids to a flawed machine."

"She's not flawed—just different." Matthew paused. "Give her a chance, Marilla."

"We'd have to put her through school, simply so she can learn the basics of interacting in society."

"So she'll go to school."

"But what is the point of buying an android, if we can't get our money's worth out of her? There is still the matter of you needing help on the farm."

"I'll hire Barry's boy out for a couple of hours during the day, and Anne can help me before and after school." He held up his hand to forestall Marilla's next protest. "We can't afford to buy a normal android. And the simple fact is: I like her." He looked at his wife. "I don't ask for much, but I'm asking for this."

Marilla harrumphed, more to cover her shock than out of any deep need to protest. This was the first time her husband had ever stood up to her and held his ground. This machine must have really gotten under his skin. "The android can stay," she stated finally, "but strictly on a trial basis. We have a three-month warranty, don't we?"

"Yes."

"Then if I'm not impressed by that time, we are returning her for a full refund. And I want no protests, Matthew. That is my condition for letting her stay now."

Matthew nodded, satisfied. He knew that despite the condition, he'd just won a great concession from his wife.

And so every morning Matthew came downstairs to the library at five to find Anne engrossed in one of his books, looking more like the child she appeared to be as she acted out the plays with enthusiasm, the dying light of the fire dancing about in her copper hair. They would talk about her latest literary discoveries of the previous night while Matthew ate his breakfast, and then their day would start, the android helping Matthew milk the cows, muck out the stables, and carry out all the hay for the animals until it was time for her to leave for school.

Within a week they had developed a comfortable routine, and Matthew was surprised to discover that for the first time in a decade he actually enjoyed getting up before the birds awoke. However, it soon became clear after a few weeks of school that Anne hadn't been able to make as favorable an impression on her classmates, who were quick to point out how different she was.

"People don't often like that which they don't understand," Marilla had told the android matter-of-factly.

But Anne had read about "kindred spirits" and how true bosom friends are accepting of all differences, and as Marilla had said, she just had to prove she was worthy of being a perfect friend.

So every day she went to school and tried to prove herself by excelling in her classwork. She had much to learn, having only known factory life before Green Gables, but it didn't take long until she was tied with Gilbert Blythe for first honors.

And still the classmates' attitude towards her didn't noticeably thaw. The android couldn't understand why. Wasn't she doing everything right?

"You think you are better than us, don't you, Miss Anne-*droid?*" was Josie Pie's snide comment after Anne won her first spelling bee. She twisted around at her desk to look directly at Anne. "Can you spell *machine?*"

Anne looked at her in puzzlement. *Was this another test?* "M-A-C-H-I...."

"Do you always have an answer for *everything?*" Josie interrupted, frustrated that she could never get a rise out of the copper-haired girl.

"Isn't the correct response to a question an answer?" she asked, still puzzled.

Josie glared at her and faced forward again, not speaking to her until their extracurricular painting class that evening. "I'm sure you are perfect at that, too," she muttered.

"I don't know," the android replied. "I've never painted before."

The class set up outside to capture the majesty of the rolling fields of Avonlea on canvas. Nestled in the tree line along the horizon, Anne could see the roof of Green Gables, and so she painted that first, her strokes precise and her measurements exact.

Then she moved to the fields, taking care to note the exact hue of the grass and blending the appropriate golden-hued green. Within 15 minutes the field was done, complete with fences drawn to scale.

While Anne was busy duplicating the trees on her canvas, the teacher went up to each student in turn to ascertain their progress and study what their diverse depictions of the one view told him about their personalities.

When he approached Anne, his eyebrows raised at the quality of the painting. Then they furrowed. "Well, it's technically perfect," he said, and he sat down to start his painting.

Diana Berry looked up from her canvas as Anne was starting to outline the clouds. The raven-haired beauty glanced at Anne's painting, her blue eyes going wide. "Oh, Anne! I wish I could paint as half as good as you do!"

"Honey, you don't need to be talented with looks like yours," Gilbert Blythe quipped from somewhere behind them. The other students snickered and the light disappeared out of Diana's eyes. She returned them to her painting.

Anne looked up from her masterpiece to discover the clouds had moved. Quickly she started painting their new position over the clouds she had already started to form.

Then she noticed that the sun had changed position. Its lower angle threw a deeper amber cast onto the field. Frantically she started to mix up a different shade of green to replace the grass she'd painted earlier.

Then she noticed that the new position of the sun meant that Green Gables was completely in shadow, rendering the cottage almost invisible to the naked eye. So Anne painstakingly painted it into a silhouette.

Then she looked up to see a salmon pink was starting to outline the bottom of the clouds, and a peach was spreading across the horizon. The sun was setting.

Her efforts to keep up with the changing colors of encroaching night meant her painting strokes increased to inhuman speed—and *still* she couldn't keep up. Every time she looked up, her painting was no longer accurate. The trees were now completely black along the horizon, and the fences cast long shadows across the field.

She stopped, at a loss for what to do. As a result of changing the colors in the sky so often and so quickly in a blur of hand and brush, the layers didn't have enough time to dry, resulting in the salmon pink blending with the earlier lighter blue shades. Her sky was now a mauve color.

It was a restful shade, throwing a slightly romantic mood over the painting, but all Anne could see was that it wasn't an accurate depiction.

Josie snickered. "It looks like Anne can't do everything right after all."

"Don't listen to her," Diana said, a little pointedly. "Josie doesn't think of anyone but herself." She looked at Anne's painting. "Why did you keep changing the colors?

Not that it looks bad," she added hastily, "but your painting looked perfectly fine before."

"The colors are all wrong."

Gilbert appeared over her shoulder, his usual nonchalant stance dissipating in his interest. "In what way?" he asked.

"We were told to paint this view." Anne gestured in front of her. "But the colors keep changing. This painting is no longer accurate."

"A painting doesn't have to be technically accurate for it to be considered a masterpiece," the teacher interjected, only his blond hair visible at the top of his canvas as he continued to paint. "It's how you interpret the view that brings the painting to life."

"I don't understand," said Anne.

"Take a look at mine," Diana offered, a little shyly.

Anne stood up and walked over, studying the painting for a long moment. "The clouds are the wrong shape."

"Not the *wrong* shape, Anne. Just a *different* shape," she replied. "It's a matter of perspective. Take a closer look."

The android tilted her head to the side, as she always did when she was thinking, and considered the clouds Diana had painted. They were perhaps a little too white. Also the strokes she used to define the texture of the clouds were too coarse to depict the lightness of the gossamer structures.

"Pretend they aren't clouds," Gilbert interjected her thoughts. "What else do you see?"

Anne considered the shapes of the clouds and nothing else, and automatically started comparing them to images in her memory banks. "They're animals!" she blurted out suddenly, Diana laughing as the android's eyes darted up to the sky. Sure enough, she could see the remnants of some of the clouds Diana had painted. If she looked closely enough, she could see what looked like a rabbit bounding over the horizon. "How did you know to do this?" she asked finally.

"I just used my imagination," Diana replied, blushing delicately at the attention.

"But androids don't have an imagination, do they, Gilbert?" Josie pointed out, twirling her hair around her finger.

"Knock it off, Josie." Gilbert replied. "Nobody's perfect. She just had to know how to look."

Anne didn't hear them. She was still trying to process what she had just learned. "So Diana's painting is better than mine, even though mine is technically more accurate."

The teacher leaned around his easel. "*Better* is not the right word. It's a more *realized* painting." He paused, trying to work out how to explain it. "Your painting shows us how you—or anyone here—phys-ically see the fields, but nothing more. It shows us nothing about *you*."

She analyzed his words carefully, and found herself, as well as her painting, lacking. "So I have failed."

"No, not necessarily." The teacher studied the android for a moment, aware that she'd probably never been confronted with failure before.

"It just means you've got more to learn." He smiled gently. "That is what school is for."

"Where do I start?"

Even Josie was struck by the earnest entreaty in the android's tone.

"Here and now," the teacher responded with a smile. "We've still got a half an hour of light."

The android sat down at her easel, unwilling to let the teacher know he had misunderstood her. She remembered what happened when the Supervisor at the factory had misunderstood her, and she didn't want to be sold again. She looked at her painting.

Where do I start?

"Do you see Green Gables in the distance?" Diana whispered into Anne's ear, leaning over in her chair. Anne nodded. "That is not merely where you live, but it's your *home*. What do you *see* when you think of home?"

Diana watched Anne's eyes blink rapidly for a few seconds, and then flitter back and forth across the painting. She reached for her paints and brush, and started mixing colors.

Diana watched, fascinated, as Anne started applying paint to the canvas once more, her speed belying her android heritage as an airship quickly took shape amongst the clouds in the painting's mauve sky.

When the flying vessel was complete, she dipped her brush in a combination of pots and leaned forward. For a minute Diana could only see the back of Anne's copper braid as the android painstakingly painted a candlelit window onto the silhouette of the cottage, but then she leaned back and dipped her brush into the black pot.

After considering the painting for a moment, the android started to paint a tiny profile of a human in the field closest to the cottage. When she also brushed in a little cattle dog beside the figure Diana realized that it was Anne's depiction of Matthew returning to Green Gables after a hard day's work on the farm.

The android's hand hesitated beside the image of the man, and Diana wondered if the android understood what a lovely—and homely—image she had just created: the light from the kitchen guiding the man home at night.

But then the android's hand darted upwards, and another silhouette started to take shape at the bow of the airship. It appeared that the figure was looking down at the cottage, and when Diana saw that the silhouette wore her hair in a braid that was lifted by the wind, Diana started in shock.

Anne had drawn herself into the painting—and she was sailing home on an *airship*, being guided home by the cottage light like a seafaring ship would a lighthouse.

Who said androids couldn't have an imagination? Diana thought triumphantly, as she looked at her new friend's painting with a smile on her face. *Anne might be a kindred spirit after all.*

Matthew pulled out his timepiece and opened the case to see where the clock hands pointed. "It's time to leave for school, Anne," he said quietly, sure that she could hear him from across the barn.

She looked up, blinking in surprise. "Usually my internal clock alerts me before now."

Matthew nodded, bemused. One of the things that endeared him the most about the android was that she could often get so swept up in her enthusiasm and curiosity for the current project she was working on that it overrode her most basic mechanical functions, like her inbuilt alarm clock. He knew that Marilla and Anne's creators considered that a manufacturing flaw, but to Matthew it seemed like a very human characteristic.

He watched her methodically put his tools back in order, and then cover the machine.

"I was nearly finished!" she complained.

"So you will finish it tonight."

"I suppose that is an acceptable conclusion," she replied.

Matthew laughed. *Was the android pouting?* "Well, my dear Anne, if this contraption of yours truly works and I never have to milk a cow again with my bare hands, then I will have the time to start teaching you chess before school tomorrow morning." He smiled at her. "Is that also an acceptable conclusion?"

It appeared to him that her eyes lit up. "More than acceptable, Matthew." She tilted her head, considering him.

Matthew blushed under her scrutiny and busied himself with closing his timepiece and running his thumb lovingly over the initials ornately carved across the lid before moving to put it away. He felt the android's curiosity before she voiced it. "It was my father's" he said quietly. He hesitated a moment, then held it out to her.

Anne appeared to understand the privilege she was being given. She took the pocket watch from Matthew with evident care, turning it around in her dainty hands to look at the initials, almost imperceptible on the old tarnished metal. She popped the lid open, and her eyes grew wide. She had never seen such a tiny machine. Behind the ornately carved brass hands, she could see the intricate wheels turn, and despite the discoloration of age, she thought it beautiful.

Matthew let the android hold his timepiece the entire way to school, the light reflecting off Anne's brass nails as she tinkered with it, drawing his attention to the advancement of her construction in comparison to his beloved pocket watch. The 19th century had seen a huge evolution in machines, and he wondered what the next century would bring if Anne was the pinnacle of this one.

The buggy started rocking more than usual, with Samuel having to navigate more ruts as a result of the storm the previous night, but when Matthew briefly glanced over at Anne he saw the pocket watch clutched protectively in her tiny hand.

She seemed almost reluctant to give it up when they reached the school, but then she heard Diana calling her and she quickly handed it over, leaping out of the buggy with her usual enthusiasm and grace. She turned to Matthew to say goodbye, and he told her he'd be there at three to pick her up.

"No need, Matthew," she said. "Gilbert Blythe said he'd walk me to the bend, and I wanted to see the new flowers that have come out since the last rain."

Matthew smiled as he watched her rush off to greet Diana, wondering if she realized how human she sounded.

He shook his head at his folly. *Of course she knows. She doesn't see herself as a machine!*

He laughed as Samuel pulled the buggy away for school, and he returned home with a smile still on his face.

"What time do you call this, Matthew Cuthbert?" Marilla asked when he walked into the kitchen to share a pot of tea with his wife before going back to work on the farm.

He didn't know why, but by Marilla's clock he was always late. He pulled out his pocket watch to check—and discovered it was no longer working.

His heart sank in his chest. His pocket watch had never failed him until today, and it was his last tangible memory of his father.

He looked at it closely and he could see that part of the clock mechanism appeared dislodged behind the face, and when he shook it gently, he could hear something metallic rattle around. It appeared that an irreplaceable component was broken in his beloved timepiece.

Marilla saw the look on his face and asked him what was wrong. After he told her, she asked, "What, if anything, did you do differently with the pocket watch today?"

He thought back on his morning. "Nothing, really. I gave it to Anne to look at, and then let her hold it while we traveled through some storm-created ruts on the way to school." He paused, considering. "Come to think of it, those ruts really were pretty rough going. I wouldn't be surprised if one of them was what did it."

Marilla wasn't convinced. "Did you watch Anne the entire time she had your timepiece, Matthew?"

"I can't say as I did," he replied, wondering what his wife was getting at. "I had to concentrate on the road on account of those bothersome ruts."

Marilla was silent for a long moment, and then she asked: "Do you think the android could have tinkered with it? She seems fascinated with the inner workings of machinery."

"Anne was fascinated by the intricacy of my pocket watch," he admitted. "But…"

"Think about it, Matthew," Marilla interrupted. "My theory makes sense. The pocket watch had never broken down in your lifetime, nor your Dad's, *until* the day you let Anne play with it."

He couldn't find any fault with her logic, but deep down in his heart he knew it wasn't true.

When Anne came home that afternoon from her walk with Gilbert Blythe, a posy of wildflowers in her hand, Marilla confronted her. "Did you fiddle with the mechanism in Matthew's pocket watch?"

Anne noted the agitated tone in her voice, and became concerned. "What's wrong with it?"

Marilla took that as an admission of a kind. "So you *know* something is wrong with it!"

"No, Marilla," Anne replied. "I honestly didn't." She looked at Matthew, who was quietly sitting in the kitchen chair, watching the exchange. He gave her a gentle smile of encouragement.

"I need a truthful answer from you, Anne," said Marilla. "Did you play with Matthew's watch until you broke it?"

"No, Marilla," said Anne truthfully, since she had no idea when it broke.

"Then who did?" demanded Marilla.

Anne simply stared at her. She'd been taught never to guess when she didn't know the answer.

Marilla glared at the android, trying to keep her temper in check. "Now listen to me carefully, Anne," she said at last, ominously enunciating every syllable. "If you don't admit that you've done wrong, and that you just lied to me, you will not be allowed to go to Diana's birthday airship flight next month."

Anne's mind quickly considered the possibilities and the consequences. If she did not admit to purposely breaking the watch, Marilla would not believe her and she would not be permitted to ride on the exotic airship. On the other hand, if she lied and admitted to breaking it, Marilla almost certainly *would* believe her and she would be allowed to go. It was very confusing: if she lied she would be rewarded, and if she told the truth she would be punished.

Which was worse—to lie and be believed, or to tell the truth and be doubted? In the end it was not the airship that was the deciding factor, but a desire to please Marilla by telling her what Anne assumed she wanted to hear and what she obviously already believed.

"I broke the watch while I was playing with it," she said at last.

Marilla stared at her a long time before speaking. Finally she said, "All right, Anne. Cuthberts always keep their word, so you will be allowed to go on the airship."

"Thank you," said Anne.

"I'm not finished yet," said Marilla harshly. "As I said, Cuthberts don't lie. You just admitted that you lied to me. Therefore, you are not and never will be a Cuthbert. I'm going to have a serious talk with Matthew after you're in bed tonight. I think we're going to return you and get our money back. You are *not* what we were promised."

Anne was still staring at the empty space where Marilla had stood long after Marilla had turned and walked away.

Deep down Anne had known she was different from everyone else in Avonlea, and that she had the means to repair the pocket watch if she only just acknowledged it. She didn't know if she had refused to accept the truth about herself and had blocked it from her mind, or she had simply been programmed to not think about it, but she had to confront it now, if she was to ever help repair the damage she had inadvertently caused.

She pulled out her carpetbag, and for the first time since she'd arrive at Green Gables she opened it up.

Inside was a batch of tools, some of them not unlike those she was using to create Matthew's milking machine, only finer in construction.

Her delicate hand reached in and sorted through them until she felt the one she needed and pulled it out, looking at it for a long moment.

She hesitated, then unlaced the top of her nightgown, looking down at the barely perceptible panel outlined on the left side of her chest. Her right hand hovered above it, implement in hand, knowing instinctively what she had to do, but unable to take the next step. Then she thought of the pain she saw in Matthew's eyes when Marilla had decreed she had to be returned to the factory, and she steeled herself, placing the implement along one side of the panel and pressing it in, hearing a tiny whir as three micro-latches started turning. A section of her popped out, and she looked at it for a long moment before carefully hooking the brass nail of her thumb into the tiny crevice and pulling it open.

I'm a machine.

The realization struck her like a punch to the stomach as she stood staring at what she had revealed, unable to process anything for some time. Although deep down she had always known, it was still a shock to see tiny brass cogs, wheels, screws and copper wires so intricately interconnected to a circuit board buried within her chest. It was a wonder to behold, even for the android.

She realized how primitive the pocket watch was in comparison, and yet she also understood its importance to Matthew, and her determination to repair it for him increased tenfold. She closed her eyes and tuned into the sounds her body made.

Tick, tick, tick, tick...

Her eyes sprung open, and she instinctively moved a bundle of copper wires that were covering the specific mechanism she needed to find. She analyzed the individual components, recognizing that some were similar those in the pocket watch.

Tick, tick, tick, tick...

She rustled around in her carpetbag and pulled out a tiny toolbox, opening it to reveal delicate jewelry-grade tools. She selected one and used it to sever the connection between the tiny mechanism and her main circuit board without a second thought.

The ticking stopped.

The android's hand froze. She felt a strong sense of loss, and she couldn't focus. She had no idea how long it took her to adjust to the change in her body, because she literally lost track of time, but she finally was able to block out the feeling that she had lost something fundamental to her being when she realized how much more she'd lose if she had to leave Green Gables.

She carefully placed the little mechanism on the table in front of her and used the firelight to study it more closely. At first she had thought she'd wasted her time, but when she put the pocket watch beside it, she was able to compare the components more easily, and she could see they were of similar composition and size; they were just finished off differently.

Then she spotted it: the part she needed.

Using the precision that only an android could command, Anne very carefully detached it and transplanted it into the pocket watch within minutes. When the last part was in place, the pocket watch sprang to life.

Tick, tick, tick, tick...

Anne clapped her hands together in delight, an affectation she'd picked up from Diana. She knew that what she achieved that night was more important than any work she'd ever done on the factory floor—or at least, it felt that way to her.

She looked at the part of herself she'd transplanted into the pocket watch, studying her handiwork, unable to find it lacking. The new part stood out from the rest of the components because it was free of tarnish, and more rose gold in color than normal brass. It also appeared more refined in composition, and she wondered if Matthew would mind the discrepancy.

She resealed her access panel and relaced the top of her nightgown before methodically packing her tools back into the carpetbag. She considered whether she should clean the brass and restore the pocket watch back to its original condition. But the cleaning agent she normally rinsed through her copper hair was in the bathroom upstairs, and she didn't want to risk waking the Cuthberts.

She picked up the pocket watch again to take it back to the kitchen where Matthew had usually kept it, and walked straight into someone.

"Anne! Give that to me immediately!" Marilla barked, standing in the doorway with a lantern in her hand. "You have been told you are no longer welcome in our house, and that means you are definitely not allowed to touch our things." She looked at the android pointedly. "Especially ones you've already broken."

Anne didn't trust herself to speak after the trouble her mouth had gotten her into earlier that day, so instead she simply held out her hand.

Marilla was taken aback by the silent acquiesce. She looked down to see that the pocket watch still open on the dainty little hand, and she wondered what other heirlooms the android had played with while her and Matthew had been asleep at night.

She retrieved the pocket watch, inspecting it to see if it came to further damage—and her heart nearly stopped.

The pocket watch was working again!

She couldn't tear her eyes away from it; she was so surprised. Then she spotted the gleaming new part at the heart of the clock mechanism, and her breath caught. "Where did you get that?" Marilla asked, looking up at Anne sharply.

The android raised her hand and placed it on her chest where a human heart would be. "Here," she said simply, her head tilting to the side.

She had used a part of herself to repair the watch! Marilla realized what a huge gesture that was. "You didn't break the watch yesterday by playing with the clock mechanism, did you?" she asked quietly.

"No."

Marilla sighed. "Then why did you say you did when I asked?"

"You told me I couldn't go on the airship for Diana's birthday celebration next month, unless I confessed to breaking it," Anne said, her big green eyes seeking Marilla's out in entreaty. "So I confessed."

"But that's lying, Anne," Marilla pointed out.

"You wouldn't believe the truth."

Marilla sighed again. "So you thought you were giving me the answer I wanted. You were trying to please me." She looked back down at the repaired pocket watch. "Let us make a deal, Anne: I will forgive you for lying, if you will forgive me for not believing you."

"What is this about forgiveness?" Matthew asked, as he, too, walked into the room.

Marilla ate some humble pie. "You were right," she admitted, and without saying any more she handed over the pocket watch.

Matthew brought the timepiece closer to his lantern to study it. That it worked again was no surprise to him. He had a feeling Anne would try to repair it after watching her dedication while building his milking machine. But what he didn't expect to see was the glint of a new component in the clock mechanism that differed in color to the rest of the watch. He looked over to Anne in shock when he recognized its construction was far more refined than the rest of the watch's components.

Anne's green eyes twinkled. "I'll never be on time for school again," she said, and Matthew realized she'd used a component from her internal clock to bring his father's beloved pocket watch back to life.

He knew what a sacrifice that must have been for the android, and his heart reached out to her, knowing that in a way he held a piece of hers within in his hand.

He walked up to her and kissed her on the forehead, much to her and Marilla's surprise. "You'll just have to learn how to tell the time like us average folks," he said as he stepped back, his voice a little gruff with emotion.

"*I'll* teach you, Anne," Marilla stated. "If you learn from Matthew, you'll never arrive anywhere on time."

Anne had always thought that sailing on an airship would give her a sense of freedom unlike any other experience in the world.

She was wrong.

Yes, it was exhilarating. Yes, she felt on top of the world—quite literally—as she leaned over the bow of the ship, the wind lifting her copper hair as the vessel passed through another cloud bank. But she soon realized that she was just a spectator watching the world pass her by. There was some peace to be discovered in that, but she had no control over that journey; she just had to enjoy the ride.

She knew now that her first true taste of freedom had been when the Station Master had released her from the cargo trunk at the train station three months ago—she just wasn't aware of it at the time. She had stepped out into a brand new world, with sensations she'd never even known had existed, yet alone experienced, and for the first time in her brief life she had the opportunity to be accepted. Appreciated.

Loved.

No longer was she being told how to perform her every action like an automated machine. She had to learn and adapt to the ramifications of her actions like everyone else, and deal with any consequences that arose. There was a great sense of freedom in being in control of her own destiny that she'd previously been denied until she'd met the Cuthberts.

Her keen android eyes searched the fields far below her until she spotted Green Gables nestled along the tree line. As she gazed at it she felt a sense of belonging that she'd never experienced before.

"We would like to adopt you," Matthew said quietly when she had hopped off the airship not long after, halting her excited rambles about how the journey through the clouds had given her such scope for the imagination.

"But you have already bought me," Anne replied, perplexed, as she considered Matthew's shy smile.

"That's true," said Marilla, "and what an expensive girl you were, to say the least." She brushed off her skirts briskly, and then looked directly at the android, who returned her gaze. "But we don't want to *own* you," she added, reaching over to take hold of Matthew's hand. "We want to know if you would *choose* to become a part of this family as the child we never had, and never knew we'd even wanted until you came into our lives."

Anne stared at both of them, and for the first time since they met her, she was speechless.

In that moment she became Anne of Green Gables.

She had finally come home.

One day multiple-Hugo-winning editor Gardner Dozois challenged Mike, who'd made half a dozen trips to Africa and was then editing a series of reprints of classic African hunting books, to write "the ultimate science fiction hunting story." Mike didn't want to just do a story in which his hunter kills bigger deadlier beasts, and finally he remembered Lewis Carroll's "The Hunting of the Snark." The resulting heart-wrenching story won a HOMer, as well as the Asimov's Readers' Poll, was a Hugo and Nebula nominee, sold to Poland, France, Israel, the Czech Republic, and is currently under option to Hollywood.

—LEZLI

Huŋtiŋg the Sŋark

BY MIKE RESNICK

(with a little help from Lewis Carroll)

B elieve me, the last thing we ever expected to find was a Snark.
And I'm just as sure we were the last thing he ever expected to meet.

I wish I could tell you we responded to the situation half as well as he did. But maybe I should start at the beginning. Trust me: I'll get to the Snark soon enough.

My name's Karamojo Bell. (Well, actually it's Daniel Mathias Bellman. I've never been within five thousand light years of the Karamojo district back on Earth. But when I found out I was a

distant descendant of the legendary hunter, I decided to appropriate his name, since I'm in the same business and I thought it might
impress the clients. Turned out I was wrong; in my entire career, I
met three people who had heard of him, and none of them went on
safari with me. But I kept it anyway. There are a lot of Daniels walking around; at least I'm the only Karamojo.)

At that time I worked for Silinger & Mahr, the oldest and best-
known firm in the safari business. True, Silinger died 63 years ago
and Mahr followed him six years later and now it's run by a faceless
corporation back on Deluros VIII, but they had better luck with their
name than I had with mine, so they never changed it.

We were the most expensive company in the business, but we
were worth it. Hundreds of worlds have been hunted out over the
millennia, but people with money will always pay to have first crack
at territory no one else has set foot on or even seen. A couple of years
ago the company purchased a ten-planet hunting concession in the
newly opened Albion Cluster, and so many of our clients wanted to
be the first to hunt virgin worlds that we actually held drawings to
see who'd get the privilege. Silinger & Mahr agreed to supply one
professional hunter per world and allow a maximum of four clients
per party, and the fee was (get ready for it!) twenty million credits. Or
eight million Maria Theresa dollars, if you don't have much faith in
the credit—and out here on the Frontier, not a lot of people do.

We pros wanted to hunt new worlds every bit as much as the
clients did. They were parceled out by seniority, and as seventh in
line, I was assigned Dodgson IV, named after the woman who'd first
charted it a dozen years ago. Nine of us had full parties. The tenth had
a party of one—an incredibly wealthy man who wasn't into sharing.

Now, understand: I didn't take out the safari on my own. I was in
charge, of course, but I had a crew of twelve blue-skinned humanoid
Dabihs from Kakkab Kastu IV. Four were gunbearers for the clients.
(I didn't have one myself; I never trusted anyone else with my weapons.) To continue: one was the cook, three were skinners (and it takes
a lot more skill than you think to skin an alien animal you've never
seen before without spoiling the pelt), and three were camp atten-
dants. The twelfth was my regular tracker, whose name—Chajinka—
always sounded like a sneeze.

We didn't really need a pilot—after all, the ship's navigational computer could start from half a galaxy away and land on top of a New Kenya shilling—but our clients were paying for luxury, and Silinger & Mahr made sure they got it. So in addition to the Dabihs, we also had our own personal pilot, Captain Kosha Mbele, who'd spent two decades flying one-man fighter ships in the war against the Sett.

The hunting party itself consisted of four business associates, all wealthy beyond my wildest dreams if not their own. There was Willard Marx, a real estate magnate who'd developed the entire Roosevelt planetary system; Jaxon Pollard, who owned matching chains of cut-rate supermarkets and upscale bakeries that did business on more than a thousand worlds; Philemon Desmond, the CEO of Far London's largest bank—with branches in maybe 200 systems—and his wife, Ramona, a justice on that planet's Supreme Court.

I don't know how the four of them met, but evidently they'd all come from the same home world and had known each other for a long time. They began pooling their money in business ventures early on, and just kept going from one success to the next. Their most recent killing had come on Silverstrike, a distant mining world. Marx was an avid hunter who had brought trophies back from half a dozen worlds, the Desmonds had always wanted to go on safari, and Pollard, who would have preferred a few weeks on Calliope or one of the other pleasure planets, finally agreed to come along so that the four of them could celebrate their latest billion together.

I took an instant dislike to Marx, who was too macho by half. Still, that wasn't a problem; I wasn't being paid to enjoy his company, just to find him a couple of prize trophies that would look good on his wall, and he seemed competent enough.

The Desmonds were an interesting pair. She was a pretty woman who went out of her way to look plain, even severe; a well-read woman who insisted on quoting everything she'd read, which made you wonder which she enjoyed more, reading in private or quoting in public. Philemon, her husband, was a mousy little man who drank too much, drugged too much, smoked too much, seemed in awe of his wife, and actually wore a tiny medal he'd won in a school track meet some thirty years earlier—probably a futile attempt to impress Mrs. Desmond, who remained singularly unimpressed.

Pollard was just a quiet, unassuming guy who'd lucked into money and didn't pretend to be any more sophisticated than he was—which, in my book, made him considerably more sophisticated than his partners. He seemed constantly amazed that they had actually talked him into coming along. He'd packed remedies for sunburn, diarrhea, insect bites, and half a hundred other things that could befall him, and jokingly worried about losing what he called his prison pallor.

We met on Braxton II, our regional headquarters, then took off on the six-day trip to Dodgson IV. All four of them elected to undergo DeepSleep, so Captain Mbele and I put them in their pods as soon as we hit light speeds, and woke them about two hours before we landed.

They were starving—I know the feeling; DeepSleep slows the metabolism to a crawl, but of course it doesn't stop it or you'd be dead, and the first thing you want to do when you wake up is eat—so Mbele shagged the Dabihs out of the galley, where they spent most of their time, and had it prepare a meal geared to human tastes. As soon as they finished eating, they began asking questions about Dodgson IV.

"We've been in orbit for the past hour, while the ship's computer has been compiling a detailed topographical map of the planet," I explained. "We'll land as soon as I find the best location for the base camp."

"So what's this world like?" asked Desmond, who had obviously failed to read all the data we'd sent to him.

"I've never set foot on it," I replied. "No one has." I smiled. "That's why you're paying so much."

"How do we know there's any game to be found there, then?" asked Marx pugnaciously.

"There's game, all right," I assured him. "The Pioneer who charted it claims her sensors pinpointed four species of carnivore and lots of herbivores, including one that goes about four tons."

"But she never landed?" he persisted.

"She had no reason to," I said. "There was no sign of sentient life, and there are millions of worlds out there still to be charted."

"She'd damned well better have been right about the animals," grumbled Marx. "I'm not paying this much to look at a bunch of trees and flowers."

"I've hunted three other oxygen worlds that Karen Dodgson charted," I said, "and they've always delivered what she promised."

"Do people actually hunt on chlorine and ammonia worlds?" asked Pollard.

"A few. It's a highly specialized endeavor. If you want to know more about it after the safari is over, I'll put you in touch with the right person back at headquarters."

"I've hunted a couple of chlorine worlds," interjected Marx.

Sure you have, I thought.

"Great sport," he added.

When you have to live with your client for a few weeks or months, you don't call him a braggart and a liar to his face, but you do file the information away for future reference.

"This Karen Dodgson—she's the one the planet's named for?" asked Ramona Desmond.

"It's a prerogative of the Pioneer Corps," I answered. "The one who charts a world gets to name it anything he or she wants." I paused and smiled. "They're not known for their modesty. Usually they name it after themselves."

"Dodgson," she said again. "Perhaps we'll find a Jabberwock, or a Cheshire Cat, or even a Snark."

"I beg your pardon?" I said.

"That's was Lewis Carroll's real name: Charles Dodgson."

"I've never heard of him," I replied.

"He wrote *Jabberwocky* and *The Hunting of the Snark,* along with the Alice books." She stared at me. "Surely you're read them."

"I'm afraid not."

"No matter," she said with a shrug. "It was just a joke. Not a very funny one."

In retrospect, I wish we'd found a Jabberwock.

"Just the place for a Snark!" the Bellman cried,
As he landed his crew with care;
Supporting each man on the top of the tide
By a finger entwined in his hair.

Dodgson IV was lush and green, with huge rolling savannahs, thick forests with trees growing hundreds of feet high, lots of large inland lakes, a trio of freshwater oceans, an atmosphere slightly richer than Galactic Standard, and a gravity that was actually a shade lighter than Standard.

While the Dabihs were setting up camp and erecting the self-contained safari Bubbles near the ship, I sent Chajinka off to collect possible foodstuffs, then took them to the ship's lab for analysis. It was even better than I'd hoped.

"I've got good news," I announced when I clambered back out of the ship. "There are at least seventeen edible plant species. The bark of those trees with the golden blossoms is also edible. The water's not totally safe, but it's close enough so that if we irradiate it it'll be just fine."

"I didn't come here to eat fruits and berries or whatever the hell Blue Boy found out there," said Marx gruffly. "Let's go hunting."

"I think it would be better for you and your friends to stay in camp for a day while Chajinka and I scout out the territory and see what's out there. Just unwind from the trip and get used to the atmosphere and the gravity."

"Why?" asked Desmond. "What's the difference if we go out today or tomorrow?"

"Once I see what we're up against, I'll be able to tell you which weapons to take. And while we know there are carnivores, we have no idea whether they're diurnal or nocturnal or both. No sense spending all day looking for a trophy that only comes out at night."

"I hadn't thought of that." Desmond shrugged. "You're the boss."

I took Captain Mbele aside and suggested he do what he could to keep them amused—tell them stories of past safaris, make them drinks, do whatever he could to entertain them while Chajinka and I did a little reconnoitering and learned what we'd be up against.

"It looks pretty normal to me," said Mbele. "A typical primitive world."

"The sensors say there's a huge biomass about two miles west of here," I replied. "With that much meat on the hoof, there should be a lot of predators. I want to see what they can do before I take four novices into the bush."

"Marx brags about all the safaris he's been on," complained Mbele. "Why not take the Great White Hunter with you?"

"Nice try," I said. "But I make the decisions once we're on the ground. You're stuck with him."

"Thanks a lot."

"Maybe he's been on other safaris, but he's a novice on Dodgson IV, and as far as I'm concerned that's all that counts."

"Well, if it comes to that, so are you."

"I'm getting paid to risk my life. He's paying for me to make sure he gets his trophies and doesn't risk *his*." I looked around. "Where the hell did Chajinka sneak off to?"

"I think he's helping the cook."

"He's got his own food," I said irritably. "He doesn't need ours." I turned in the direction of the cooking Bubble and shouted: "Chajinka, get your blue ass over here!"

The Dabih looked up at the sound of my voice, smiled, and pointed to his ears.

"Then get your goddamned t-pack!" I said. "We've got work to do."

He smiled again, wandered off, and returned a moment later with his spear and his t-pack, the translating mechanism that allowed Man and Dabih (actually, Man and just about anything, with the proper programming) to converse with one another in Terran.

"Ugly little creature," remarked Mbele, indicating Chajinka.

"I didn't pick him for his looks."

"Is he really that good?"

"The little bastard could track a billiard ball down a crowded highway," I replied. "And he's got more guts than most Men I know."

"You don't say," said Mbele in tones that indicated he still considered Dabihs one step up—if that—from the animals we had come to hunt.

"His form is ungainly—his intellect small—"
(So the Bellman would often remark)—
"But his courage is perfect! And that, after all,
Is the thing that one needs with a Snark."

I'm not much for foot-slogging when transportation is available, but it was going to take the Dabihs at least a day to assemble the safari vehicle and there was no sense hanging around camp waiting for it. So off we went, Chajinka and me, heading due west toward a water hole the computer had mapped. We weren't out to shoot anything, just to see what there was and what kind of weaponry our clients would need when we went out hunting the next morning.

It took us a little more than an hour to reach the water hole, and once there we hid behind some heavy bush about fifty yards away from it. There was a small herd of brown-and-white herbivores slaking their thirst, and as they left, a pair of huge red animals, four or five tons apiece, came down to drink. Then there were four or five more small herds of various types of grass-eaters. I had just managed to get comfortable when I heard a slight scrabbling noise. I turned and saw Chajinka pick up a slimy five-inch green worm, study its writhing body for a moment, then pop it into his mouth and swallow it. He appeared thoughtful for a moment, as if savoring the taste, then nodded his head in approval, and began looking for more.

Once upon a time that would have disgusted me, but I'd been with Chajinka for more than a decade and I was used to his eating habits. I kept looking for predators, and finally asked if he'd spotted any.

He waited for the t-pack to translate, then shook his head. "Night eaters, maybe," he whispered back.

"I never saw a world where *all* the carnivores were nocturnal," I answered. "There have to be some diurnal hunters, and this is the spot they should be concentrating on."

"Then where are they?"

"You're the tracker," I said. "You tell me."

He sighed deeply—a frightening sound if you're not used to Dabihs. A few of the animals at the water hole spooked and ran off thirty or forty yards, raising an enormous cloud of reddish dust. When they couldn't spot where the noise had come from, they warily returned to finish drinking.

"You wait here," he whispered. "I will find the predators."

I nodded my agreement. I'd watched Chajinka stalk animals on a hundred worlds, and I knew that I'd just be a hindrance. He could travel as silently as any predator, and he could find cover where I would swear none existed. If he had to freeze, he could stand or squat motionless for up to fifteen minutes. If an insect was crawling across his face, he wouldn't even shut an eye if it was in the insect's path. So maybe he regarded worms and insects as delicacies, and maybe he had only the vaguest notion of personal hygiene, but in his element— and we were in it now—there was no one of any species better suited for the job.

I sat down, adjusted my contact lenses to Telescopic, and scanned the horizon for the better part of ten minutes, going through a couple of smokeless cigarettes in the process. Lots of animals, all herbivores, came by to drink. Almost too many, I decided, because at this rate the water hole would be nothing but a bed of mud in a few days.

I was just about to start on a third cigarette when Chajinka was beside me again, tapping me on the shoulder.

"Come with me," he said.

"You found something?"

He didn't answer, but straightened up and walked out into the open, making no attempt to hide his presence. The animals at the water hole began bleating and bellowing in panic and raced off, some low to the ground, some zigzagging with every stride, and some with enormous leaps. Soon all of them vanished in the thick cloud of dust they had raised.

I followed him for about half a mile, and then we came to it: a dead catlike animal, obviously a predator. It had a tan pelt, and I estimated its weight at 300 pounds. It had the teeth of a killer, and its front and back claws were clearly made for rending the flesh of its prey. Its broad tail was covered with bony spikes. It was too muscular to be built for sustained speed, but its powerful shoulders and haunches looked deadly efficient for short charges of up to one hundred yards.

"Dead maybe seven hours," said Chajinka. "Maybe eight."

I didn't mind that it was dead. I minded that its skull and body were crushed. And I especially minded that there'd been no attempt to eat it.

"Read the signs," I said. "Tell me what happened."

"Brown cat," said Chajinka, indicating the dead animal, "made a kill this morning. His stomach is still full. He was looking for a place to lie up, out of the sun. Something killed him."

"*What* killed him?"

He pointed to some oblong tracks, not much larger than a human's. "This one is the killer."

"Where did he go after he killed the brown cat?"

He examined the ground once more, then pointed to the northeast. "That way."

"Can we find him before dark?"

Chajinka shook his head. "He left a long time ago. Four, five, six hours."

"Let's go back to the water hole," I said. "I want you to see if he left any tracks there."

Our presence frightened yet another herd of herbivores away, and Chajinka examined the ground.

Finally he straightened up. "Too many animals have come and gone."

"Make a big circle around the water hole," I said. "Maybe a quarter mile. See if there are any tracks there."

He did as I ordered, and I fell into step behind him. We'd walked perhaps half the circumference when he stopped.

"Interesting," he said.

"What is?"

"There were brown cats here early this morning," he said, pointing to the ground. "Then the killer of the brown cat came along—you see, here, his print overlays that of a cat—and they fled." He paused. "An entire family of brown cats—at least four, perhaps five—fled from a single animal that hunts alone."

"You're sure he's a solitary hunter?"

He studied the ground again. "Yes. He walks alone. Very interesting."

It was more than interesting.

There was a lone animal out there that was higher on the food chain than the 300-pound brown cats. It had frightened away an entire pod of large predators, and—this was the part I didn't like—it didn't kill just for food.

Hunters read signs, and they listen to their trackers, but mostly they tend to trust their instincts. We'd been on Dodgson IV less than five hours, and I was already getting a bad feeling.

"I kind of expected you'd be bringing back a little something exotic for dinner," remarked Jaxon Pollard when we returned to camp.

"Or perhaps a trophy," chimed in Ramona Desmond.

"I've got enough trophies, and you'll want to shoot your own."

"You don't sound like a very enthusiastic hunter," she said.

"You're paying to do the hunting," I replied. "My job is to back you up and step in if things get out of hand. As far as I'm concerned, the ideal safari is one on which I don't fire a single shot."

"Sounds good to me," said Marx. "What are we going after tomorrow?"

"I'm not sure."

"You're not sure?" he repeated. "What the hell were you doing all afternoon?"

"Scouting the area."

"This is like pulling teeth," complained Marx. "What did you find?"

"I think we may have found signs of Mrs. Desmond's Snark, for lack of a better name."

Suddenly everyone was interested.

"A Snark?" said Ramona Desmond delightedly. "What did it look like?"

"I don't know," I replied. "It's bipedal, but I've no idea how many limbs it has—probably four. More than that is pretty rare in large animals anywhere in the galaxy. Based on the depth of the tracks, Chajinka thinks it may go anywhere from 250 to 400 pounds."

"That's not so much," said Marx. "I've hunted bigger."

"I'm not through," I said. "In a land filled with game, it seems to have scared the other predators out of the area." I paused. "Well, actually, that could be a misstatement."

"You mean it hasn't scared them off?" asked Ramona, now thoroughly confused.

"No, they're gone. But I called them *other* predators, and I don't know for a fact that our Snark is a predator. He killed a huge, catlike creature, but he didn't eat it."

"What does that imply?" asked Ramona.

I shrugged. "I'm not sure. It could be that he was defending his territory. Or...." I let the sentence hang while I considered its implications.

"Or what?"

"Or he could simply enjoy killing things."

"That makes two of us," said Marx with a smile. "We'll go out and kill ourselves a Snark tomorrow morning."

"Not tomorrow," I said firmly.

"Why the hell not?" he asked pugnaciously.

"I make it a rule never to go after dangerous game until I know more about it than it knows about me," I answered. "Tomorrow we'll go out shooting meat for the pot and see if we can learn a little more about the Snark."

"I'm not paying millions of credits to shoot a bunch of cud-chewing alien cattle!" snapped Marx. "You've found something that practically screams 'Superb Hunting!' I vote that we go after it in the morning."

"I admire your enthusiasm and your courage, Mr. Marx," I said. "But this isn't a democracy. I've got the only vote that counts, and since it's my job to return you all safe and sound at the end of this safari, we're not going after the Snark until we know more about it."

He didn't say another word, but I could tell that at that moment he'd have been just as happy to shoot me as the Snark.

Before we set out the next morning, I inspected the party's weapons.

"Nice laser rifle," I said, examining Desmond's brand new pride and joy.

"It ought to be," he said. "It cost fourteen thousand credits. It's got night sights, a vision enhancer, an anti-shake stock...."

"Bring out your projectile rifle and your shotgun, too," I said. "We have to test all the weapons."

"But I'm only going to use *this* rifle," he insisted.

I almost hated to break the news to him.

"In my professional opinion, Dodgson IV has a B3 biosystem," I said. "I already registered my findings via subspace transmission from the ship last night." He looked confused. "For sport hunting purposes, that means you have to use a non-explosive-projectile weapon with a maximum of a .450 grain bullet until the classification is changed."

"But—"

"Look," I interrupted. "We have fusion grenades that can literally blow this planet apart. We have intelligent bullets that will find an animal at a distance of ten miles, respond to evasive maneuvering, and not contact the target until an instant kill is guaranteed. We've got molecular imploders that can turn an enemy brigade into jelly. Given the game we're after, none of them would qualify as sport hunting. I know, we're only talking about a laser rifle in your case, but you don't want to start off the safari by breaking the law, and I'm sure as a sportsman you want to give the animal an even break."

He looked dubious, especially about the even break part, but finally he went back to his Bubble and brought out the rest of his arsenal.

I gathered the four of them around me.

"Your weapons have been packed away for a week," I said. "Their settings may have been affected by the ship's acceleration, and this world's gravity is different, however minimally, from your own. So before we start, I want to give everyone a chance to adjust their sights." *And,* I added to myself, *let's see if any of you can hit a non-threatening target at 40 yards, just so I'll know what I'm up against.*

"I'll set up targets in the hollow down by the river," I continued, "and I'll ask you to come down one at a time." *No sense letting the poorer shots get humiliated in front of the better ones—always assuming there are any better ones.*

I took a set of the most basic targets out of the cargo hold. Once I reached the hollow, I placed four of them where I wanted them, activated the antigrav devices, and when they were gently bobbing and weaving about six feet above the ground, I called for Marx, who showed up a moment later.

"Okay, Mr. Marx," I said. "Have you adjusted your sights?"

"I *always* take care of my weapons," he said as if the question had been an insult.

"Then let's see what you can do."

He smiled confidently, raised his rifle, looked along the sights, pulled the trigger, and blew two targets to pieces, then repeated the procedure with his shotgun.

"Nice shooting," I said.

"Thanks," he replied with a look that said: *of course* I'm a crack shot. I told you so, didn't I?

Desmond was next. He raised his rifle to his shoulder, took careful aim, and missed, then missed three more times.

I took the rifle, lined up the sights, and fired. The bullet went high and to the right, burying itself in a tree trunk. I adjusted the sights and took another shot. This time I hit a target dead center.

"Okay, try it now," I said, handing the rifle back to Desmond.

He missed four more times. He missed sitting. He missed prone. He missed using a rest for the barrel. Then he tried the shotgun, and missed twice more before he finally nailed a target. Then, for good measure, he totally misused his laser rifle, trying to pinpoint the beam rather than sweep the area, and missed yet again. We were both relieved when his session ended.

His wife was a little better; she hit the target on her third try with the rifle and her second with the shotgun. She swept the area with her laser rifle, wiping out all the remaining targets.

Pollard should have been next, but he didn't show up, and I went back to camp to get him. He was sitting down with the others, sipping a cup of coffee.

"You're next, Mr. Pollard," I said.

"I'm just going to take holos," he replied, holding up his camera.

"You're sure, Jaxon?" asked Desmond.

"I don't think I'd enjoy killing things," he replied.

"Then what the hell are you doing here?" demanded Marx.

Pollard smiled. "I'm here because you nagged incessantly, Willard. Besides, I've never been on a safari before, and I enjoy taking holographs."

"All right," I said. "But I don't want you wandering more than twenty yards from me at any time."

"No problem," said Pollard. "I don't want *them* killing me any more than I want to kill *them*."

I told his gunbearer to stay behind and help with the camp and the cooking. You'd have thought I'd slapped him in the face, but he agreed to do as he was ordered.

We clambered into the vehicle and got to the water hole in about half an hour. Within five minutes Marx had coolly and efficiently brought down a pair of spiral-horned tan-and-brown herbivores with one bullet each. Then, exercising his right to name any species that he was the first to shoot, he dubbed them Marx's Gazelles.

"What now?" asked Desmond. "We certainly don't need any more meat for the next few days."

"I'll send the vehicle back to camp for the skinners. They'll bring back the heads and pelts as well as the best cuts of meat, and I'll have them tie the rest of the carcasses to some nearby trees."

"Why?"

"Bait," said Marx.

"Mr. Marx is right. *Something* will come along to feed on them. The smell of blood might bring the catlike predators back. Or, if we're lucky, maybe the Snark will come back and we'll be able to learn a little more about him."

"And what do *we* do in the meantime?" asked Desmond in petulant tones.

"It's up to you," I said. "We can stay here until the vehicle returns, we can march back to camp, or we can footslog to that swamp about four miles to the north and see if there's anything interesting up there."

"Like a Snark?" asked Ramona.

"Five Men and four Dabihs walking across four miles of open savannah aren't about to sneak up and surprise anything. But we're not part of the ecological system. None of the animals will be programmed to recognize us as predators, so there's always a chance—if he's there to begin with—that the Snark will stick around out of curiosity or just plain stupidity."

It was the answer they wanted to hear, so they decided to march to the swamp. Pollard must have taken fifty holos along the way. Desmond complained about the heat, the humidity, the terrain, and the insects. Ramona stuck a chip that read the text of a book into her ear and didn't utter a word until we reached the swamp. Marx just lowered his head and walked.

When we got there we came upon a small herd of herbivores, very impressive-looking beasts, going about 500 pounds apiece. The males possessed fabulous horns, perhaps 60 inches long, with a triple twist in them. The horns looked like they were made of crystal, and they acted as a prism, separating the sunlight into a series of tiny rainbows.

"My God, look at them!" said Pollard, taking holographs as fast as he could.

"They're magnificent!" whispered Ramona Desmond.

"I'd like one of those," said Marx, studying the herd.

"You took the gazelles," I noted. "Mr. Desmond has first shot."

"I don't want it," said Desmond nervously.

"All right," I said. "Mrs. Desmond, you have first shot."

"I'd never kill anything so beautiful," she replied.

"No," muttered Desmond so softly that she couldn't hear him. "You'd just throw them into jail."

"Then it's Mr. Marx's shot," I said. "I'd suggest you take the fellow on the far right. He doesn't have the longest horns, but he's got the best-matched set. Let's get a little closer." I turned to the others as Marx took his rifle from his gunbearer and loaded it. "You stay here."

I signaled to Chajinka to take a circuitous approach. Marx, displaying the proper crouching walk, followed him, and I brought up the rear. (A hunter learns early on *never* to get between a client and the game. Either that, or he keeps a prosthetic ear company in business.)

When we'd gotten to within thirty yards, I decided we were close enough and nodded to Marx. He slowly raised his rifle and took aim. I could tell he was going for a heart shot rather than take the chance of ruining the head. It was a good strategy, always assuming that the heart was where he thought it was.

Marx took a deep breath, let it out slowly, and began squeezing the trigger.

And just as he did so, a brilliantly colored avian flew past, shrieking wildly. The horned buck jumped, startled, just as Marx's rifle exploded. The rest of the herd bolted in all directions at the sound of the shot, and before Marx could get off a second shot the buck bellowed in pain, spun around, and vanished into the nearby bush.

"Come on!" said Marx excitedly, jumping up and running after the buck. "I know I hit him! He won't get far!"

I grabbed him as he hurtled past. "You're not going anywhere, Mr. Marx!"

"What are you talking about?" he demanded.

"There's a large dangerous wounded animal in the bush," I said. "I can't let you go in after it."

"I'm as good a shot as you are!" he snapped. "It was just a fluke that that goddamned bird startled it. You know that!"

"Look," I said. "I'm not thrilled going into heavy bush after a wounded animal that's carrying a pair of five-foot swords on its head, but that's what I get paid to do. I can't look for him and keep an eye on you as well."

"But—"

"You say you've been on safari before," I said. "That means you know the rules."

He muttered and he cursed, but he *did* know the rules, and he rejoined the rest of the party while Chajinka and I vanished into the bush in search of our wounded prey.

The swamp smelled of rotting vegetation. We followed the blood spoor on leaves and bushes through two hundred yards of mud that sucked at the Dabih's feet and my boots, and then, suddenly, it vanished. I saw a little hillock a few yards off to the right, where the grass was crushed flat, small branches were broken, and flowers were broken off their stems. Chajinka studied the signs for a full minute, then looked up.

"The Snark," he said.

"What are you talking about?"

"He was hiding, watching us," answered Chajinka. He pointed to the ground. "The wounded animal lay down here. You see the blood? The Snark was over there. Those are his tracks. When the animal lay down, the Snark saw it was too weak to get up again, but still danger-ous. He circled behind it. See—here is where he went. Then he leaped upon it and killed it."

"How?"

Chajinka shrugged. "I cannot tell. But he lifted it and carried it off."

"*Could* he lift an animal that big?"

"He did."

"He can't be more that a few hundred yards ahead of us," I said. "What do you think? Can we catch up with him?"

"You and I? Yes."

Every now and then, when my blood was up, Chajinka had to remind me that I wasn't hunting for my own pleasure. Yes, was the implication, he and I could catch up with the Snark. Marx might not be a hindrance. But there was no way we could take Pollard and the Desmonds through the swamp, keep an eye out for predators, and hope to make up any ground on the Snark—and of course I couldn't leave them alone while we went after the Snark with Marx.

"All right," I said with a sigh. "Let's get back and tell them what happened."

Marx went ballistic. He ranted and cursed for a good three minutes, and by the end of it I felt he was ready to declare a blood feud against this trophy thief.

When he finally calmed down, I left Chajinka behind to see if he could learn anything more about the Snark while the rest of us began marching back to the water hole, where the vehicle was waiting for us.

"We have sailed many months, we have sailed many weeks,
(Four weeks to the month you may mark),
But never as yet ('tis your Captain who speaks)
Have we caught the least glimpse of a Snark!"

Mbele had himself a good laugh when we got back to camp, hot and tired and hungry.

"You keep talking about the Snark as if it exists!" he said in amusement. "It's an imaginary beast in a children's poem."

"Snark is just a convenient name for it," I said. "We can call it anything you like."

"Call it absent," he said. "No one's seen it."

"Right," I said. "And I suppose when you close your eyes, the whole galaxy vanishes."

"I never thought about it," admitted Mbele. "But it probably does." He paused thoughtfully. "At least, I certainly hope so. It makes me feel necessary."

"Look!" I exploded. "There's a dead 300-pound killer cat out there, and a missing antelope that was even bigger!" I glared at him. "*I* didn't kill one and steal the other. Did *you?*"

He swallowed his next rejoinder and gave me a wide berth for the rest of the day.

Chajinka trotted into camp the next morning and signaled to me. I walked over and joined him.

"Did you learn anything?" I asked.

"It is an interesting animal," he said.

I grimaced, for as everyone knows, the Dabihs are masters of understatement.

"Come, listen, my men, while I tell you again
The five unmistakable marks
By which you may know, wheresoever you go,
The warranted genuine Snarks."

I gathered the hunting party around me.

"Well," I announced, "we know a little more about the Snark now than we did yesterday." I paused to watch their reactions. Everyone except Desmond seemed interested; Desmond looked like he wished he were anywhere else.

"Chajinka has been to the tree where we tied the dead meat animals," I continued.

"And?" said Marx.

"The ropes were untied. Not cut or torn apart or bitten through; untied. So we know that the Snark either has fingers, or some damned effective appendages. And some meat was missing from the carcasses."

"All right," said Ramona. "We know he can untie knots. What else?"

"We know he's a carnivore," I said. "We weren't sure about that yesterday."

"So what?" asked Marx. "There are millions of carnivores in the galaxy. Nothing unique about that."

"It means he won't stray far from the game herds. They're his supermarket."

"Maybe he only has to eat once every few months," said Marx, unimpressed.

"No," I said. "That's the third thing we've learned: he's got to eat just about as often as we do."

"How do we know that?" asked Ramona.

"According to Chajinka, he approached the meat very cautiously, but his tracks show that he trotted away once he'd eaten his fill. The trail disappeared after a mile, but we know that he trotted that whole distance."

"Ah!" said Ramona. "I see."

"I sure as hell don't," complained her husband.

"Anything that can sustain that pace, that kind of drain on its energy, has to eat just about every day." I paused. "And we know a fourth thing."

"What is that?" she asked.

"He's not afraid of us," I said. "He had to know we were the ones who killed those meat animals. Our tracks and scent were all over the place, and of course there were the ropes. He knows that we're a party of at least nine—five, if you discount Chajinka and the three gunbearers, and he has no reason to discount them. And yet, hours after learning all that, he hasn't left the area." I paused. "That leads to a fifth conclusion. He's not very bright; he didn't understand that Marx's gun was what wounded the animal he killed yesterday—because if he realized we could kill from a distance, he'd *be* afraid of us."

"You deduce all that just from a few tracks and the signs that Chajinka saw?" asked Desmond skeptically.

"Reading signs and interpreting what they mean is what hunting's all about," I explained. "Shooting is just the final step."

"So do we go after him now?" asked Marx eagerly.

I shook my head. "I've already sent Chajinka back out to see if he can find the creature's lair. If he's like most carnivores, he'll want to lie up after he eats. If we know where to look for him, we'll save a lot of time and effort. It makes more sense to wait for Chajinka to report back, and then go after the Snark in the morning."

"It seems so odd," said Ramona. "We've never seen this creature, and yet we've already reasoned out that he's incredibly formidable."

"Of course he's formidable," I said.

"You say that as if *everything* is formidable," she said with a condescending smile.

"That's the first axiom on safari," I replied. "Everything bites."

"If this thing is as dangerous as you make it seem," said Desmond hesitantly, "are we permitted to use more…well, sophisticated weapons?"

"Show a little guts, Philemon," said Marx contemptuously.

"I'm a banker, not a goddamned Allan Quatermain!" shot back Desmond.

"If you're afraid, stay in camp," said Marx. "Me, I can't wait to get him in my sights."

"You didn't answer my question, Mr. Bell," persisted Desmond.

Mbele pulled out the Statute Book and began reading aloud. "Unless, in the hunter's judgment, the weapons you are using are inadequate for killing the prey, you must use the weapons that have been approved for the world in question."

"So if he presents a serious threat, we can use pulse guns and molecular imploders and the like?"

"Have you ever seen a molecular imploder in action?" I asked. "Aim it at a 50-story building and you turn the whole thing into pudding in about three seconds."

"What about pulse guns?" he persisted.

"There's not a lot of trophy left when one of those babies hit the target," I said.

"We need *something*, damn it!" whined Desmond.

"We have more than enough firepower to bring down any animal on this planet," I said, getting annoyed with him. "I don't mean to be blunt, but there's a difference between an inadequate hunter and an inadequate weapon."

"You can say that again!" muttered Marx.

"That was *very* blunt, Mr. Bell," said Desmond, getting up and walking to his Bubble. His wife stared at him expressionlessly, then pulled out her book and began reading.

"That's what you get for being honest," said Marx, making no attempt to hide his amusement. "I just hope this Snark is half the creature you make it out to be."

I'll settle for half, I thought uneasily.

Chajinka, who was sitting on the hood of the safari vehicle, raised his spear, which was my signal to stop.

He jumped down, bent over, examined the grasses for a few seconds, then trotted off to his left, eyes glued to the ground.

I climbed out and grabbed my rifle.

"You wait here," I said to the four humans. The Dabih gunbearers, who clung to handles and footholds on the back of the vehicle when it was moving, had released their grips and were now standing just behind it.

"Whose shot it is?" asked Marx.

"Let me think," I said. "You shot that big buck yesterday, and Mrs. Desmond killed the boar-like thing with the big tusks just before that. So Mr. Desmond has the first shot today."

"I'm not getting out of the vehicle," said Desmond.

"It's against regulations to shoot from the safety of the vehicle," I pointed out.

"Fuck your regulations and fuck you!" hollered Desmond. "I don't want the first shot! I don't want *any* shot! I don't even know what the hell I'm doing on this stupid safari!"

"Goddammit, Philemon!" hissed Marx fiercely.

"What is it?" asked Desmond, startled.

"If there was anything there, Mr. Desmond," I explained, trying to control my temper, "you just gave it more than ample reason to run hell for leather in the opposite direction. You *never* yell during a hunt."

I walked away in disgust and joined Chajinka beneath a small tree. He was standing beside a young dead herbivore whose skull had been crushed.

"Snark," he said, pointing to the skull.

"When?" I asked.

He pulled back the dead animal's lips to examine its gums, felt the inside of its ears, examined other parts for a few seconds.

"Five hours," he said. "Maybe six."

"The middle of the night."

"Yes."

> *"Its habit of getting up late you'll agree*
> *That it carries too far, when I say*
> *That it frequently breakfasts at five-o'clock tea,*
> *And dines on the following day."*

"Can you pick up his trail?" I asked Chajinka.

He looked around, then gave the Dabih equivalent of a frown. "It vanishes," he said at last, pointing to a spot ten feet away.

"You mean some animals obliterated his tracks after he made them?"

He shrugged. "No tracks at all. Not his, not anyone's."

"Why not?"

He had no answer.

I stared at the ground for a long moment. "Okay," I said at last. "Let's get back to the vehicle."

He resumed his customary position on the hood, while I sat behind the control panel and thought.

"Well?" asked Marx. "Did it have something to do with the Snark?"

"Yeah," I said, still puzzled by the absence of any tracks. "He made a kill during the night. His prey was an animal built for what I would call evasive maneuvering. That means he's got excellent nocturnal vision and good motor skills."

"So he's a night hunter?" asked Ramona.

"No, I wouldn't say that," I replied. "He killed the crystal-horned buck at midday, so like most predators he's also an opportunist; when a meal is there for the taking, he grabs it. Anyway, if we can't find his lair, we're probably going to have to build a blind, sit motionless with our guns, hang some fresh bait every evening, and hope it interests him."

"That's not *real* hunting!" scoffed Marx.

"There's no way we can go chasing after him in the dark," I responded.

"I'm not chasing *anything* in the dark!" said Desmond adamantly. "You want to do it, you do it without me."

"Don't be such a coward!" said Marx.

"Fuck you, Willard!" Desmond retorted.

"Bold words," said Marx. "Why don't you take some of that bravery and aim it at the animals?"

"I hate it here!" snapped Desmond. "I think we should go back to camp."

"And do what?" asked Marx sarcastically.

"And consider our options," he replied. "It's a big planet. Maybe we could take off and land on one of the other continents—one without any Snarks on it."

"Nonsense!" said Marx. "We came here to hunt big game. Well, now we've found it."

"I don't know *what* we've found," said Desmond, halfway between anger and panic, "and neither do you."

"That's what makes it such good sport and so exciting," said Marx.

"Exciting is watching sports on the holo," Desmond shot back. "*This* is *dangerous*."

"Same damned thing," muttered Marx.

We spent the next two days searching unsuccessfully for any sign of the Snark. For a while I thought he had moved out of the area and considered moving our base camp, but then Chajinka found some relatively fresh tracks, perhaps three hours old. So we didn't move the camp after all—but we also didn't find the creature.

Then, on the third afternoon of the search, as we were taking a break, sitting in the shade of a huge tree with purple and gold flowers, we heard a strange sound off in the distance.

"Thunder?" asked Marx.

"Doesn't seem likely," replied Pollard. "There's not a cloud in the sky."

"Well, it's *something*," continued Marx.

Ramona frowned. "And it's getting closer. Well, louder, anyway."

On a hunch, I set my lenses to Telescopic, and it was a damned lucky thing I did.

"*Everybody! Up into the tree—fast!*" I shouted.

"But—"

"No arguments! Get going!"

They weren't the most agile tree-climbers I'd ever encountered, but when they were finally able to see what I had seen, they managed to get clear of the ground in one hell of a hurry. A minute later a few thousand Marx's Gazelles thundered past.

I waited for the dust to settle, then lowered myself to the ground and scanned the horizon.

"Okay, it's safe to come down now," I announced.

"Why didn't we climb into the vehicle?" asked Ramona, getting out of the tree and checking her hands for cuts.

"It's an open vehicle, Mrs. Desmond," I pointed out. "You could have wound up with a fractured skull as they jumped over it—or with a gazelle in your lap if one of them was a poor jumper."

"Point taken."

"What the hell would cause something like that?" asked Pollard, staring after the stampeding herd as he brushed himself off.

"I'd say a predator made a sloppy kill, or maybe blew one entirely."

"How do you figure that?"

"Because this is the first time we've seen a stampede…so we can assume that when they're killed quickly and efficiently, the gazelles just move out of the predator's range and then go back to grazing. It's when the predator misses his prey, or wounds it, and then races after it into the middle of the herd that they panic."

"You think it's one of the big cats?" asked Pollard.

"It's possible."

"I'd love to get some holos of those cats on a kill."

"You may get your wish, Mr. Pollard," I said. "We'll backtrack to where the stampede started and hope we get lucky."

"That suits me just fine," said Marx, patting his rifle.

We headed southwest in the vehicle until the terrain became too rough, then left it behind and started walking as the landscape changed from hilly and tree-covered to heavily forested. Chajinka trotted ahead of us, eyes on the ground, spotting things even I couldn't see, and finally he came to a stop.

"What it is?" I asked, catching up with him.

He pointed straight ahead into the dense foliage. "He is there."

"He?"

"The Snark," he said, pointing to a single track.

"How deep is the cover?" I asked. "How do you know he didn't run right through it?"

He pointed to the bushes, which were covered with thorns. "He cannot run through this without pain."

"You've never seen him," said Ramona, joining us. "How do you know?"

"If it did not rip his flesh, he would be a forest creature, created by God to live here," answered Chajinka, as if explaining it to a child. "But we know that he hunts plains game. A forest dweller with thick, heavy skin and bones could not move swiftly enough. So this is not his home—it is his hiding place."

I thought there was a good chance that it was more than his hiding place, that it could very well be his fortress. It was damned near impenetrable, and the forest floor was covered with dry leaves, so no one was going to sneak up on him without giving him plenty of warning.

"What are we waiting for?" asked Marx, approaching with Desmond. He stopped long enough to take his rifle from his gunbearer.

"We're waiting until I can figure out the best way to go about it," I responded.

"We walk in and blow him away," said Marx. "What's so hard about that?"

I shook my head. "This is *his* terrain. He knows every inch of it. You're going to make a lot of noise walking in there, and the way the upper terraces of the trees are intertwined, I've got a feeling that it could be dark as night 600 yards into the forest."

"So we'll use infrared scopes on our guns," said Marx.

I kept staring at the thick foliage. "I don't like it," I said. "He's got every advantage."

"But *we've* got the weapons," persisted Marx.

"With minimal visibility and maneuverability, they won't do you much good."

"Bullshit!" spat Marx. "We're wasting time. Let's go in after him."

"The four of you are my responsibility," I replied. "I can't risk your safety by letting you go in there. Within a couple of minutes you could be out of touch with me and with each other. You'll be making noise with every step you take, and if I'm right about the light, before long you could be standing right next to him without seeing him. And we haven't explored any Dodgson forests yet—he might not be the only danger. There could be everything from arboreal killer cats to poisonous insects to 50-foot-long snakes with an attitude."

"So what do you propose?" asked Marx.

"A blind makes the most sense," I said. "But it could take half a day to build one, and who the hell knows where he'll be by then?" I paused. "All right. The three of you with weapons will spread out. Mr. Pollard, stand well behind them. Chajinka and I will go into the bush and try to flush him out."

"I thought you said it was too dangerous," said Ramona.

"Let me amend that," I answered. "It's too dangerous for amateurs."

"If there's a chance that he can harm you, why don't we just forget about it?" she continued.

"I appreciate your concern," I began, "but—"

"I'm not being totally altruistic. What happens to us if he kills you?"

"You'll return to base camp and tell Mbele what happened. He'll radio a subspace message to headquarters, and Silinger & Mahr will decide whether to give you a refund or take you to another planet with a new hunter."

"You make it sound so...so businesslike," she said distastefully.

"It's my business," I replied.

"Why did you ever become a hunter?"

I shrugged. "Why did you become a judge?"

"I have a passion for order," she said.

"So do I," I replied.

"You find order in killing things?"

"I find order in nature. Death is just a part of it." I paused. "Now, Mr. Marx," I said, turning back to him, "I want you to..."

He wasn't there.

"Where the hell did he go?" I demanded.

No one seemed to know, not even Chajinka. Then his gunbearer approached me.

"Boss, Marx went *there*." He pointed to the forest, then ruefully held up the backup rifle. "He did not wait for me."

"*Shit!*" I muttered. "It's bad enough that I've got to go in after the Snark! Now I stand a hell of a good chance of getting blown away by that macho bastard!"

"Why would he shoot you?" asked Ramona.

"He'll hear me before he sees me," I answered. "He's running on adrenaline. He'll be sure I'm the Snark."

"Then stay out here."

"I wish I could," I said truthfully. "But it's my job to protect him whether he wants me to or not."

That particular argument became academic about five seconds later, when we heard a shot, and then a long, agonized scream.

A *human* scream.

"You two stand about 200 yards apart," I said to the Desmonds. "Shoot anything that comes out of there that doesn't look like me or a Dabih!" Then, to Chajinka: "Let's go!"

The Dabih led the way into the forest. Then, as it started getting thicker and darker, we lost Marx's trail. "We're more likely to find him if we split up," I whispered. "You go left, I'll go right."

I kept my gun at the ready, wishing I'd inserted my infrared lenses into my eyes that morning. After a minute I couldn't hear Chajinka anymore, which meant when I finally heard footsteps I was going to have to hold my fire until I could tell whether it was the Dabih or the Snark.

It's no secret that hunters hate going into the bush after a wounded animal. Well, let me tell you something: going into the bush after an *un*wounded animal is even less appealing. Sweat ran down into my eyes, insects crawled inside my shoes and socks and up my shirtsleeves, and my gun seemed to have tripled in weight. I could barely see ten feet in front of me, and if Marx had yelled for help from 50 yards away, I probably would be five minutes locating him.

But Marx was past yelling for help. I was suddenly able to make out the figure of a man lying on the ground. I approached him cautiously, seeing Snarks—whatever they looked like—behind every tree.

Finally I reached him and knelt down to examine him. His throat had been slashed open, and his innards were pouring out of a gaping hole in his belly. He was probably dead before he hit the ground.

"*Chajinka!*" I hollered. There was no response.

I called his name every thirty seconds, and finally, after about five minutes, I heard a body shuffling through the thick bush, its translated, monotone voice saying, "Don't shoot! Don't shoot!"

"Get over here!" I said.

He joined me a moment later. "Snark," he said, looking at Marx's corpse.

"For sure?" I asked.

"For sure."

"All right," I said. "Help me carry his body back out of here."

Then, suddenly, we heard two rifle shots.

"Damn!" I bellowed. "He's broken out!"

"Perhaps he will be dead," said Chajinka, leading the way back out of the forest. "There were two shots."

When we finally got into the open, we found Philemon Desmond sitting on the ground, hyperventilating, his whole body shaking. Ramona and Pollard stood a few yards away, staring at him—she with open contempt, he with a certain degree of sympathy.

"What happened?" I demanded.

"He burst out of the woods and came right at me!" said Desmond in a shaky voice.

"We heard two shots. Did you hit him?"

"I don't think so." He began shaking all over. "No, I definitely didn't."

"How the hell could you miss?" I shouted. "He couldn't have been twenty yards away!"

"I've never killed anything before!" Desmond yelled back.

I scanned the hilly countryside. There was no sign of the Snark, and there had to be a good five hundred hiding places just within my field of vision.

"Wonderful!" I muttered. "Just wonderful!"

The Bellman looked uffish, and wrinkled his brow.
"If only you'd spoken before!
It's excessively awkward to mention it now,
With the Snark, so to speak, at the door!"

We dragged Marx's body out of the forest and loaded it into the back of the safari vehicle.

"My God!" whined Desmond. "He's dead! He was the only one of us who knew the first damned thing about hunting, and he's dead! We've got to get out of here!"

"He was also a friend," said Ramona. "You might spare a little of your self-pity for *him*."

"Ramona!" said Pollard harshly.

"I'm sorry," she said with a total lack of sincerity.

Pollard had been staring at Marx's body since we brought it out of the forest. "Jesus, he's a mess!" he said at last. "Did he suffer much?"

111

"No," I assured him. "Not with wounds like those—he would have gone into shock immediately."

"Well, we can be thankful for that, I suppose," said Pollard. He finally tore his eyes away from the body and turned to me. "What now?"

"Now it's not a matter of sport anymore," I said, morbidly wondering whether the authorities would revoke my license for losing a client, or simply suspend it. "He's killed one of us. He's got to die."

"I thought that was the whole purpose of the safari."

"The purpose was a sporting stalk, with the odds all on the game's side. Now the purpose is to kill him as quickly and efficiently as we can."

"That sounds like revenge," noted Ramona.

"Practicality," I corrected her. "Now that he knows how easy it is to kill an armed man, we don't want him to get into the habit."

"How do you stop him?"

"There are ways," I said. "I'll use every trick I know—and I know a lifetime's worth of them—before he has a chance to kill again." I paused. "Now, so I'll know which traps to set, I want you to tell me what he actually looks like."

"Like a huge red ape with big glaring eyes," said Pollard.

"No," said Ramona. "He looked more like a brown bear, but with longer legs."

"He was sleek," offered Pollard.

Ramona disagreed again. "No, he was shaggy."

"Wonderful," I muttered. "I trust you at least took a couple of holos, Mr. Pollard?"

He shook his head. "I was so surprised when he burst out of there that I totally forgot the camera," he admitted shamefacedly.

"Well, that's an enormous help," I said disgustedly. I turned to Desmond. "How about you?"

"I don't know," he whimpered. Suddenly he shuddered. "He looked like Death!"

"You must forgive Philemon," said Ramona, with an expression that said *she* wasn't about to forgive him. "He's really very good at investments and mergers and even hostile takeovers. He's just not very competent at *physical* things." She patted his medal. "Except running."

Marx had a wife and three grown children back on Roosevelt III, and his friends felt sure they'd want him shipped home, so we put his body in a vacuum container and stuck it in the cargo hold.

After that was done, Chajinka and I went to work. We set seven traps, then went back to camp and waited.

Early the next morning we went out to see what we'd accomplished.

That was when I learned that the Snark had a sardonic sense of humor.

Each of the traps contained a dead animal. But lest we mistakenly think that *we* had anything to do with it, each one had its head staved in.

The son of a bitch was actually mocking us.

> *"For the Snark's a peculiar creature, that won't*
> *Be caught in a commonplace way.*
> *Do all that you know, and try all that you don't:*
> *Not a chance must be wasted today!"*

I awoke the next morning to the sound of vaguely familiar alien jabbering. It took me a minute to clear my head and identify what I was hearing. Then I raced out of my Bubble and almost bumped into Chajinka, who was running to meet me.

"What's going on?" I demanded.

He responded in his native tongue.

"Where's your t-pack?" I asked.

He jabbered at me. I couldn't understand a word of it.

Finally he pulled me over to the area where the Dabihs ate and slept, and pointed to the shapeless pile of metal and plastic and computer chips. Sometime during the night the Snark had silently entered the camp and destroyed all the t-packs.

I kept wondering: was he just lucky in his choice, or could he possibly have *known* how much we needed them?

Mbele, awakened by the same sounds, quickly emerged from his Bubble.

"What the hell is going on?" he asked.

"See for yourself," I said.

"Jesus!" he said. "Can any of the Dabihs speak Terran?"

I shook my head. "If they could, they wouldn't need t-packs, would they?"

"Was it the Snark?"

I grimaced. "Who else?"

"So what do you do now?"

"First, I try to figure out whether it was mischief or malice, and whether he had any idea what havoc it would cause."

"You think he might be a little smarter than your average bear in the woods?"

"I don't know. He lives like an animal, he acts like an animal, and he hunts like an animal. But in a short space of time he's killed Marx, and he's seen to it that the five remaining Men can't communicate with the twelve Dabihs." I forced a wry smile to my mouth. "That's not bad for a dumb animal, is it?"

"You'd better wake the others and let them know what's happened," said Mbele.

"I know," I said. I kicked one of the broken t-packs up against a tree. "Shit!"

I woke the Desmonds and Pollard and told them what had occurred. I thought Philemon Desmond might faint. The others were a little more useful.

"How long ago did this happen?" asked Pollard.

"Chajinka could probably give you a more accurate estimate, but I can't speak to him. My best guess is about two hours."

"So if we go after him, he's two hours ahead of us?"

"That's right."

"We'd better kill him quickly," said Ramona. "He could come back any time, now that he knows where our camp is."

"Give me a laser rifle," added Pollard. "I haven't fired a gun since I was a kid at camp, but how the hell hard can it be to sweep the area with a beam?"

"You look a little under the weather, Mr. Desmond," I said. "Perhaps you'd like to stay in camp."

Actually, he looked incredibly grateful for the out I'd given him. Then his wife ruined it all by adding that he'd just be in the way.

"I'm going," he said.

"It's really not necessary," I said.

"I paid. I'm going."

And that was that.

"There's no sense taking gunbearers," I said as the four of us walked to the safari vehicle. "We can't talk to them, and besides, the rules don't apply in this case. If we see him, we'll take him from the safety of the vehicle, and it'll give you something solid to rest your rifles on while you're sweeping the area." They climbed onto their seats. "Wait here a minute."

I went back, found Mbele, and told him that we were going after the Snark, and that he should use the Dabihs to set up some kind of defensive perimeter. Then I signaled to Chajinka to join me. A moment later he had taken his customary position on the hood of the vehicle, and we were off in pursuit of the Snark.

The trail led due northeast, past the savannah, toward rolling country and a large, lightly forested valley. Two or three times I thought we'd spot him just over the next hill, but he was a cagey bastard, and by midafternoon we still hadn't sighted him.

As dusk fell Chajinka couldn't read the signs from the vehicle, so he jumped off and began trotting along, eyes glued to the ground. When we entered the valley, he was following the trail so slowly that Ramona and Pollard got out and walked along with him while I followed in the vehicle and Desmond stayed huddled in the back of it.

> *But the valley grew narrow and narrower still,*
> *And the evening got darker and colder,*
> *Till (merely from nervousness, not from good will)*
> *They marched along shoulder to shoulder.*

Night fell with no sign of the Snark. I didn't want to chance damaging the vehicle by driving over that terrain in the dark, so we slept until sunrise, and then drove back to base camp, reaching it just before noon.

Nobody was prepared for the sight that awaited us.

The eleven Dabihs we'd left behind were sprawled dead on the ground in grotesquely contorted positions, each with his throat shredded or his intestines ripped out. Dismembered arms and legs were everywhere, and the place was swimming in blood. Dead staring eyes greeted us accusingly, as if to say: "Where were you when we needed you?"

The stench was worse than the sight. Ramona gagged and began vomiting. Desmond whimpered and curled up into a fetal ball on the floor of the vehicle so he wouldn't have to look at the carnage. Pollard froze like a statue; then, after a moment, he too began vomiting.

I'd seen a lot of death in my time. So had Chajinka. But neither of us had ever seen anything remotely like this. There hadn't been much of a struggle. It doesn't take a 400-pound predator very long to wipe out a bunch of unarmed 90-pound Dabihs. My guess was that it was over in less than a minute.

"What the hell happened here?" asked Pollard, gesturing weakly toward all the blood-soaked dismembered bodies when he finally was able to speak.

"The method employed I would gladly explain,
While I have it so clear in my head.
If I had but the time and you had but the brain—
But much yet remains to be said."

"Where's Mbele?" I asked, finally getting past the shock of what I was looking at and realizing that he wasn't among them.

Before anyone could answer, I raced to the hatch and entered the ship, rifle at the ready, half-expecting to be pounced on by the Snark at any moment.

I found what was left of Captain Mbele in the control room. His head had been torn from his body, and his stomach was ripped open. The floor, the bulkheads, even the viewscreen were all drenched with his blood.

"Is he there?" called Ramona from the ground.

"Stay out!" I yelled.

Then I searched every inch of the ship, looking for the Snark. I could feel my heart pounding as I explored each section, but there was no sign of him.

I went back to the control room and began checking it over thoroughly. The Snark didn't know what made the ship work, or even what it was, but he knew it belonged to his enemies, and he did a lot of damage. Some of it—to the pilot's chair and the DeepSleep pods and the auxiliary screens—didn't matter. Some of it—to the fusion ignition and the navigational computer and the subspace radio—mattered a *lot*.

I continued going through the ship, assessing the damage. He'd ripped up a couple of beds in his fury, but the most serious destruction was to the galley. I had a feeling that nothing in it would ever work again.

I went back outside and confronted the party.

"Did you find Captain Mbele?" asked Ramona.

"Yes. He's in the ship." She started walking to the hatch. I grabbed her arm. "Trust me: you don't want to see him."

"That's it!" screamed Desmond. "We were crazy to come here! I want out! Not tomorrow, not later! *Now!*"

"I second the motion," agreed Ramona. "Let's get the hell off this planet before it kills any more of us."

"That's not possible," I said grimly. "The Snark did some serious damage to the ship."

"How long will it take to fix it?" asked Pollard.

"If I was a skilled spacecraft mechanic with a full set of tools and all the replacement parts I needed, maybe a week," I answered. "But I'm a hunter who doesn't know how to fix a broken spaceship. I wouldn't know where to begin."

"You mean we're stranded?" asked Ramona.

"For the time being," I said.

"What do you mean, 'for the time being'?" shrieked Desmond hysterically. "We're here forever! We're dead! We're all dead!"

I grabbed him and shook him, and when he wouldn't stop screaming I slapped him, hard, on the face.

"That won't help!" I said angrily.

"We'll never get off this goddamned dirtball!" he bleated.

"Yes we will," I said. "Mbele had to check in with Silinger & Mahr every week. When they don't hear from us, they'll send a rescue party. All we have to do is stay alive until they get here."

"They'll never come!" moaned Desmond. "We're all going to die!"

"Stop your whining!" I snapped. *This is just what I needed now*, I thought disgustedly; *we're surrounded by dismembered corpses, the very ground is soaked with blood, the Snark's probably still nearby, and this ass-hole is losing it.* "We have work to do!" They all looked at me. "I want the three of you to start digging a mass grave for the eleven Dabihs. When that's done, I want us to burn everything—every tree, every bush, everything—to get rid of the smell of blood so it doesn't attract any predators. What we can't burn, we'll bury."

"And what are *you* going to be doing?" demanded Desmond, who had at least regained some shred of composure.

"I'm going to bring what's left of Mbele out of the ship and clean up all the blood," I said bluntly. "Unless you'd rather do it." I thought he was going to faint. "Then, if I can make myself understood to Chajinka, he and I will try to secure the area."

"How?" asked Ramona.

"We got some devices that are sensitive to movement and body heat. Maybe we can rig up some kind of alarm system. Chajinka and I can hide them around the perimeter of the camp. If we finish before you do, we'll pitch in and help with the grave. Now get busy—the sooner we finish, the sooner we can lock ourselves in the ship and decide on our next move."

"*Is* there a next move?" asked Pollard.

"Always," I replied.

It took me almost four hours to clean Mbele's blood and innards from the control room. I put what was left of him into a vacuum pouch, then hefted it to my shoulder and carried it outside.

I found Chajinka helping with the grave. I called him over and showed him, with an elaborate pantomime, what I had in mind, and a few moments later we were planting the sensing devices around the perimeter of our camp. I saw no reason to stay in the Bubbles with such a dangerous enemy on the loose, so I collapsed them and moved them back into the cargo hold. The grave still wasn't done, so Chajinka and I helped finish the job. Desmond wouldn't touch any of the corpses, and Ramona looked like she was going be get sick again, so the Dabih, Pollard and I dragged the corpses and spare body parts to the grave, I added the pouch containing Mbele's remains, and after we four humans and Chajinka filled it in, I read the Bible over it.

"Now what?" asked Ramona, dirty and on the verge of physical collapse.

"Now we burn everything, bury any remaining dried blood, and then we move into the ship," I said.

"And just wait to be rescued?"

I shook my head. "It could be weeks, even a month, before a rescue party arrives. We're going to need meat, and since we've no way to refrigerate it with the galley destroyed, it means we'll probably have to go hunting every day, or at least every other day."

"I see," she said.

"And I'm going to kill the Snark," I said.

"Why don't we just wait for the rescue party and not take any chances?" suggested Ramona fearfully.

"It's killed thirteen beings who were under my protection," I said grimly. "I'm going to kill him if it's the last thing I do."

"Maybe Philemon should give you his laser rifle," Ramona suggested. "He's not very good with it anyway."

Desmond glared at her, but made no reply.

"He may need it," I said. "Besides, I'm happy with my own weapon."

"Where will you hunt for it?" asked Pollard.

"Right in this general area," I answered. "He has no reason to leave it."

"We can't just sit around like bait and wait for him!" whined Desmond. "In all the time we've been on the planet you've never even seen him—but he's killed Marx and Mbele and our Dabihs. He comes into camp whenever he wants! He sabotages our t-packs and our ship! We'll need an army to kill him!"

"If he comes back, you'll be safe inside the ship," I said.

"Locking himself in the ship didn't help Captain Mbele," noted Ramona.

"He didn't close the hatch. As I read the signs, he saw what was happening and raced into the ship for a gun. The Snark caught him before he found it." I paused. "He knew better than to be out here without a weapon."

"So now it's *his* fault that this monster killed him?" shouted Desmond. "Let's not blame the hunter who fucked up! Let's blame the victim!"

That's when I lost it. "One more word out of you and there'll be another killing!" I shouted back at him.

Pollard stepped between us. "Stop it!" he snapped. "The creature's out there! Don't do his work for him!"

We both calmed down after that, and finally went into the ship. There was no food, but everyone was so physically and emotionally exhausted that it didn't matter. Half an hour later we were all sound asleep.

Each morning Chajinka and I walked across the scorched, empty field that had so recently been covered with vegetation. We would climb into the safari vehicle and prepare to go out to bag the day's food—and even though there was no longer any place to hide near the ship, I constantly had the uneasy feeling that *he* was watching us, measuring our strength, biding his time.

We never went more than four miles from camp. I didn't shoot the choicest animals, just the closest. Then we'd cut off the strips of meat we thought we'd need and leave the carcass for the scavengers. We'd return to camp, and after breakfast we'd set out on foot to look for signs of the Snark.

I knew he was nearby, knew it as surely as I knew my own name, but we couldn't find any physical sign of him. I warned the others not to leave the ship without their weapons, preferably not to leave it at all, and under no circumstance were they to go more than thirty yards away from it unless they were in my company.

By the fifth day after the massacre everyone was getting tired of red meat, so I decided to take Chajinka down to the river, and see if we could spear a few fish.

"Can I come with you?" asked Ramona, appearing just inside the hatch. "I'm starting to feel distinctly claustrophobic."

I couldn't see any reason why not. Hell, she was safer with Chajinka and me than back at the ship.

"Bring your rifle," I said.

She disappeared inside the ship, then emerged with a laser rifle a moment later.

"I'm ready."

"Let's go," I said.

We marched through heavy bush to the river.

"All the local animals must come down here to drink," noted Ramona. "Wouldn't it be easier to do your hunting right here rather than go out in the safari vehicle each morning?"

"We'd attract too many scavengers," I explained. "And since Chajinka and I come down here twice a day to bring water back to the ship, why cause ourselves any problems?"

"I see." She paused. "Are there any carnivores in the river—the kind that might eat a human?"

"I haven't seen any," I replied. "But I sure as hell wouldn't recommend taking a swim."

When we reached the river, Chajinka grabbed a large branch and beat the water. When he was sure it was safe, he waded out, thigh-deep, and held his spear above his head, poised to strike, while we watched him in total silence. He stayed motionless for almost two full minutes, then suddenly stabbed the water and came away with a large, wriggling fish.

He grinned and said something that I couldn't understand, then clambered onto the bank, picked up a rock, and smashed it down on the fish's head. It stopped moving, and he went back into the water.

"Two more and we'll have our dinner," I remarked.

"He's really something," she said. "Where did you find him?"

"I inherited him."

"I beg your pardon?"

"He was the tracker for the hunter I apprenticed under," I explained. "When he retired, he left me his client list—and Chajinka."

Suddenly there was a yell of triumph from Chajinka. He held up his spear, and there was a huge fish, maybe 25 pounds, squirming at the end of it. The Dabih himself didn't weigh much more than 85 pounds, the current was strong and the footing was slippery. Suddenly he fell over backward and vanished beneath the surface of the water.

He emerged again a second later, but without the spear and the fish. I saw them floating downstream a good ten yards from him. There was no sense telling him where to look; he couldn't understand a word I said without a t-pack. So I waded into the water and went after the spear myself. It became chest-deep very quickly, and I had to fight the current, but I finally reached the spear and waded back to shore. Chajinka climbed out a moment later with an embarrassed grin on his face. He made another incomprehensible comment, then brained the fish as he had done with the first one.

"See?" I said sardonically. "Even fishing can be exciting with you're on safari."

There was no answer. I spun around. Ramona Desmond was nowhere to be seen.

So the Snark pronounced sentence, the Judge being quite
Too nervous to utter a word.
When it rose to its feet, there was silence like night,
And the fall of a pin might be heard.

I squatted down next to her corpse. There was no blood; he'd noiselessly broken her neck and left her where she'd fallen.

"He was watching us the whole time," I said furiously. "He waited until she was alone, then grabbed her and pulled her into the bush." A chilling thought occurred to me. "I wonder who's hunting who?"

Chajinka muttered something incomprehensible.

"All right," I said at last. "Let's take her back to camp."

I lifted Ramona's body to my shoulder and signaled him to follow me.

Desmond raced out of the ship when he saw us. He began flagellating himself and pulling tufts of his hair out, screaming nonsense words at the top of his lungs.

"What the hell is happening?" asked Pollard, clambering out through the hatch. Then he saw the body. He had to work to keep his voice under control. "Oh, Jesus! Oh, Jesus!" he kept repeating. When he'd finally calmed down, he said, "It's more than an animal! It's like some vengeful alien god come to life!"

Chajinka went into the cargo hold and emerged with a shovel.

Pollard stared at Desmond, who was still raving. "I'll help with the grave."

"Thanks," I said. "I think I'd better get Desmond to his cabin and give him a sedative."

I walked over and put a hand on his shoulder.

"It was *your* fault!" he screamed. "*You* were supposed to protect her and you let it kill her!"

I couldn't deny it, so I just kept urging him gently toward the ship.

And then, between one second and the next, he snapped. I could see it in his face. His eyes went wide, the muscles in his jaw began twitching, even the tenor of his voice changed.

"That thing is going to learn what it means to kill the wife of the most powerful man on Far London!" He looked off into the bush and hollered: "I'm Philemon Desmond, goddammit, and I'm through being terrified by some ignorant fucking beast! Do you hear me? It's over! You're dead meat!"

"Come on, Mr. Desmond," I said softly, pushing him toward the ship.

"Who the hell are you?" he demanded, and I could tell that he really didn't recognize me.

I was about to humor him with an answer when everything went black and the ground came up to meet me.

And the Banker, inspired with a courage so new
It was a matter for general remark,
Rushed madly ahead and was lost to their view
In his zeal to discover the Snark.

Pollard sloshed some water on my face. I gasped for breath, then sat up and put a hand to my head. It came away covered with blood.

"Are you all right?" he asked, kneeling down next to me, and I saw that Chajinka was behind him.

"What happened?"

"I'm not sure," he said. "We were just starting to dig the grave when I heard Desmond suddenly stop gibbering. Then he whacked you on the head with something, and ran off."

"I never saw it coming," I groaned, blinking my eyes furiously. "Where did he go?"

"I don't know." He pointed to the southwest. "That way, I think."

"*Shit!*" I said. "The Snark is still in the area!"

I tried to get to my feet, but was overwhelmed by pain and dizziness, and sat back down, hard.

"Take it easy," he said. "You've probably got a hell of a concussion. Where's the first aid kit? Maybe I can at least stop the bleeding."

I told him where to find it, then concentrated on trying to focus my eyes.

When Pollard returned and began working on my head, I asked, "Did you see if he at least took his laser rifle with him?"

"If he didn't have it when he hit you, he didn't stop to get it."

"Goddammit!"

"I guess that means he doesn't have it."

"Wonderful," I muttered, wincing as he did something to the back of my head. "So he's unarmed, running through the bush, and screaming at the top of his lungs."

"All done," said Pollard, standing up. "It's not a pretty job, but at least the bleeding's stopped. How do you feel?"

"Groggy," I said. "Help me up."

Once I was on my feet, I looked around. "Where's my rifle?"

"Right here," said Pollard, picking it up and handing it to me. "But you're in no shape to go after Desmond."

"I'm not going after Desmond," I mumbled. "I'm going after *him*!" I signaled Chajinka to join me and set off unsteadily to the southwest. "Lock yourself in the ship."

"I'll finish burying Ramona first."

"*Don't!*"

"But—"

"Unless you're prepared to fend him off with a shovel if he shows up, do what I said."

"I can't leave her body out for the scavengers," Pollard protested.

"Take her with you. Spray her with the preservatives we use for trophies and stash her in the cargo hold. We'll bury her when I get back."

"*If* you get back," he corrected me. "You look like you can barely stand on your feet."

"I'll be back," I promised him. "I'm still a hunter, and he's still just an animal."

"Yeah—he's just an animal. That's why there's just you, me and Chajinka left alive."

Desmond didn't get very far—not that I ever expected him to. We found him half a mile away, his skull crushed. I carried him back to camp and buried him next to his wife.

"That bastard's been one step ahead of us from the start," said Pollard bitterly as we sat down next to the ship and slaked our thirst with some lukewarm water. Chajinka sat a few yards away, motionless as a statue, watching and listening for any sign of the Snark.

"He's smarter than I thought," I admitted. "Or luckier."

"Nothing is that lucky," said Pollard. "He must be intelligent."

"Absolutely," I agreed.

Pollard's eyes went wide. "Wait a minute!" he said sharply. "If you *knew* he was intelligent, what the hell were we doing hunting him in the first place?"

"There's a difference between intelligence and sentience," I said. "We know he's intelligent. We don't know that he's sentient."

He looked puzzled. "I thought they were the same thing."

I shook my head. "Back on Earth, chimpanzees were intelligent enough to create crude tools, and to pass that knowledge on from one generation to the next—but no one ever claimed they were sentient. The fact that the Snark can hide his trail, spot my traps and elude us makes him intelligent. It doesn't make him sentient."

"On the other hand, it doesn't prove he's *not* sentient," said Pollard stubbornly.

"No, it doesn't."

"So what do we do?"

"We kill him," I answered.

"Even if he's sentient?"

"What do you do when someone murders fifteen sentient beings?" I said. "If he's a Man, you execute him. If he's an animal, you track him down and kill him. Either way, the result is the same."

"All right," said Pollard dubiously. "We kill him. How?"

"We leave the ship and go after him."

"Why?" he demanded. "We're safe in the ship!"

"Tell that to Mbele and the Desmonds and the Dabihs," I shot back. "As long as we stay here, he knows where we are and we don't know where *he* is. That means he's the hunter and we're the prey. If we leave camp and pick up his trail before he picks up ours, we go back to being the hunters again." I got to my feet. "In fact, the sooner we start, the better."

He wasn't happy about it, but he had no choice but to come along, since the alternative was to remain behind alone. After we loaded the vehicle I patted the hood, waited for Chajinka to jump onto it, and then we drove to the spot where we'd found Desmond's body.

The Dabih picked up the trail, and we began tracking the Snark. I wanted him so bad I could taste it. It wasn't just revenge for all the Men and Dabihs he'd killed. It wasn't even a matter of professional pride. It was because I knew this was my last hunt, that I'd never get my license back after losing fifteen sentient beings who were under my protection.

The trail led back to the camp, where the Snark had watched us bury Desmond's body. It had kept out of sight until we drove off, and then began moving in a northwesterly direction. We tracked it until late afternoon, when we found ourselves about eight miles from the ship.

"There's no sense going back for the night," I told Pollard. "We might never pick up the trail again."

"Isn't he likely to double back to the camp?"

"Not while we're out here, he isn't," I said with absolutely certainty. "This isn't a hunt any longer—it's a war. Neither of us will quit until the other's dead."

He looked at me much the way I'd looked at Desmond earlier in the day. Finally he spoke up: "We can't track him at night."

"I know," I replied. "We'll each keep watch for three hours—you, me and Chajinka—and we'll start again as soon as it's light enough."

I sat the first watch, and I was so keyed up that I couldn't get to sleep, so I sat through Pollard's watch as well before I woke Chajinka and managed a three-hour nap. As soon as it was light, we started following the trail again.

By noon we were approaching a small canyon. Then, suddenly, I saw a flicker of motion off in the distance. I stopped the vehicle and activated my Telescopic lenses.

He was more than a mile away, and he had his back to us, but I knew I'd finally gotten my first look at the Snark.

Erect and sublime, for one moment of time,
In the next, that wild figure they saw
(As if stung by a spasm) plunge into a chasm,
While they waited and listened in awe.

I drove to the edge of the canyon. Chajinka hopped off the hood, and Pollard and I joined him a moment later.

"You're sure you saw him?" asked Pollard.

"I'm sure," I said. "Bipedal. Rust-colored. Looks almost like a cross between a bear and a gorilla, at least from this distance."

"Yeah, that's him all right." He peered down into the canyon. "And he climbed down there?"

"That's right," I said.

"I assume we're going after him?"

"There's no reason to believe he'll come out anywhere near here," I said. "If we wait, we'll lose him."

"It's looks pretty rocky," he said. "Can we pick up his trail?"

"Chajinka will find it."

Pollard sighed deeply. "What the hell," he said with a shrug. "I'm not going to wait here alone while the two of you go after him. I figure I'll be safer with you—providing I don't break my neck on the terrain."

I motioned for Chajinka to lead the way down, since he was far more sure-footed than any human. He walked along the edge of the precipice for perhaps fifty yards, then came to a crude path we were able to follow for the better part of an hour. Then we were on the canyon floor next to a narrow stream where we slaked our thirst, hoping the water wouldn't make us too sick, as we'd left the irradiation tablets back at the ship.

We rested briefly, then took up the hunt again. Chajinka was able to find a trail where I would have sworn none existed. By early afternoon the floor of the canyon was no longer flat, and we had to follow a winding path over and around a series of rock formations. Pollard was game, but he was out of shape. He kept falling behind, actually dropping out of sight a couple of times, which forced us to stop and wait for him to catch up.

127

When he dropped behind yet again, I wanted to ask him if he needed a break. I didn't dare shout and give away our position to the Snark, so I compromised by signaling Chajinka to slow his pace until Pollard caught up with us.

He didn't—and after a few minutes we went back to see what was the matter.

I couldn't find him. It was like he had vanished off the face of the planet.

They hunted till darkness came on, but they found
Not a button, or feather, or mark,
By which they could tell that they stood on the ground
Where the Baker had met with the Snark.

We spent half an hour looking for Pollard. There was no trace of him, and eventually we were forced to admit that somehow the Snark had turned back on his trail and circled around us or hid and waited for us to pass by. Either way, it was obvious that he'd managed to get Pollard.

I knew it was futile to keep looking for him, so I signaled Chajinka to continue searching for the Snark. We hiked over the rocky canyon floor until at last we came to a steep wall.

"We go up, or we go back," I said, looking at the wall. "Which will it be?"

He stared at me expectantly, waiting for me to signal him which way to go.

I looked back the way we'd come, then up in the direction of the path we were following—

—and as I looked up, I saw a large object hurtling down toward me!

I pushed Chajinka out of the way and threw myself to my left, rolling as I hit the ground. The object landed five feet away with a bone-jarring *thud!*—and I saw that it was Pollard's body.

I looked up, and there was the Snark standing on a ledge, glaring down at me. Our eyes met, and then he turned and began racing up the canyon wall.

"Are you all right?" I asked Chajinka, who was just getting to his feet.

He brushed himself off, then made a digging motion and looked questioningly at me.

We didn't have any shovels, and it would take hours to dig even a shallow grave in the rocky ground using our hands. If we left Pollard's body where it was, it would be eaten by scavengers—but if we took the time to bury him, we'd lose the Snark.

"Leave him here to his fate—it is getting so late!"
The Bellman exclaimed in a fright.
"We have lost half the day. Any further delay,
And we sha'n't catch a Snark before night."

When we got halfway up the wall, I stopped and looked back. Alien raptors were circling high in the sky. Then the first of them landed next to Pollard and began pulling away bits of his flesh. I turned away and concentrated on the Snark.

It took an hour to reach the top, and then Chajinka spent a few minutes picking up the Snark's trail again. We followed it for another hour, and the landscape slowly changed, gradually becoming lush and green.

And then something strange happened. The trail suddenly became easy to follow.

Almost *too* easy.

We tracked him for another half hour. I sensed that he was near, and I was ready to fire at anything that moved. The humidity made my hands sweat so much that I didn't trust them not to slip on the stock and barrel, so I signaled Chajinka that I wanted to take a brief break.

I took a sip from my canteen. Then, as I leaned against a tree, wiping the moisture from my rifle, I saw a movement half a mile away.

It was *him!*

I pulled my rifle to my shoulder and took aim—but we were too far away. I leaped to my feet and began running after him. He turned, faced me for just an instant, and vanished into the bush.

When we got to where he'd been, we found that his trail led due north, and we began following it. At one point we stopped so I could remove a stinging insect from inside my boot—and suddenly I caught sight of him again. He roared and disappeared again into the heavy foliage as I raced after him.

It was almost as if the son of a bitch was *taunting* us, and I wondered: is he leading us into a trap?

And then I had a sudden flash of insight.

Rather than leading us *into* a trap, was he leading us *away* from something?

It didn't make much sense, but somewhere deep in my gut it felt right.

"Stop!" I ordered Chajinka.

He didn't know the word, but the tone of my voice brought him up short.

I pointed to the south. "This way," I said.

The Dabih frowned and pointed toward the Snark, saying something in his own tongue.

"I know he's there," I said. "But come this way anyway."

I began walking south. I had taken no more than four or five steps when Chajinka was at my side, jabbering again, and pulling my arm, trying to make me follow the Snark.

"No!" I said harshly. It certainly wasn't the word, so it must have been the tone. Whatever the reason, he shrugged, looked at me as if I was crazy, and fell into step behind me. He couldn't very well lead, since there was no trail and he didn't know where we were going. Neither did I, for that matter, but my every instinct said the Snark didn't want me going this direction, and that was reason enough to do it.

We'd walked for about fifteen minutes when I heard a hideous roar off to my left. It was the Snark, much closer this time, appearing from a new direction. He showed himself briefly, then raced off.

"I *knew* it!" I whispered excitedly to Chajinka, who just looked confused when I continued to ignore the Snark.

As we kept moving south, the Snark became bolder and bolder, finally getting within a hundred yards of us, but never showing himself long enough for me to get a shot off.

I could feel Chajinka getting tenser and tenser, and finally, when the Snark roared from thirty yards away, the little Dabih raised his spear above his head and raced after him.

"*No!*" I cried. "He'll kill you!"

I tried to grab him, but he was much too quick for me. I followed him into the eight-foot-high grasslike vegetation. It was a damned stupid thing to do: I couldn't see Chajinka, I couldn't see the Snark, and I had no room to maneuver or even sidestep if there was a charge. But he was my friend—probably, if I was honest, my *only* friend—and I couldn't let him face the Snark alone.

Suddenly I heard the sounds of a scuffle. There was some growling, Chajinka yelled once, and then all was silent.

I went in the direction I thought the sounds had come from, pushing the heavy grasses aside. Then I was making my way through thornbush, and the thorns ripped at my arms and legs. I paid no attention, but kept looking for Chajinka.

I found him in a clearing. He'd put up the fight of his life—his wounds attested to that—but even with his spear he was no match for a 400-pound predator. He recognized me, tried to say something that I wouldn't have understood anyway, and died just as I reached his side.

I knew I couldn't stay in the heavy bush with the Snark still around. This was *his* terrain. So I made my way back to the trail and continued to the south. The Snark roared from cover, but didn't show himself.

After another quarter mile I came to a huge tree with a hollow trunk. I was about to walk around it when I heard a high-pitched whimpering coming from inside it. I approached it carefully, my rifle ready, the safety off—

—and suddenly the Snark broke out of cover no more than fifteen yards away and charged me with an ear-splitting roar.

He was on me so fast that I didn't have time to get off a shot. He swiped at me with a mighty paw. I ducked and turned away, but the blow caught me on the shoulder and sent me flying. I landed on my back, scrambled to my feet, and saw him standing maybe ten feet away. My rifle was on the ground right next to him.

He charged again. This time I was ready. I dove beneath his claws, rolled as I hit the ground, got my hands on my weapon, and got off a single shot as he turned to come at me again.

"Got you, you bastard!" I yelled in triumph.

At first I thought I might have hit him too high in the chest to prove fatal, but he collapsed instantly, blood spurting from the wound—and I noticed that he had a festering wound on his side, doubtless from Marx's shot a week ago. I watched him for a moment, then decided to "pay the insurance," the minimal cost of a second bullet, to make sure he didn't get back up and do any damage before he died. I walked over to stick the muzzle of my rifle in his ear, found that I didn't have a clear shot, and reached out to nudge his head around with my toe.

I felt something like an electric surge within my head, and suddenly, though I'd never experienced anything remotely like it before, I knew I was in telepathic communication with the dying Snark.

Why did you come to my land to kill me? he asked, more puzzled than angry.

I jumped back, shocked—and lost communication with him. Obviously it could only happen when we were in physical contact. I squatted down and took his paw in my hands, and felt his fear and pain.

Then he was dead, and I stood up and stared down at him, my entire universe turned upside down—because during the brief moment that I had shared his thoughts, I learned what had *really* happened.

The Snark's race, sentient but non-technological, was never numerous, and had been wiped out by a virulent disease. Through some fluke, he alone survived it. The others had died decades ago, and he had led a life of terrifying loneliness ever since.

He knew our party was on Dodgson IV the very first day we landed. He was more than willing to share his hunting ground with us, and made no attempt to harm us or scare us off.

He had thought the killing of the crystal-horned buck was a gift of friendship; he didn't understand that he was stealing Marx's trophy because the concept of trophies was completely alien to him. He killed Marx only after Marx wounded him.

Even then he was willing to forgive us. Those dead animals we found in my traps were his notion of a peace offering.

He couldn't believe that we really wanted to kill him, so he decided he would visit the camp and try to communicate with us. When he got there, he mistook the Dabihs' t-packs for weapons and destroyed them. Then, certain that this would be seen as an act of aggression even though he hadn't harmed anyone, he left before we woke up.

He came back to try one last time to make peace with us. This time he made no attempt to enter the camp unseen. He marched right in, fully prepared to be questioned and examined by these new races. But what he *wasn't* prepared for was being attacked by the Dabihs. Fighting in self-defense, he made short work of them. Mbele raced into the ship, either to hide or to get a weapon. He knew first-hand what Marx's weapon had done to him at fifty yards, and he didn't dare let Mbele shoot at him from the safety of the ship, so he raced into it and killed him before he could find a weapon.

After that it was war. He didn't know why we wanted to kill him, but he no longer doubted that we did…and while there was a time when he would have welcomed an end to his unhappy, solitary existence, he now had a reason, indeed a driving urge, to stay alive at all costs…

…because he wasn't a *he* at all; he was an *it*. The Snark was an asexual animal that reproduced by budding. Its final thought was one of enormous regret, not that it would die, for it understood the cycles of life and death, but that now its offspring would die as well.

I stared down at the Snark's body, my momentary feeling of triumph replaced by an overwhelming sense of guilt. What I had thought was my triumph had become nothing less than genocide in the space of a few seconds.

I heard the whimpering again, and I walked back to the hollow tree trunk and looked in. There, trembling and shrinking back from me, was a very small, very helpless version of the Snark.

I reached out to it, and it uttered a tiny, high-pitched growl as it huddled against the back of the trunk.

I spoke gently, moved very slowly, and reached out again. This time it stared at my hand for a long moment, and finally, hesitantly, reached out to touch it. The instant we made contact I was able to feel its all-encompassing terror.

Do not be afraid, little one, I said silently. *Whatever happens, I will protect you. I owe you that much.*

Its fear vanished, for you cannot lie when you are telepathically linked, and a moment later it emerged from its hiding place.

I looked off into the distance. Men would be coming soon. The rescue party would touch down in the next week or two. They'd find Marx's body in the hold, and they'd exhume the Desmonds and Mbele and the eleven Dabihs. They'd read the Captain's diary and know that all this carnage was caused by an animal called a Snark.

And since they were a hunting company, they'd immediately outfit a safari to kill the Snark quickly and efficiently. No argument could possibly deter them, not after losing an entire party of Men and Dabihs.

But they would be in for a surprise, because *this* Snark not only knew the terrain, but knew how Men thought and acted, and was armed with Man's weapons.

The infant reached out to me and uttered a single word. I tried to repeat it, laughed at how badly I mispronounced it, took the tiny creature in my arms, and went off into the bush to learn a little more about being a Father Snark while there was still time.

In the midst of the word he was trying to say,
In the midst of his laughter and glee,
He had softly and suddenly vanished away—
For the Snark was a Boojum, you see.

I had written a story for Kevin J. Anderson's Blood Lite, *an anthology of funny horror stories, and when Kevin got a contract from Simon & Schuster for a second book in the series, he invited me again. I invited Lezli to collaborate, and we brainstormed "The Close Shave," where not all the magical creatures of the night were tall, dark and handsome—or deadly.*

—MIKE

The Close Shave

BY MIKE RESNICK & LEZLI ROBYN

I t's 2:30 in the morning, and The Close Shave is starting to fill up. Which figures. After all, how many places can you go for a trim and a shave in the middle of the night?

Basil is in the chair now. I knew him back before he changed, when he went to bed after the eleven o'clock news like normal people, when he howled at a pretty girl it was because all the guys did. But that was, oh, maybe five years ago—before that mangy-looking dog bit him.

Otis is reading the newspaper. I knew him back in the old days too. I can remember when he'd pick up a paper to see if the Geldings had finally drafted a linebacker, or if Can't Miss was running the next day, or if Pharaohs' cheerleaders had been arrested for indecent exposure again—important stuff like that. These days—well, these nights—all he reads are the obituaries.

Morton just comes to hang out. I mean, there isn't a hair on his whole body, or any skin either, now that I think of it. He's just bone as far as the eye can see. Looks kind of like a refugee from Halloween. He never bothers anyone—I think he's just lonely—and to be honest the main reason I let him sit there is the hope that sooner or later he'll buy a can of pop from the machine I keep in the corner and I'll see where it goes once it passes through his…let me see; *lips* is the wrong word, and he hasn't got any gums either. Through his teeth, I guess.

Harold comes by once a week, maybe a little more often, usually for a shave. While he's here he always asks for a shampoo. I keep telling him that I don't shampoo snakes, and although he claims they're perfectly harmless, that they *like* soap and water, the one time I sat him in the chair and leaned him back and got ready to shampoo some of the slime off the snakes, one of them gave me a great big reptilian smile, and it had teeth—*sharp* teeth—and from that day to this I don't give shampoos to male medusas (or female medusas either, though none has asked yet.)

"Take a little off the top, Sam," says Basil.

"Right," I say, brushing it out a bit to make it easier to cut.

"And the sides."

"Got it," I say.

"And the chin."

"That's a shave," I say. "It'll be an extra five-spot."

"I thought we were friends, Sam," he says in hurt tones.

"I am your friend all day long," I respond. "But when I open up The Close Shave at ten o'clock at night, I am your barber for the next eight hours, and never the twain shall meet."

"Okay, trim the mustache and beard," says Basil with a shrug. "And maybe the neck and the forearms and the backs of the hands."

I just stare at him.

"All right, just a trim and a shave."

I lay out my equipment, because Basil's hair isn't like most people's (which figures; it's been a long time since anyone mistook Basil for a people) when suddenly he lets out a howl that damned near shatters my front window.

"Come on, Basil," I say. "How can I have cut you? I haven't even started working on you yet."

This is followed by another, more plaintive howl.

"Basil, what the hell is it?"

He points through the window to Hepzibah McCoy's second-floor apartment across the street.

"She's getting undressed and she forgot to pull her shade down again!" says Basil, emitting a third howl.

"You're a werewolf," I say. "Can't you just wolf whistle?"

"Oh, the litters I could have with her!" says Basil.

"Maybe she doesn't like the hairy type," offers Morton, who is all bone and as unhairy as a billiard ball (and less colorful as well.) Otis keeps telling him that he should wear pants, but I cannot imagine why, and neither can Morton. Besides, I figure his waistline comes in at a quick three inches. Do you know how hard it is to find a belt that size?

"You guys are so normal," says Harold in bored tones. "A girl with gazongas like that, if she's still on the loose and living alone, maybe she wants something a little unusual."

Three high-pitched voices say "Absolutely!" "For sure!" and "You betcha!" and I look around to see who is talking, but I don't spot anyone.

"Who said that?" I demand.

"Me and my two pals," says one of the purple snakes that is growing out of Harold's head. "Wanna make something of it?"

"Harold," I say, "your hair is talking to me."

"It talks to me all the time, mate," he says with a shrug as his mild Australian accent comes through. Then he adds, "Except when I comb it. Then it just screams bloody murder."

Well, his hair starts arguing among itself about which of them Hepzibah McCoy would most love to run her fingers through, and I pick up my scissors and go to work on Basil, and everything is going along nicely when suddenly he turns his head.

"She has gone into the bathroom for her shower!" he announces to the room at large. And a second later he makes another announcement, which is "*Ouch!*"

"I am sorry, Basil," I say, "but I am not *very* sorry, because you are an adult and you know better than to make sudden movements when someone is working your mane over with a scissors. I will get a styptic pencil, or a bandage, or some concrete mortar, and you will be good as new in just a minute."

Otis has been sniffing the air, and now he is staring hypnotically at the drop of blood on Basil's neck, and his pupils are dilated and his hands start shaking and suddenly there is a little bit of drool on his chin.

"*Blood!*" he whispers.

"Control yourself, Otis," I say sharply.

"*Blood!*" he repeats.

"You don't know who he's eaten lately, or what diseases they might have been carrying," I say. "Just lean back and relax."

"*Blood!*" he hisses, standing up abruptly.

"Otis," I say, "this is as boring and one-sided a conversation as I have had in quite some time. Now you sit there and behave yourself or I'm going get really annoyed with you—and don't you dare turn into a bat! Do you know how hard it is to shave you when you're hanging upside down from the ceiling?"

Otis starts pouting, feigns disinterest, and again buries his nose in the late edition's obituary column. I return to taming Basil's mane, but then the bell on my door rings and so I turn, expecting to greet another of my regulars. Instead, the unexpected walks in: a human.

"Hello," I say. "Welcome to The Close Shave."

"Good evening," he says.

Morton fidgets, creaking slightly, while Basil growls softly under his breath.

"Do you need a trim?" I ask, not knowing what else to say—it has been years since a human required my services, especially at this time of night.

"No," he says. "I am looking for a medusa."

Harold looks up in surprise, his hair slithering around in excitement.

Then the man says the unthinkable—at least to me. "I want to die," he states. "I heard that I could find you here. I require your assistance."

"Why?" asks Morton gently.

"Death is overrated," intones Otis morbidly. "Do you know how much harder it is to keep these teeth from decaying since I became undead?" he continues, displaying his fangs to Morton, who is still looking (can I say looking? What with him having no eyes and all) at the man in the doorway.

"Be quiet, Otis," I say. I turn to the newcomer. "Why do you want to die?"

"Because life is not worth living," he answers in a voice top-heavy with self-pity.

Otis licks his lips somewhat seductively. "Well, if *that's* the way you feel about it...."

"Otis," I say, "how many times have I told you: you don't bite the customers."

"But he *wants* me to," says Otis, almost keeping the whine out of his voice.

"No," says the man. "I've tried that, and it didn't work. Apparently vampires can't drink my blood."

"I view that as a personal challenge," replies Otis.

"They can't drink mine either," pipes in Morton, always wanting to fit in.

Basil, no longer growling, speaks up. "Morton, you don't *have* any blood."

"We're getting off topic," Harold states suddenly. "The crux of the matter is, I'm a pacifist." He shrugs. "I won't kill anyone—with or without their permission."

"Why didn't you tell me that before?" I complain, thinking of all those times I'd refused the money to wash his slimy hair for fear of hungry little teeth.

"I like to see you squirm," he says, grinning as his hair slithers around him like a halo.

Well, the man has stayed quiet throughout this entire little exchange, but now he clears his throat. "You misunderstood me. I don't expect *you* to kill me. I just want your permission to let one of your snake companions bite me." He sighs heavily. "Maybe *that* will work."

"Pick me!" "No, choose me!" "What about me?" is the chorus that instantly responds to his request as little snake heads jump up and down in childish enthusiasm.

"Oh, in that case, be my guest," says Harold with another shrug. "I'm not responsible for their moral choices. I'm from Australia, so my snakes are amongst the most poisonous in the world, however,"—he raises a hand, immediately stilling the writhing snakes—"I suggest you ask Cecil. He's got the biggest fangs."

The other snakes sigh and sink back down to float around Harold's head in dejection as the man walks over and raises his wrist to Cecil. A dainty little head reaches out and sinks its teeth into the man—

—and a few seconds later the head pulls back, its slimy body wracked by sobs.

"He hurt me!" squeals Cecil. "He broke my fangs!"

"Is there such a thing as a dentist for snakes?" asks Otis, looking up from his newspaper to watch Harold trying to console his hair.

Out of the corner of my eye I see the man sink into one of my barber chairs, despair written all over his face. "I can't even die properly," he laments.

"Why do you want to die at all?" asks Basil.

"I'm tired," says the man.

"That seems a little severe," says Basil. "Whenever I'm tired I take a nap."

"I have been tired for two thousand years," says the man.

Everybody allows that two thousand years is a long time to be tired, and even fifteen hundred is no picnic if push comes to shove.

"Have you got a name?" I ask.

He kind of half-smiles and half-snorts. "I've had 134 of them."

"I knew a Juan Domingo Pedro Jesus Riccardo Jose Felipe Sanchez," I say. "He could grow a beard while he was signing his name. But I never met anyone with 134 names."

"I haven't had them all at once," he explains. "I meant that I've had 134 over the centuries."

"Who *are* you?" I ask.

"I'm the guy who should have kept his mouth shut on Golgotha," he says.

"Golgotha?" asks Morton. "Isn't that out by Des Moines?"

"No," says Basil. "I think it's on the California coast, just south of San Jose."

Cecil slithers down to the vicinity of Harold's ear. "You want to tell them, or should I?"

"Golgotha is where Jesus was crucified," says Harold. He stares at the man. "Only one person who was there should still be around. Gentlemen, say hello to the Wandering Jew."

"Really?" asks Morton.

The man nods his head.

"No wonder you're tired," continues Morton. "That's a *lot* of wandering." He stares at the man. "So do we call you Wandering or Jew?"

"I change my name to fit in with my surroundings," he answers. "This is 21st century New York. Call me Goldberg."

"Okay, Goldberg," said Basil, starting to look a shade more human as the moon goes behind a cloud. "So you want to kill yourself. Tell us about it."

"It's not as easy as you would think," says Goldberg, frowning.

"Telling us?"

"Killing myself."

"Sure it is," says Basil. "A silver bullet to the heart will do it every time."

Goldberg shakes his head. "Not mine. It's been tried."

"Don't listen to him," interjects Otis. "What does a dumb animal know, meaning no offense. If you want to die, get someone to drive a wooden stake through your heart."

Goldberg looks even more unhappy. "It doesn't work."

"All right, then," says Otis. "Go out to the beach in a thong at high noon."

"I don't burn," says Goldberg miserably. "Or react to poison." He looks at Cecil. "Or get sick. Or get cut. No matter how creative I get, I just can't die."

"How creative *do* you get?" asks Morton.

"King Arthur tried to stab me with Excalibur once," begins Goldberg. "He couldn't pierce my skin. Robespierre sentenced me to the guillotine; the blade broke on my neck. Tamerlane spurred his favorite horse and tried to run me down; the horse bounced off and was never the same again." Goldberg shakes his head sadly. "So I figure if one man can't bring me eternal peace, maybe a bunch can. I show up, ready to be sliced to ribbons, at Rosebud River—and Custer makes his last stand at the Little Big Horn fifteen miles upstream that same afternoon. I intercept a message that the D-Day invasion is set for

Pas de Calais, and I'm there with the Nazi army ready to be blown sky-high—and it turns out that the message was *supposed* to be intercepted, and the invasion takes place at Normandy." He signed deeply. "It's been like that for centuries."

"I still say just take a long nap," says Basil. "Whenever I'm bored that's what I do."

"Have *you* been bored for centuries?" asks Goldberg.

"Ten minutes is usually my limit," admits Basil.

"Maybe you should travel the world and see the sights," suggests Harold.

"I've been traveling the world for two thousand years," answers Goldberg. "I'm the Wandering Jew, remember?"

"You must have seen some fascinating things," offers Morton. "Notre Dame, the Taj Mahal, the Forbidden City...."

Goldberg shrugged. "Common. Pedestrian."

"Oh?" says Harold. "What *has* impressed you?"

Goldberg thinks for a minute. "There was a town hall in the mountains of Tibet. Held about eighty people. Very pretty." He frowns. "Destroyed in a landslide in, let me see, 582 AD—or was it 583?"

"Still, if you've been wandering for a couple of thousand years, give or take, you must have seen a lot of things," allows Morton. "What was the most interesting sight you ever saw?"

Goldberg gets a faraway look on his face, but he doesn't answer.

We stare at him for a minute, and then Basil says, "You go into catatonic trances a lot, do you?"

"I was just remembering," says Goldberg.

"The most interesting sight?"

"The most beautiful."

"What was it?"

"She wasn't an *it*," says Goldberg. "At least I don't think so."

"She?" repeats Basil. "This just became a lot more interesting."

"It's tragic," replies Goldberg, a tear trickling down his cheek. "She's the real reason I want to kill myself."

"That's funny," says Basil. "I almost never want to kill myself when I see a beautiful woman. I just want to kill all the guys in the vicinity." He turns to Otis. "How about you?"

"I can't kill myself," answers Otis. "I'm *already* dead."

"We're getting away from the subject here," says Harold.

"What was the subject?" asks Otis.

"The most beautiful woman Goldberg ever saw."

"That's right," says Otis. He turns to Goldberg. "So tell us about her."

"She was the most beautiful, the sexiest, the most exquisite creature in the history of the human race," says Goldberg, and everyone perks up when he uses the word 'creature.' "And I should know. I've been here for enough of its history."

"I'm sure glad you don't speak in superlatives," I say.

"She was absolute perfection," continues Goldberg.

"You say 'was' and not 'is'," notes Basil.

"Well, he did met her centuries ago," chimes in Harold.

"Millennia," Goldberg corrects him.

"How did she die?" asks Otis, who has a professional fascination with such things.

"I don't know if she *is* dead," says Goldberg.

"Not a lot of women make it past their two thousandth birthday," I say.

"She is not a lot of women," says Goldberg. "She is the most perfect woman who ever lived, with a face that could launch twice as many ships as Helen's, and a body that would be the envy of every Playmate."

"A woman that perfect should be pretty famous by now," suggests Basil.

"The two don't necessarily go together," said Goldberg. "The model for Mona Lisa was a frump. No one ever heard of her good-looking kid sister."

"So has this perfect female got a name?"

"Of course she does," says Goldberg.

"You gonna tell us, or do we have to guess?" I say.

"Her name is Salome."

"Like as in danced before the king?" asks Harold.

Goldberg nods his head.

"I've always wanted to see the Dance of the Seven Veils," says Basil. "How was it?"

"Heavenly!" sighs Goldberg. "And it was the Dance of the Five Veils. They cleaned it up for the history books."

"I don't recall reading anything about Salome after the dance," continues Basil. "Maybe she died back then."

Goldberg shakes his head. "I saw her again in Rome, and then Athens, but I never got close enough to talk to her."

"Then why haven't we heard about her, if she's all that sexy and beautiful, and a good dancer to boot?"

"You have," says Goldberg. "H. Rider Haggard wrote her up as Ayesha, Edgar Rice Burroughs disguised her as La of Opar, Kurt Weil put her in a musical as Venus, John Cleland named her Fanny Hill and described her perfectly.... She has appeared many times, thinly disguised, down through the ages."

"And just as thinly dressed," notes Harold.

"I saw her briefly, from afar, in Persia in the 5th Century," continues Goldberg. "Then I spotted her in Mecca in the 11th century, Greece in the 12th, India in the 14th, China in the 16th, but I could never get close enough to speak to her. Since then I've seen her in Tahiti, Kenya, England, Russia, Brazil, New Zealand, and Passaic, New Jersey."

"Well, it does explain your wandering," says Morton.

"I can't go on. Two thousand years, and I still haven't gotten close enough to meet her or touch her. It's been 107 years since I last saw her. She was just across the river in Jersey, the perfect woman—and a capricious Fate hasn't let me get within fifty feet of her in two millennia. She's lost to me, and I want to end it all." Another tear rolls down his cheek as Cecil and the other snakes watch in fascination. "If I can't kill myself, maybe I'll just destroy the world."

"*Can* you?" I ask.

"You think blowing up the world is the sole province of jihadists?" he shoots back. "Every mad scientist and rejected suitor wants to at one time or another."

"With the whole world to wander, what are you doing here in New York?" I ask. "Are you following some lead?"

"No," he answers miserably.

"Then why here?" I persist.

"Your delis make the best blintzes and knishes," says Goldberg.

"Makes sense," Basil chimes in. "If you're going to be miserable, at least be well-fed and miserable."

"He should let the *yenta* I married cook for him," I say. "That'll take ten years off of anyone's life."

"Yeah, marriage is a death sentence for any man," agrees Harold, grinning.

"A death sentence just isn't what it used to be in the good old days," notes Otis.

Just as he says it, a bearded old man who knows a little something about death sentences enters the shop, dressed in a black robe and carrying a sickle. "That's hardly my fault," he says. "I keep taking them. It's *you* who keeps bringing them back."

"Who are you?" asks Basil.

"The sickle doesn't give it away?" says the old man.

"You're the Grim Reaper?" continues Basil.

The old man nods.

"That's a hell of a moniker to be stuck with," offers Harold.

"I enjoy my work," he says, "but even *I* don't think I'd care to be known as the Jolly Reaper."

"You're really him?" asks Goldberg, who's been staring at him since he entered the shop.

"I'm really him," answers the Grim Reaper. "Sam will vouch for me. I often come here on my break. It's the one place in town where I can avoid temptation. I'll be leaving in a few minutes."

"Take me with you!" shouts Goldberg.

"Don't be silly," says the Grim Reaper. "You're off-limits to me, you know that."

"Can't you try?"

"If I get any closer to you than I am right now, I get a migraine like you wouldn't believe, plus an attack of nausea. You've been cursed, pal."

"Maybe it's worn off," suggests Goldberg hopefully. "When's the last time you tried to take me?"

"Sumatra, 1749 AD," answers the Grim Reaper. "Took me a whole week to recover, and it was close to a century before I could eat blowfish again."

"Won't you try once more?" says Goldberg. "Please?"

"It's not going to work."

"*Please?*" repeats Goldberg more desperately.

The Grim Reaper shrugs. "What the hell." He begins approaching Goldberg. Then, suddenly, he grabs his stomach. "I'm gonna be sick! Sam, where's your bathroom?"

I point to the back room, and he makes a beeline toward it.

"Some Grim Reaper!" snorts Otis.

"You heard him," I say. "Goldberg is cursed."

"My wife isn't," complains Otis. "She's uncursed *and* undead."

"Then why do you always complain about her?" asks Basil.

"Because she's also unforgiving," answers Otis. "I mean, it's not as if I can walk into a restaurant and order a quart of blood. So of course I find nourishment in nubile young women. Their skin is softer, their blood is richer, their screams are more exciting. *And they don't make demands on me.*" A pause, coupled with a frown. "I should never have bitten her that third time…but I was so *hungry.* Now I can't get rid of her." He turns to the back room and raises his voice. *"And some people are no damned help at all!"*

"You weren't listening," notes Morton. "He *took* her. *You* took her back."

"Details, details!" mutters Otis.

"If she bothers you that much, kill her again," suggests Basil. "I'll bet if you run a wooden stake through her heart, the Reaper will accept her."

Suddenly Otis's entire demeanor changes. "I'm kind of used to her," he says. "And she tastes so good."

"Well, then?"

"If only she'd stop reading all those idiot vampire romance novels and assuming I'm like that every time I go out, we'd get along fine."

"When's the last time you brought her a present to show you cared?" asks Morton.

"I took her to the dressing room after the hockey game last week and gave her first choice," says Otis. "I got the leftovers. How's *that* for a present?"

"That's nice," says Morton in a voice that sounds less than sincere. "But when's the last time you brought her flowers?"

"She can't eat flowers," replies Otis.

"Neither can the other fifty million women who get them from time to time," says Morton.

"Right, mate," Harold chimes in. "She's more than just an appetite, you know."

Otis looks thoughtful for a moment. "Okay," he says at last. "I'll give it a shot." Then: "Live ones or dead ones?"

Morton sighs. "Talk to some florists. They'll figure it out."

Basil starts howling again. There's no sense asking why, because the moon is full in the sky and his humanity is buried beneath a wolf's exterior. I look out the shop window, and sure enough there is the incredibly shapely silhouette of Hepzibah McCoy closing her curtains. I find myself sympathizing with Basil; that is one hell of a view to be deprived of.

Everyone but Goldberg is looking mournfully at Hepzibah Mc-Coy's darkened window. Goldberg is gazing intently at my bleach bottles. He senses my curiosity and glances up with a small smile.

"Tried that," he states simply.

"Acid?"

"It just cleanses my insides."

"Jump into any active volcanoes lately?" I ask wryly.

He sighs deeply. "Not since Pompeii."

The subject seems hopeless, so I turn my attention back to Basil's ears. Then I hear the most enticing voice I have ever heard, but it does not sound like it is in an enticing mood.

"What does a girl have to do to get a good night's sleep around here?"

I turn to see the most luscious creature I have ever laid eyes on standing in my doorway. My heart starts pounding. My throat goes dry. My palms start sweating. She is to the average beautiful woman what Shaquille O'Neal is to the average midget. My first thought is that the Church should hire her, because once a man sees her there is no way he cannot believe in God.

Basil starts panting and drooling at the sight of her, so I cuff him over the head. It is a reflex action, because I am still unable to pull any coherent thoughts together.

Morton hops out of his chair with an enthusiasm I've never seen in him before, and instantly offers it to her. This makes me realize that she might actually be a patron, and that in turn brings me back to the here and now.

"Hello," I hear myself say in a shaky voice. "Welcome to The Close Shave."

She doesn't immediately respond, but instead runs her hands sensuously along the arm of my leather chair before turning back to me, all business. "How hard can it be for you to find a muzzle for your mutt?" she asks, glaring briefly at Basil before turning her hypnotic gaze my way again. "Every time I go near the window he howls...and my bed is beside the window." She pouts, and I feel my heart beating in triple time. "It's late," she continues, "and I need my beauty sleep." She puts her hands on her hips to emphasize her comment, but all it does is emphasize her small waist leading up and down to the generous curves that her flimsy dressing gown has slid open to reveal.

"You don't need any beauty sleep, Sheila," states Harold suddenly, with a little too much warmth in his tone. "That I can guarantee."

She throws him a cold glance—at odds with the heat radiating out from her body—and states, "I'm known as Hepzibah, not Sheila."

"Don't get your knickers in a knot, love," says Harold. "Sheila is just an Aussie word for girl."

"You think *this*"—she opens up her robe—"is the body of a mere girl?"

I'm frozen to the spot, staring. So is Morton, and Basil, and everyone else. Well, everyone except Harold's snakes.

"You're all woman to me!" one yells.

"Let me show you what a night of sleaze and slime can be like!" yells another, as they all squirm excitedly.

Hepzibah smiles, and walks—well, undulates—over to Harold, all her parts moving in thrillingly perfect sync. She reaches out a hand to run her fingers through Harold's hair, causing snake after snake to shudder delicately. "I like excitement," she whispers to them, "and different experiences. Do you think you could...*amuse* me?"

"Absolutely!" "You betcha" "In a heartbeat!" say three of them.

"How pathetic," says another.

Hepzibah's hand stills, and there is a dangerous glint in her beautiful eyes. "Who said that?" she asks softly, but with deadly intent.

One defiant snake slithers out in front of the rest. "I did," comes the reply in a distinctly feminine voice. "I'm sick of the vulgar display my brothers make of themselves whenever they see a cute bit of tail."

She pokes Hepzibah's hand in disgust. "It's degrading, and embarrassing—and it gives us a bad name."

"Like biting and killing people haven't contributed to that bad reputation," observes Basil wryly, the moon having slid behind an incoming storm cloud.

"It's you!" comes an awestruck voice and we all turn to see who belongs to it—and believe me, turning away from Hepzibah even for a second takes a major effort of will. And it so happens that the voice belongs to Goldberg, who is staring wide-eyed at her. "After all these years, it's Salome!"

She gives him a good hard look. "I know you," she said. "You're that guy who hooted and hollered louder than anyone when I did my dance."

Goldberg nods his head. He tries to say something, but his voice starts to break.

"Two thousand years and your throat is *still* hoarse from all that screaming?" she says with a smile. "I consider that a high compliment."

"You're as beautiful as ever," he manages to say.

Which is an understatement, because she is even more beautiful now than when she entered the shop, but I decide not to contradict him, and besides my throat is so dry I probably can't get the words out.

Just then the Grim Reaper emerges from the back room.

"Don't be afraid," said Goldberg. "I won't let him touch you."

The Reaper takes one look at her, grabs his stomach, bellows, *"You're* here, too? I'm gonna be sick again!" and runs back to the bathroom.

"Too?" she repeats, looking at Goldberg with renewed interest. "You're immortal?"

He nods.

"Well," she says, "we have a lot to talk about."

"You'll actually talk to me?" said Goldberg, barely able to contain his excitement.

"Talking's not my long and strong suit," she replies in sultry tones. "But we can *start* by talking."

Basil has to repress another howl. Harold's lady snake looks shocked. Morton tenses, which is harder than you think for a skeleton. Otis merely salivates.

"So do I call you Hepzibah or Salome?" asks Goldberg.

She shrugs, and Basil and Harold almost faint before the last of the shrug fades from view. "Or Eve, or Lilith, or Helen, or…"

She goes on and on, and I begin to see that this is not only the most beautiful and exotic creature in the history of this and every other universe, but also a well-named one (or at least a multiply-named one). Not only that, but she's got a real head on her shoulders or she couldn't remember more than half those names.

"It was Salome I fell in love with, so it is Salome I shall call you," says Goldberg. He continues staring at her, his mouth open (which is not always a good idea in New York City, as you never know what might fly into it). "What are you doing here?"

"Telling this wolf to shut up and let me sleep," she answers.

"I mean, in New York. I have been searching for you for two millennia, and this is the closest I've ever gotten."

"Really?" she says. "I'm flattered." Which is wrong, because take my word for it, she isn't anything with the word "flat" in it. "Who are you?" she continues.

"I am a man who has been cursed with wanderlust," answers Goldberg. "A man who has loved you for two thousand years and has forsaken all other women."

"*All* other women?" says Salome, clearly pleased.

"Yes," he says. "Just as I know you have kept yourself pure for me."

"Well, within reason," she says with another shrug.

"I am doomed to wander the world," says Goldberg. "Please tell me I no longer have to do so alone."

"To tell the truth, I *am* getting tired of New York," she says. "Sure, I'll come away with you."

"I'll wait here and count the minutes while you pack your clothes," says Goldberg.

"You've counted enough minutes," says Salome. "Besides, who needs clothes?"

Basil starts whining piteously.

"Then shall we leave right now?" asks Goldberg.

"Why not?" she said, linking her arm in his. "Where shall we go?"

"The Riviera is beautiful this time of year," says Goldberg.

She shakes her head. "I was just there last summer. How about Tahiti?"

"It's not what it was back in Gauguin's time," he answers as they walk slowly toward the door. "How about a fling at the gaming tables in Monaco?"

"Been there, done that," she replies. "Perhaps dinner at Maxim's after we tour the Louvre?"

They are still trying to find a place they haven't both been, or at least aren't tired of, when they walk into the night and out of sight.

"Are they gone?" rasps the Grim Reaper from the back room.

"Yeah, you can come out now," I say.

He comes back into the shop and glares at me. "You got any more surprises for me, an honest hardworking guy who's never done you any harm...*yet*," he concludes meaningfully.

"Not that I'm aware of," I say. "You want a trim while you're here?"

He shakes his head and walks to the door. "This has been a very upsetting experience. I've got to go out and find some stale air to breathe."

As he leaves, Harvey the Yeti, his shaggy fur dripping ice water, brushes by him on the way in. The Reaper mutters something, and Harvey yells after him: "Yeah? Well, I'm not half as abominable as a guy who takes our starting quarterback three weeks before the playoffs!"

"Hi, Harvey," I say as Basil gets up and the yeti takes his place. "What can I do for you?"

"I've come for a blow-dry" he says in his deep gravelly voice. "I've got a hot date with a fire nymph in a couple of hours." He looks around the room. "I've never dated one before. Anyone got any tips?"

A moment later Otis is telling him how to find a fire nymph's jugular, Basil is explaining which cut of her goes best with mashed potatoes and glazes carrots, and Harold's snakes want to know why a fire nymph would prefer a yeti to them.

It's just another night at The Close Shave.

When Kevin invited us to re-visit the wonderful all-night barber shop we created in "The Close Shave" for Simon & Schuster's Blood Lite III *anthology, we responded with "Making the Cut," perhaps our funniest collaboration to date.*

—MIKE

Making the Cut
(A Close Shave story)

BY MIKE RESNICK & LEZLI ROBYN

It's been a busy night at The Close Shave. I've already given a trim and a shampoo to Harvey the Yeti, of whom there is an awful lot to trim and wash. Mildred the Lamia comes in looking for Leonard her almost-husband, and decides to have some feathers plucked while she is here, and as the clock strikes midnight I am giving Basil his nightly shave and trim. He hands me a pair of books, one on dog grooming and one an illustrated copy of Kipling's *Jungle Book*, and suggests that he wants to look exactly like Akila, the leader of the pack, and I point out that everything I do is ephemeral because come morning he will look like an aging, overweight Mowgli again.

In fact," I say, "if the moon goes behind a cloud, you will probably forget to be a wolf even while I am trimming your whiskers."

"What do you know about werewolves?" he says contemptuously. "We're a unique and noble race."

"Unique, noble and hairy," I say. "Now be quiet and hold still or I'll wind up nicking you."

"What do I care?" he demands. "We werewolves are made of stern stuff."

"*You* may not care," I reply. "But *he* does."

I gesture toward Otis, who is sitting there reading the obituary column, as usual. His fangs are pressing against his lips as if they may burst through at any moment.

"Otis is my friend," says Basil. "He would never drink my blood."

"Not unless I was thirsty," agrees Otis.

"When are you thirsty?" I ask.

"All the time," admits Otis.

"Well, *I* would never drink your blood," chimes in Morton, which I find very disappointing. Morton is all bone as far as the eye can see. He looks like a refuge from a medical class or maybe a Halloween party, and I have been waiting for him to eat or drink something for fourteen years now, just so I can see where it goes once he swallows it.

"What's the matter with my blood?" demands Basil.

"Nothing," says Otis "I will defend your blood for as long as it lasts." He stares at Basil. "I think it would go well with a jelly donut."

The door opens and a pretty woman with auburn curls as soft as fairy floss, dressed in slacks and a blouse, enters.

"Can I help you?" I ask.

She holds up a page she's torn from a newspaper. Otis sees that it's not another obituary column and pays her no further attention. "I'm answering your ad for a manicurist."

"You *did* see the part about the unusual clientele?" I ask.

"How unusual can they be?" she asks.

"Go to work on Basil here," I say, stepping aside, "and then tell me."

She pulls up a stool, I roll the manicuring tray over to her, and she takes Basil's paw in her hands.

"Claws," she says, frowning. "He has claws."

"And dew claws," I add, pointing to the curved claw growing out of each wrist.

She shrugs. "What the hell, I need the work."

"Don't cut the quicks," says Basil, stifling a whine.

"Or at least alert me if you do," adds Otis.

154

"This is some place, this barber shop," she says. "By the way, my name's Mavis."

I am about to ask her what her last name is, or how much she thinks I am paying her, but just then three elderly ladies, all wearing hats, and each carrying a hatpin in her withered fingers, burst into the shop.

"Damn!" mutters one of them. "He's not here!"

"Let's go, girls!" says another to her two companions, who haven't been girls since Sherman took a little stroll through Georgia. "He can't have gotten too far."

And just like that, they're back on the sidewalk and rushing down the block.

"This happens a lot, does it?" asks Mavis.

"Actually, we're hardly ever visited by old ladies brandishing hatpins," I tell her.

"I want a raise," she says.

"You've been here less than three minutes," I note.

"I want one anyway."

"You don't even know what I'm paying you."

"If I'm going to work on werewolves and skeletons, it's not enough," says Mavis.

"Okay," I agree. "When you're right, you're right. You've got a raise."

"Good," she says, going back to work on Basil's claws. I make a mental note that someday I must figure out what I'm paying her. At the moment, she doesn't seem to care, as long as it's more than it was when she walked in the door.

And speaking of walking in the door, she has barely begun to work on Basil in earnest when the door opens and in walks a burly figure. I assume it is a man, because it walks on two legs and wears shoes and socks. But it also wears a floor-length overcoat with the collar turned up, and a scarf wrapped around most of its face, and a slouch hat covering the rest of it, and while assuming it is a man is a safe assumption anywhere else, here at The Close Shave it is very little better than an even-money proposition.

It walks to the coat tree, where Morton and Otis have hung their overcoats—Basil doesn't need one with all that fur, and besides he can't find one to fit him when he's busy being a wolf—and it peeks out through the front window.

"Are they coming back?" it says in a deep masculine voice.

"Who did you have reference to?" I ask.

"The old biddies with the hatpins," it says.

"No, they seemed in a hurry to go up the street," says Basil.

"Good!" it says with a sigh of relief. "Do you mind if I stay here for a few minutes, just in case?"

"Just in case they come back?" I ask.

"Just in case they're still on the street looking for me."

"What did you do to them?" asks Otis, who takes a professional curiosity in such things.

"Nothing!" it says passionately. It takes its hat and coat off, and I can see that it's a man. Or at least it used to be. He's got an awful lot of wounds on him, even a few bullet holes, but no blood and no scabs, and his skin is mostly gray. And all he's wearing under the coat is a pair of colorful gold briefs.

"I know you!" exclaims Mavis. "You're Loathsome Lamont! I saw you wrestle last month!"

He nods his head wearily. "Yeah, that's me."

"What *did* you do to those sweet old ladies?" persists Otis.

"Not a thing!" insists Lamont.

"Then why do they want you?"

"They want to stick their hatpins in me," says Lamont.

"For no reason at all?" says Otis dubiously.

"I'm a rassler," answers Lamont. "What other reason do they need? Most of our audience is excitable little old ladies with hatpins. If we ever stop, half the hatpin manufacturers in the world will go broke. I mean, who else *uses* hatpins these days?"

"But why are you hiding from them?" asks Morton. "Not to put too fine a point on it, you're a zombie. You can't feel pain."

"What does that have to do with anything?" says Lamont.

"Hold on," I say. "Now even *I'm* confused."

"Look," explains Lamont. "I'm a Bad Guy." I can almost hear the capital letters. "I don't want to be, I want everyone to cheer me, but"—a bitter expression crosses his lifeless face—"there's a prejudice against zombies. So I bite and I kick and I choke, and at least once a match I hit my opponent with a chair from ringside. It's all in good fun, and no one ever gets hurt. I mean, after all, we're *rasslers*."

"I always thought the matches were fixed," says Morton.

"They're not *fixed*," Lamont corrects him. "They're *scripted*, like any other dramatic performance." A wistful expression crosses his face. "I'd give anything to be the Good Guy for a change. Lancelot Lamont, they could call me, or Lamont the Lustrous. Even Lamont the Lovable would be okay. But no," he concludes unhappily, "I have to be Loathsome Lamont. I blame it on anti-zombie prejudice in high places."

"I don't want to interrupt a mournful tale of self-pity," I say," but why are you here at all?"

"I was choking the life out of Handsome Harry, same as always—we were going to meet later for a beer—and then he twisted out of it, applied a reverse Mongolian death grip, and threw me out of the ring, just like we practiced it in the gym yesterday."

"And the little old ladies threatened you with their hatpins and you ran away," concludes Morton. "But why? You're already dead. Nothing can hurt you."

"But *they* don't know it," answers Lamont. "They stick me, and I howl in anguish, and it makes their evening."

"Why do I think this story is not going where I thought it was going?" muses Otis aloud.

"When I was doubled up on the floor in mock agony, I was keeping an eye on *my* fans, and some *other* little old lady—I think she was there to abuse Horrible Hubert—stuck a hatpin in my back, and I didn't react. The woman immediately started screaming that I was a fake and that I didn't feel pain, and my loyal fans shouted her down and then decided to prove that of course it hurt when they stuck their hatpins into me…but there were so many of them I knew I couldn't react to every one of them, so I ran to the locker room, grabbed my coat and hat, and fled into the night."

And Otis, Basil, Morton, Mavis, and I all ask in unison: *"Why?"*

"They're my *fans*," he explains. "I couldn't break their sweet, bloodthirsty, little-old-lady hearts by disappointing them." A very dry tear tries to roll down his cheek. "I never want to disappoint *anyone*."

Mavis walks over and runs her hand through Lamont's unkempt hair, ignoring the pieces of scalp that flake off. He looks up at her with an expression I have only seen on abused puppies.

"Aw, you poor thing," says Mavis, who is adapting to The Close Shave quicker than I'd expected.

"All I ever wanted was to be a hero," says Lamont, his lower lip trembling. "Just once in my life—well, in my death—I want to hear cheers instead of boos. I want my fans to send me the roses, not the thorns. Is that so much to ask?"

"Hey, pal, we all have problems," says Basil, who is even less sympathetic as a wolf than he is as a man.

"You're a magnificent carnivore, very near the top of the food chain," replies Lamont. "What problems could you possibly have?"

"Do you know how few sheep are running loose in Central Park?" shoots back Basil. "I hang out behind an all-night hot dog stand begging for scraps. And the two times I actually find lady werewolves, they're not in heat."

"But you can still resort to dating humans," Lamont points out.

"Hey!" shouts Mavis suddenly. "*Resort?* Like a *last* resort?"

"Oh, no offense intended at all, Madam!" apologizes Lamont.

She glares at him. "*Madam?*"

"*Miss,*" stammers Lamont. "I mean *Miss.*"

She arches an auburn eyebrow.

Lamont blushes—which is to say he turns a deeper shade of gray. "I would never insult a lovely lady like you."

She preens, twirling a lock of hair on an impeccably manicured finger, and then throws him a smile as a reward. From his reaction I get the distinct impression that Lamont doesn't get many smiles *or* rewards.

"So why do you want to be a hero?" I ask when Lamont is through with his version of a blush.

"Why, indeed?" adds Otis, deigning to look up from his obituary columns, "when it's so much *sexier* being bad?"

Lamont blinks, and it is obvious that he has never considered this angle before. "But I look like the walking dead. In fact, I *am* the walking dead. What could be sexy about that?"

Otis glances up at the zombie, amused, then folds up the newspaper and looks speculatively at Mavis. He lets his gaze slide down from her face to the curve of her neck, suggestively licking his blood red lips. She shudders delicately, and unconsciously tilts her head to expose more of her neck.

Otis stands, and even I am transfixed by the elegance in the gesture; I've never seen him display his vampiric charms before. He glides over to Mavis while she stares at him as if hypnotized. He keeps eye contact for a long moment before moving around to stand behind her, sliding his hand up her arm as he does so, until he's pulling her hair away from the side of her neck. He leans in, his lips a hairsbreadth from the aortic artery throbbing in her neck. "It's the danger they find intoxicating," he says at last, baring his fangs. "Not only do we court death, but our natural instinct is to take away life. And yet a night with us can lead to immortality, and maybe even eternal love…." He looks up at Lamont and winks. "Women love that romantic claptrap. They don't realize that vampire males want the same thing as human males."

What's that?" asks Morton, who long since ceased being any kind of a male.

"Poor fellow," says Otis with obvious sympathy. "I think I'll leave it to your imagination."

"But I haven't had an imagination in decades," protests Morton.

"Then perhaps I'll show you after all," replies Otis.

The sight of a vampire literally drooling all over my newest employee suddenly brings me back to the here and now, and I realize how vulnerable Mavis is. While supernatural creatures such as werewolves and zombies are immune to a vampire's charms, human minds and hearts are very susceptible to manipulation. I see how the situation could become *very* bloody in an instant, and my insurance doesn't cover death from vampire attack.

"Otis, I don't think Edna's going to approve of this," I say, hoping mention of his insanely jealous wife will help snap him out of it.

"Omigod!" he rasps. "Is that *yenta* on the way in?" His eyes dart to the front of the shop, searching frantically for a full minute before relaxing. "So I wanted a little nosh," he says weakly. "Sue me."

"Try that again and I just might!" snaps Mavis, who is suddenly animated again.

Otis sighs and his eyes lose their hypnotic red glow as he pulls himself away from Mavis, severing their connection. He turns to me and asks in a half-whining, half-supplicating tone, "Not even a little taste?"

"You know the ground rules," I tell him. "No blood gets spilled in The Close Shave unless it's caused by my razor."

Otis sighs in the overly tragic fashion that only a self-centered vampire can approximate. His fangs retract and he makes his way back to his customary seat to bury himself in the obituary columns once again.

Mavis watches him until she's sure he isn't a threat anymore, then turns to me, her impeccably manicured hands now resting pointedly on her hips. "Somehow I intuit that working here could be very hazardous to my health," she states.

Now it's my turn to sigh. "So I'll give you another raise."

Mavis flashes me a triumphant smile, which is more than a little bit curious, or at least premature, as I have never once mentioned her starting salary. "Wonderful!" she says, and then turns back to the barber's chair. "Now, Basil, tell me how you let your paws get into such a disgraceful state." She sits across from the werewolf again, and opens up her beautician's bag, pulling out various implements—more than a few of them looking like small medieval torture devices—as well as a curious container of cream. While Basil complains about the damage the concrete causes his claws when he runs with the pack at night, Mavis starts to rub the cream onto his paws. "You just need to moisturize every day to keep your skin supple," she tells him. "That's all there is to it."

"I wish," laments Morton, who hasn't had any skin since before Mavis was born.

"What's the point?" asks Lamont. "I use anti-dandruff shampoo, and you can see how well that works." He shakes his head, and it's as if it starts snowing. Flakes of dead skin start falling everywhere.

"Walk around with a couple of talkative snakes for hair, constantly yammering in your ear, and then see if you complain about something as trivial as flaky skin."

We all turn to where the voice is coming from and see Harold, one of my regular clients, walk through the door.

"I thought you were going on a walkabout," says Otis.

The Australian medusa shrugs. "It wasn't worth the hissing and whining," he says, taking his usual seat. "If it wasn't one damned snake, it was another. Cecil kept me awake all night, bitching about his broken fangs. As for the rest...." He grimaces. "Are we there yet?

Are we there yet?" Then he mutters an obscenity. "When are they going to understand there is no tangible *there* on a walkabout, even in Central Park?"

"Are they dangerous?" asks Mavis quietly, carefully observing the undulations of the snakes.

"Don't be frightened," says Morton. "They're harmless."

"Even if you're not a skeleton?" asks Mavis dubiously.

"Don't listen to him!" cries one of Harold's snakes in a squeaky little voice as it stretches out to its full five inches. "I'm as vicious as they come!"

"Me, too!" says another, and then another. And suddenly they are all bouncing up and down to get the manicurist's attention, and baring their fangs to impress her.

Mavis's face blanches to a shade lighter than Otis—which is quite a feat, as Otis hasn't seen the sun for half a century—and I realize that if I'm not careful I could lose an employee, a commodity in which The Close Shave does not exactly abound. Mavis has been here twenty minutes, which is already longer that the previous four lasted.

"Harold is a pacifist," I say reassuringly.

"But *I'm* not!" says Cecil, the biggest of the snakes.

"Big deal," snorts Otis contemptuously. "I'll lay plenty of seven-to-five that you can't even bite your way through a balloon."

"Don't get him started on his broken fangs," says Harold plaintively. "It's all he talks about."

"But it hurtssss," Cecil hisses, his head hanging low.

"Maybe Mavis has a tooth file amongst her instruments," I suggest.

Her auburn curls bob around her face as she shakes her head. "I'll have to order one." She looks at me, head tilting. "The Close Shave will pay for it, right?"

"Yes," I say. Then I turn to Harold and add: "If Harold pays for the dental service."

Harold's face hardens. "I'm not even talking to Cecil this week."

I shrug. "There's your answer."

Suddenly Morton stands up and walks over to the vending machine. He puts some coins into it and out pops a Coke.

I can barely contain my excitement. Finally, fourteen years after putting that vending machine on the shop floor in the hope that

Morton would someday use it, I am going to see where liquid goes when it passes through his teeth.

Lamont sighs. "Boy, that looks good," he says wistfully.

"So have one," I say.

He indicates his glittering trunks. "I was in such a hurry to leave the arena that my pants—and my money—are still in the locker room."

"Here, have mine," offers Morton.

"Thanks," says Lamont, taking it from him.

I wait for him to buy another.

He doesn't.

"Boy, am I thirsty!" I say finally. "You must be thirsty, too, Morton."

Morton shrugs, and I swear I can hear his bones creak. "Not really. The urge has passed. Besides, I don't have any more money."

I try not to sound desperate. "The least I can do is give you another can, on the house, for being so generous."

"No need," says Morton, as polite as ever. "I've been meaning to go on a diet anyway."

I almost do a double take at the thought of a skeleton on a diet. "What the hell," I say in desperation. "I'll buy you a diet pop."

"It's bad for the teeth," answers Morton, giving me a full skeletal grin.

I stand there for a minute, not trusting myself to speak. Otis looks up at me from his obituary columns, clearly amused, and I swear Harold's snakes are hissing in laughter.

I turn to the medusa, exasperated. "What the hell *are* you doing here anyway?"

"I've come for a shave and a shampoo."

"Please, not a shampoo!" begs one of the snakes. "It gets in our eyes! We'll be good from now on, I promise!"

"It's wet!" cries another. "My Uncle Nate drowned during a shampoo!"

"Oh, aren't they just adorable!" exclaims Mavis, no longer wary of the terrified creatures.

The snakes all turn to Mavis. "Save ussss!" they hiss in unison.

"We promise not to bite," says Cecil. "Probably," he adds very softly.

I'm about to point out that Cecil can't bite anyone anyway, when Mavis's face softens into a smile. "How about this," she says. "I'm busy

162

with another client at the moment"—she gestures to Basil—"but if you boys behave, I'll wash you afterwards." She raises her hand to stall any protests. "I promise not to immerse any of you in water. I'll just rub you with a wet soapy cloth to get you clean."

The snakes start writhing in excitement.

"You can do *anything* you want to us, Sweetie!" one of them exclaims, pulling himself erect.

"Anything at all," agrees another.

"Okay, it's a deal," says Mavis. She turns back to Basil and starts working on his cuticles. Suddenly he yelps in pain.

"Don't be a crybaby," she admonishes him, "I've barely touched you."

He growls.

"Basil!" I warn him.

"But it *hurts!*" he whimpers.

"You're not a cub anymore," I say. "Man up!"

"Or wolf up," adds Morton helpfully.

Basil sinks back down in the chair, and Mavis starts to work on him again. Not a minute has gone by before he's howling in pain. "Oh, I'm so sorry, Basil!" she exclaims. "I'm not used to working on werewolves."

Otis drops his newspaper, now alert, his nostrils twitching. "*Blood!*" he intones.

I look over and see that Mavis has cut Basil near his dew claw.

"The cream *burns!*" howls the werewolf.

"What's in it?" asks Lamont, walking over and looking at Basil's arm.

"It's a secret recipe that's been used by my family for decades. I know it uses chimera blood, and firebird feathers, and just a dollop of chopped liver. My Uncle Saul, who is a Wizard of the 3rd Order, created it." She sniffs it. "I always thought it had cream cheese as well."

"Is it *supposed* to burn?" I ask, surprised to find myself genuinely worried for Basil.

"Only if I nick him," she responds. "It softens hard dry skin, and I suppose that includes nails, though in all my years as a manicurist I've never nicked a dew claw before." She pauses, then adds thoughtfully: "In fact, I've never *seen* a dew claw before. Well, except on my puppy."

"You have a puppy?" asks Lamont, suddenly interested.

"She's the cutest little thing you ever saw," says Mavis.

"Bring her to my next match at the arena," says Lamont. "I could pretend I'm going to eat her, and when I'm just two seconds away from biting her head off, Heroic Horace can whack me over the head with that rubber bat of his and throw me out of the ring." "Where all your little old ladies will jab you with hatpins," says Morton. "Are you sure you want that?"

"I hadn't thought that far ahead," admits Lamont, and suddenly he's depressed again.

"*Ouch,* goddammit!" snarls Basil.

"Don't be such a crybaby," I say. "You're giving werewolves a bad name."

"She's cutting me to bits, and you're giving me stupid little homilies!" moans Basil.

Mavis examines his paw, frowning. "I didn't cut a quick," she announces.

"You must have," insists Basil.

She shakes her head. "There's no blood."

"Damn!" grumbles Otis. "It's not fair to get a fellow's hopes up like that."

"You haven't been a fellow in 50 years," I tell him.

"No," concludes Mavis after checking his paw again. "I never touched a quick."

"Then you cut into my skin," says Basil accusingly.

"I most certainly did not," replies Mavis. "There's not a mark on it."

"It's not my skin anyway," sulks Basil. "It's my claw."

"You don't have any feeling in your claw," insists Mavis. "I put a tiny nick in the top of it, but you only have feeling in your quick, and I never touched it."

"Well, it hurts like hell," complains Basil.

"All right, all right," mutters Mavis. "Let me rub a little cream on it, just to make sure you don't get infected while you're running in the park."

She rubs the cream on, and only gravity keeps Basil from jumping right through the ceiling. His howl is so loud that I think he's going to shatter my front window, but fortunately it survives intact, though the mirror behind the chair develops two large cracks in it, and one of my fillings falls out.

"She's murdering me!" screams Basil.

She frowns. "It must be the chopped liver."

"Aw, come on, pal," says Lamont. "I was watching her, and all she did was dab a little cream on a claw."

"Yeah," says Basil bitterly. "And all Lizzie Borden did was trim her father's mustache!"

"If you were acting, I'd say you have the makings of a pro rassler," says Lamont. He frowns. "But you sound like you mean it."

"I do. I was fine until she rubbed that cream on me."

"I think I've got it," says Mavis. "Uncle Saul always complained that he really wanted the feathers of a harpy, but they are almost impossible to find without a qualified tracker, so he had to settle for some equally rare firebird feathers. Obviously the combined ingredients indeed softens the skin—its intended purpose—but the substituted ingredient also increases sensitivity exponentially." She shook her head. "No wonder the cream burns."

Lamont's gaze goes from Basil's claw to the cream and back to the claw. Finally he turns to Mavis and extends his hand. "Would you rub some of that on my hand, please?"

She shrugs and dabs the back of his hand with it.

"Can't feel a thing," says Lamont, who is clearly disappointed.

"I can't feel it on my other three claws," says Basil. "Just where she nicked me."

Lamont holds his hand out. "Bite it."

"No way!" says Basil. "That stuff hurts enough on the *outside* of my body."

"Otis?" says Lamont, extending his hand in the vampire's direction.

"I wish I could accommodate you," answers Otis. "But you don't have any blood. I don't think my metabolism could handle that."

"Ah, what the hell," says Harold, getting to his feet. He walks over, takes Lamont's hand, and lays it on his head. "Dig in, boys."

Each of the snakes takes a bite—well, all except Cecil, who really needs the services of a dentist with a background in herpetology, or maybe a herpetologist with a background in dentistry—and suddenly Lamont shrieks even louder than Basil did.

"What happened?" I ask.

"I feel *pain!*" he exclaims with a huge grin. "Isn't it wonderful?"

Not surprisingly, not a single person in the shop—not even any of the snakes—agrees with him.

"Don't you see?" continues Lamont. "I'll rub this all over my body before a match, and then I won't have to pretend anymore!"

"You *want* to be in pain?" asks Mavis.

"It's for my fans," he answers. "Especially the little old ladies. They've kept me in business since I came back from...well...you know. This is the least I can do for them." A pause. "Maybe I'd better give it a field test."

He takes off his coat and has Mavis rub her cream all over his back, his eyes lighting up in both pleasure and pain as the cream bit into the wounds the little hatpin ladies had inflicted after his match. "You can get more of this stuff, right?" he asks, through gritted teeth.

"Uncle Saul left us five gallons of it," she assures him. "And if we run out, I'm sure I can convince him to leave the mausoleum for one night and make more. He's always complaining about how cramped he feels in his tomb anyway."

Lamont walks to the door. "Wish me luck."

We all do, and then he's out in the street.

"Well, I'll be damned," says Otis, looking up from the paper. "Horatio Throop died."

"Who was Horatio Throop?" asks Morton.

"The cop who tracked me down after I bit every girl at the Our Lady of Unseemly Passions Flower Festival over in Brooklyn. Put six slugs into me at point-blank range. Of course they didn't do any damage at all, except to the watch I had in a vest pocket. They didn't believe his story at headquarters and fired him for being drunk or maybe delusional. We became quite good friends after that. Whenever he was depressed he'd give me a phone call, come on over, empty his revolver into me, and then he'd feel all better."

Just then Ursula the Undine enters the shop. She is only three feet tall, bald as an egg, and totally without fingernails, so I know she's not here on business.

"I don't mean to bother you," she says breathlessly, "but there's quite a commotion going on out there. I almost got trampled to death!"

"Oh?" I say.

166

"Yes," she continues. "A bunch of wild-eyed old ladies are chasing some poor guy down the street, jabbing him with hatpins. He's screaming in pain, but as he passes me he's smiling the biggest damned smile you ever saw."

"Mavis," I say as Ursula works up the courage to go back outside, "it looks like you just may have a client for life."

"Which in this case," adds Otis, "means quite a bit more than usual."

We sold "Shame" to Analog *magazine, and also to Greece. It took us two evenings, start to finish. ("Evening" is a subjective term; we were still living ten thousand miles—and fourteen hours—apart.)*

—MIKE

Shame

BY MIKE RESNICK & LEZLI ROBYN

F ar out on the rim of the galaxy there is a pastoral world, golden-hued, with lush green fields, crystal clear rivers and streams, color-ful avians, gorgeous blossoms.

It used to be a colony world. Fairview, they called it. There's still a town there, though no one's lived in it for…well, for a long time now. There's a church, with a steeple you can see from just about anywhere, and a general store that's stood empty for close to sixty years. Same with the saloon, and the restaurant, and the bank, and the bubble-domed boarding houses.

There's really only one thing of note to see on Fairview. It's right in the center of the small town square, and you don't know it's there until you're almost upon it.

It's an old-fashion gallows, complete with a rope noose. And hanging from the noose, its body swaying and gently spinning with every breeze, is something dead, something that looks like a man from a distance, but the closer you get, the more you realize that you're looking at something very strange and very *alien*.

It's been dead a long time, this *something* that hangs in the town square. I don't know what its skin looked like in life, but it's all leathery now, and any color it might have had has been burned away.

Oh—and there's the sign. *That* gets your attention even more than what's hanging from the gallows. It's propped up against the base of it—well, bonded or nailed there, or it would long since have blown away. It's almost as high as a man's waist, and maybe twice as long as it is high.

And on it, in bold letters more than two feet high, all capitals, is a single word:

SHAME

You see it, and you know there has to be a story behind it. So I looked around the empty town, and sure enough, I found one old man, toothless, bent over with the weight of his years, almost as leathered as the body on the gallows, and he told me the tale of what happened on Fairview.

He had a name (said the old man), but no one could pronounce it. Most folks just called him Boy, or sometimes Satan because of the reddish tint to his skin and those hooves that passed for feet. He wasn't native to Fairview—hell, Fairview didn't *have* no natives. As I hear tell, he got here right after the first wave of colonists, and spent his time digging for something in the rocky outcrops just beyond where they built the town. The geological surveys said there wasn't nothing out there worth the effort he was going to, but who knows what's valuable to an alien?

He wasn't what you'd call eloquent or articulate, but he spoke a kind of Terran, enough to make himself understood. We figured he'd been dropped off on Fairview, since there wasn't any sign of his ship, and that'd mean someday he'd be picked up, but truth to tell nobody gave it much thought since he didn't spend time around the human centers much. Never entered a bar or a restaurant, and the general store sure didn't have anything he could use. We never did learn what he ate, but whatever it was he must have found it out there where he was digging.

I'm not aware that anyone ever had a grudge against him. No one tried to befriend him neither. He was just too different, if you know what I mean. He lived alone, kept to himself, didn't bother anyone, didn't talk much to anyone, didn't pay us any more attention than we paid him.

Not until Charlie Drumm came along, anyway.

He showed up one day, put his robots to work building him a house on the outskirts of town, made friends nice and quick with anyone who gave him half a chance, spent his first few weeks buying drinks for anyone who was thirsty, even took to attending our little church. That church probably wasn't pulling a dozen people on a Sunday morning, but then Charlie started going and people decided that if a man they all admired could go humble himself before God, maybe it wasn't such a bad idea after all.

He did one thing that caused more than a few eyebrows to raise, because no one could figure out *why* he did it. He actually went out of his way to make friends with the alien, and spent a lot of time visiting him out in the foothills. He even invited him into his own home. Might have been some trouble if he'd been anyone but Charlie Drumm. You know the rules: you just don't invite an alien into your house, no matter what.

Before long they'd become fast friends. You didn't see the one in town without the other. Charlie would vanish for three or four days at a time, then come back and tell us about the trip he'd taken with Satan, off to some new mountain looking for whatever the hell it was Satan looked for. Or Satan would be in town every day, and sleep in at Charlie's place.

I still remember the night Charlie walked into the tavern with his arm around Satan's shoulders, waved hello to everyone, and sidled right up to the bar. Now, we didn't have no rules forbidding aliens to join us in the bars. We just figured that nine out of ten couldn't handle our drinkin' stuff, and the tenth would have sense enough to know when he wasn't wanted.

"I'll have Barillian whiskey and a chaser," Charlie announced.

The barkeep headed off to get it.

"Hang on a second," said Charlie. "You haven't asked my friend what he wants."

The barkeep walked over, with an expression on his face like you might see if his shorts were too tight, and said, "What'll it be, boy?"

"Just a minute," said Charlie. "He's got a name. Probably you can't pronounce it, so you can call him Satan, which is what I hear a lot of folks calling him. But he's not a boy, yours or anyone else's, and I don't want to hear anyone calling my friend Boy again."

I don't think anyone but Charlie could have said that without starting a fight that would involve everyone in the bar. The barkeep looked around to see if anyone was about to throw a punch, or maybe a chair, and when they didn't his face got even more pained, and he said, "What can I fix you, sir?"

"Water," said Satan in that gravelly, mush-mouthed voice of his.

"Water's pretty expensive on Fairview," said the barkeep.

"The hell it is," said Charlie. "And I want you to put it on my bill."

And that was that. They waited for their drinks, then wandered over to a table in a corner, probably so no one could sneak up behind them. Pretty soon conversations started up again, and by the end of the evening hardly anyone paid them any attention.

They came back the next night, and the night after that, and by week's end it was like Satan had always been a customer. A couple of men even started up conversations with him when Charlie was off in the john, but he didn't have much to say. In fact, the major topic of conversation when him and Charlie weren't around was what the hell they could find to spend all those hours talking about.

I guess Charlie had been here maybe four months when news of the Skeletons started coming through. No one knew what they looked like or why they were called Skeletons—no one in town, anyway—but word had it that they'd been attacking mining colonies for the better part of a year, plundering any kind of fissionable materials they could find.

We didn't worry overmuch about it. We were an agricultural and trading world. The only mining anyone did, and I don't know if mining is even the right word, was Satan digging out there in the hills, and he didn't glow when he'd walk through town at night, so we figured there was nothing radioactive out there. We knew that sooner or later the navy would dope out where the Skeletons were going to strike next and be waiting for them, and we'd hear about it on the subspace radio when they'd sent the last of 'em off to hell.

Still, we did a lot of talking about it at the tavern, wondering what a critter called a Skeleton looked like. Jake Mundy thought they were probably just real skinny things, maybe like a six-foot man who weighs 75 pounds, but Christian Duran argued that maybe they had eyes set so deep in their heads that they looking like skulls with gaping eyeholes. I remember that Roz Waterson even suggested that they were big fat blimp-like creatures, and someone with a sense of humor had dubbed 'em Skeletons.

Finally Charlie spoke up from where he was sitting with Satan.

"You're all wrong," he said. "They're bipeds like us, but they've got exoskeletons."

"You ever seen one?" asked Jake Mundy.

"Once or twice," answered Charlie.

"And you're sure they were Skeletons?"

"You get one look at one, you'll know there's nothing else you could call them," said Charlie.

Well, as you can imagine, the whole tavern wanted to know more, but Charlie just finished his beer, announced it was getting late, and he and Satan got up to leave.

"Hey, Satan," said Roz Waterson. "Have *you* ever seen a Skeleton?"

He turned to her. "It is possible," he answered her.

"If they're that distinctive, how could you not know?" she said.

"I saw many races before I came here," he replied.

Before she could ask any more questions the two of them—him and Charlie—had left the place, and we spent the next couple of hours trying to figure out how a two-legged alien with an exoskeleton would appear. We even used the tavern's computer—it was more complex than anything we were carrying around with us—to try to create a holo of one, but no one could decide who was right, and we figured we'd better pack it in for the night before we got into a fight over it. So we all went to bed still wondering what a Skeleton looked like.

Turned out we didn't have that long to wait before we found out.

It was the crack of dawn not a fortnight later when them Skel-etons landed on Fairview and rousted us out of our beds. They rounded us up like animals and put us in the church—the only place big enough to hold us all—and demanded we take them to Charlie Drumm. That's when we realized how little we knew about Charlie, including why the Skeletons were searching for him.

They looked mighty scary if I say so myself, and given how well-armed they were there was no doubt in anyone's mind that they meant business. But we protected our own, and Charlie was one of us by then, so we told them that there was no one named Charlie in our town. And it wasn't really a lie, either; he'd left three days earlier with Satan on one of their jaunts.

Of course, they didn't take our word for it. They ransacked our homes looking for him, and then used them bone-covered hands of theirs to rough some of us up a little, but not one of us squealed on Charlie. The interrogation went on for most of the day and finally, when we thought that they were ready to give up and go looking for him on some other world, Satan happened to walk through the door.

He may have looked like the devil entering our church, but he was *our* alien, and he was Charlie's friend to boot, so when the Skeletons surrounded him and asked about Charlie, we were sure that he would follow our example and keep his trap shut—and he did.

Even when they leaned on him, all he told was that he was just a down-on-his-luck prospector who had come to the church to pray for a better yield in his mines. Now, since they specialized in raiding mining worlds, he had to have known that the Skeletons ears would prick up at that. They demanded to see his yield, threatening that if it wasn't good enough to compensate them for a wasted trip they'd kill him. So off they went, Satan leading the parade, and suddenly the rest of us were forgotten.

I might not have liked him, but I had to grudgingly admit that he'd led the Skeletons away from us, and I was a little worried about him. Satan might have looked demonic, but he didn't have a patch on these raiders with their spiky exoskeletons and glowing reptilian eyes.

We waited in the church until nightfall, not knowing if they'd gone yet, and not wanting to provoke any of them if they hadn't. I mean, hell, what could a handful of farmers do against a shipload of armed raiders? It was best to just let them take what they wanted, and bide our time until they left.

So when three of our five moons had risen for the night, we used the moonlight to guide us quietly back to our homes, and we discovered how destructive the Skeletons had been. There wasn't a piece of furniture left unturned, and all of our root cellars had been looted of anything of value. I figured it would take us the next two seasons worth of crops just to get our stores back up, but at least they'd believed us about not knowing Charlie. It looked to us like they'd gone.

We were wrong.

We decided that a few of us would hike out to Charlie's house to see if he was all right—and I have to admit we were mighty curious to find out why they were looking for him in the first place.

The one thing we never expected to see as we came over the rise was Satan leading an armed group of Skeletons right up to Charlie's front door. We also didn't expect to see him to stand there motionless as they dragged Charlie out of the house, but that's what happened. They half-dragged and half-carried him to their scout ship. We couldn't do anything but watch: hell, we were outnumbered and outgunned. But no sooner had the ship taken off than we were running down the hill to Charlie's house.

I still remember the look in Satan's eyes as he saw us close in on him: it was like a deer caught in a vehicle's headlights back on Old Earth. But he didn't make any attempt to run away: he looked like all the fight had gone out of him—if he ever had any in the first place.

We questioned him all night, trying to get a straight answer out of him with words, with fists, with other things—but never once did he explain to why he'd led the Skeletons right up to Charlie's house when he *knew* Charlie was inside it, or what they'd given him to betray the one man who'd befriended him.

Jake Mundy and a couple of others wanted to kill him on the spot, but we were civilized men and we decided we had to have a trial. There was no way we were going let him set foot in our church again, so we held the trial in the only other place big enough for all the townsfolk to gather under one roof: the bar. We trussed him up to keep him from running away, and sat him at the very same corner table he and Charlie had shared a drink at. He looked uncomfortable as hell, beaten and bruised as he was, but that didn't bother any of us, not after what he'd done.

The trial took less than five minutes. A bunch of us had seen him lead the Skeletons to Charlie, so all we really had to do was vote him guilty and work out his sentence. We didn't have the facility or the resources to confine him for the rest of his life (which could have been a few hundred years for all anyone knew), and we sure as hell weren't going to slap him on the wrist and turn him loose. I think even before the trial began everyone knew what the sentence would be.

We gave him a chance before we passed sentence to speak in his own defense, and he wouldn't say a word. We gave him another chance when we put the noose around his neck right in the middle of the town square, and again he didn't say anything, but just stared silently at us.

I wanted him to say *something*. Maybe just that he was sorry, or even that he hated all Men and he was glad of what he'd done. I just wanted to know *why* he did it, but he stayed stoic and silent to the end.

Took him a long time to die, twitching and dangling at the end of the rope, but nobody looked away, not even the womenfolk or the kids. I suppose we could have shot up or poisoned him, but somehow hanging seemed right for what he'd done.

And after he'd finished kicking and was just hanging there, limp and dead, Roz Waterson and a couple of other women brought out a sign with **SHAME** written on it in big black letters, and propped it up against the gallows.

They were both still there—the alien and the sign—when I went outside the next morning, and by mutual consent the townspeople let them stay there permanently, to remind everyone what happens when you betray a friend.

Over the next few months avians pecked his eyes out, and his skin dried out and turned leathery, and he didn't smell anymore, and when a newcomer would land on the planet, or a friend would visit, we always made sure they saw Satan hanging there, and told them the story of how one colony, at least, had dispensed justice when it was called for.

And then, four months later, came a visitor no one expected—Charlie Drumm. Most of us figured he wouldn't last the night aboard the Skeletons' ship, and even the most optimistic figured he'd be dead within a week—either he'd be killed after giving them whatever they wanted from him, or he'd die keeping it from them—but there he was, staring at Satan's body twisting in the wind.

Then he stormed into the bar and demanded to know what had happened. After we'd told not, not without a certain amount of pride in our actions, he just stood there silently for a couple of minutes, and when we thought he might maybe have gone catatonic, he uttered a single word:

"Fools!" We looked at him like whatever he'd suffered at the hands of the Skeletons had unhinged him.

"Fools!" he repeated. "He was worth any twenty of you!"

"What the hell are you talking about?" demanded Christian Duran. "Did he turn you over to the Skeletons or didn't he?"

"On my orders," responded Drumm, trying to control his temper

"On your orders?" repeated Jake Mundy. "Just who the hell are you?"

"I'm an officer who's been fighting the goddamned Skeletons for five years!" he snapped. "They've been after me for almost two years. We found a way to let them know that I was here."

"Let me get this straight," I said. "You *wanted* to be captured?"

"I had a subspace transmitter sealed inside a false wisdom tooth. When they delivered me to their flagship, they led our navy right to it."

"Are you saying Satan worked for our navy too?" demanded Jake Mundy. "Because if he did, he's the first alien I ever heard of to do so."

"No," said Charlie. "He worked for his own government, but we had a common cause: they're at war with the Skeletons too. I *told* him to let them bribe or threaten him into giving me up."

"Why didn't he tell us when he had the chance?"

"There could have been a fifth columnist here," said Charlie. "This wouldn't be the first world."

"You should have confided in one of us," said Christian Duran bitterly. "After all, we're *men*—and he was just an alien."

"I know," said Charlie with no attempt to hide his contempt. "His race doesn't hold kangaroo courts and lynchings."

He walked outside, strode over to were Satan was hanging, stared at the **SHAME** sign, and spat on it. Then he was gone, and that's the last any of us ever saw of Charlie Drumm.

By nightfall every colonist on Fairview knew the story, knew what we had done. And suddenly it seemed like that sign was there to remind us of ourselves, not of Satan, and no one had the guts to take it down

One by one people started leaving the planet; they just didn't want to live with what we'd done. Within a year only sixteen people were left, in two years only seven, and in three years there was just me. I stuck around because I thought *someone* ought to be here to tell the true story of what happened, because when you see that body still hanging there and the sign beneath it, you can misinterpret it as easily as we misinterpreted what we saw all those years ago.

"That's the story," said the old man. "I've been telling it to anyone who'd listen, maybe two or three visitors a year, for close to forty years now, but my time's just about up, and I'm going back to my home world to spend my last few months or years there and be buried in my family plot." He paused. "It's a pity the truth's going to be forgotten again, but I did what I could, probably not enough to rub all the grime off my soul, but maybe some of it anyway."

After he left I pulled out of my pocket computer and ran a check on Charlie Drumm. Turns out he was Lieutenant Colonel Andrew Charles Drumm, twice decorated for bravery in the Skeleton War, died in action in the Lammix Campaign. I couldn't find anything about Satan, but I did learn one interesting thing: Charlie Drumm left his estate to a charitable institution on the planet Malakawn II, which was inhabited by a red-skinned race that, though hooved, was bipedal.

That night I moved my gear into Charlie's deserted house. Sooner or later visitors will touch down on Fairview and see what was still on display in the town square, and somebody has to be here to tell them the true story.

"Soulmates" was our second collaboration, based on an abandoned start of Mike's that had been sitting around his desk for years. He told me that if I could work out what was wrong with it and suggest how it should be reconceived, we could collaborate on quite a potentially powerful story. We sold it to Asimov's, the top short sf market at the time, and very shortly also sold it to Russia, China, the Czech Republic, Poland, Italy, Bulgaria, Slovakia, and Spain. It won the Ictineu Award for Best Story Translated into Catalan, and was a nominee for Australia's Aurealis Award and Spain's Ignotus Award.

—LEZLI

Soulmates

BY MIKE RESNICK & LEZLI ROBYN

Have you ever killed someone you love—I mean, *really* love? I did.

I did it as surely as if I'd fired a bullet into her brain, and the fact that it was perfectly legal, that everyone at the hospital told me I'd done a humane thing by giving them permission to pull the plug, didn't make me feel any better. I'd lived with Kathy for twenty-six years, been married to her for all but the first ten months. We'd been through a lot together: two miscarriages, a bankruptcy, a trial separation twelve years ago—and then the car crash. They said she'd be a vegetable, that she'd never think or walk or even move again. I let her hang on for almost two months, until the insurance started running out, and then I killed her.

Other people have made that decision and they learn to live with it. I thought I could, too. I'd never been much of a drinker, but I started about four months after she died. Not much at first, then more every day until I'd reach the point, later and later each time, where I couldn't see her face staring up at me anymore.

I figured it was just a matter of time before I got fired—and you have to be pretty messed up to be fired as a night watchman at Global Enterprises. Hell, I didn't even know what they made, or at least not everything they made. There were five large connected buildings, and a watchman for each. We'd show up at ten o'clock at night, and leave when the first shift showed up at seven in the morning—one man and maybe sixty robots per building.

Yeah, being sacked was imminent. Problem was, once you've been fired from a job like this, there's nothing left but slow starvation. If you can't watch sixty pre-programmed robots and make sure the building didn't blow up, what the hell *can* you do?

I still remember the night I met Mose.

I let the Spy Eye scan my retina and bone structure, and after it let me in I went directly to the bottle I'd hidden in the back of the washroom. By midnight I'd almost forgotten what Kathy looked like on that last day—I suppose she looked pretty, like she always did, but *innocent* was the word that came to mind—and I was making my rounds. I knew that Bill Nettles—he was head man on the night shift—had his suspicions about my drinking and would be checking up on me, so I made up my mind to ease off the booze a little. But I had to get rid of Kathy's face, so I took one more drink, and then next thing I knew I was trying to get up off the floor, but my legs weren't working.

I reached out for something to steady myself, to lean against as I tried to stand, and what I found was a metal pillar, and a foot away was another one. Finally my eyes started focusing, and I saw that what I had latched onto were the titanium legs of a robot that had walked over when it heard me cursing or singing or whatever the hell I was doing.

"Get me on my feet!" I grated, and two strong metal hands lifted me to my feet.

"Are you all right, sir?" asked the robot in a voice that wasn't quite a mechanical monotone. "Shall I summon help?"

"*No!*" I half-snapped, half-shouted. "No help!"

"But you seem to be in physical distress."

"I'll be fine," I said. "Just help me to my desk, and stay with me for a few minutes until I sober up."

"I do not understand the term, sir," it said.

"Don't worry about it," I told him. "Just help me."

"Yes, sir."

"Have you got an ID?" I asked as he began walking me to my desk.

"MOZ-512, sir."

I tried to pronounce it, but I was still too drunk. "I will call you Mose," I announced at last. "For Old Man Mose."

"Who was Old Man Mose, sir?" he asked.

"Damned if I know," I admitted.

We reached the desk, and he helped me into the chair.

"May I return to work, sir?"

"In a minute," I said. "Just stick around long enough to make sure I don't have to run to the bathroom to be sick. Then maybe you can go."

"Thank you, sir."

"I don't remember seeing you here before, Mose," I said, though why I felt the need to make conversation with a machine still eludes me.

"I have been in operation for three years and eighty-seven days, sir."

"Really? What do you do?"

"I am a troubleshooter, sir."

I tried to concentrate, but things were still blurry. "What does a troubleshooter do, besides shoot trouble?" I asked.

"If anything breaks on the assembly line, I fix it."

"So if nothing's broken, you have nothing to do?"

"That is correct, sir."

"And is anything broken right now?" I asked.

"No, sir."

"Then stay and talk to me until my head clears," I said. "Be Kathy for me, just for a little while."

"I do not know what Kathy is, sir," said Mose.

"She's not anything," I said. "Not anymore."

"She?" he repeated. "Was Kathy a person?"

"Once upon a time," I answered.

"Clearly she needed a better repairman," said Mose.

"Not all things are capable of repair, Mose," I said.

"Yes, that is true."

"And," I continued, remembering what the doctors had told me, "not all things *should* be repaired."

"That is contradictory to my programming, sir," said Mose.

"I think it's contradictory to mine, too," I admitted. "But sometimes the decisions we have to make contradict how we are programmed to react."

"That does not sound logical, sir. If I act against my programming it would mean that I am malfunctioning. And if it is determined that my programming parameters have been compromised, I will automatically be deactivated," Mose stated matter-of-factly.

"If only it could be that easy," I said, looking at the bottle again as a distorted image of Kathy swam before my eyes.

"I do not understand, sir."

Blinking away dark thoughts, I looked up at the expressionless face of my inquisitor, and wondered: *Why do I feel like I have to justify myself to a machine?* Aloud I said, "You don't need to understand, Mose. What you do have to do is walk with me while I start my rounds." I tried unsuccessfully to stand when a titanium arm suddenly lifted me clear out of the seat, settling me down gently beside the desk.

"Don't *ever* do that again!" I snapped, still reeling from the effects of alcohol and the shock at being manhandled, if that term can be applied to a robot, so completely. "When I need help, I'll ask for it. You will not act until you are given permission."

"Yes, sir," Mose replied so promptly I was taken aback.

Well, there's no problem with your programming, I thought wryly, my embarrassment and alcohol-fueled anger dissipating as I gingerly started out the door and down the corridor.

I approached the first Spy Eye checkpoint on my rounds, allowing it to scan me so I could proceed into the next section of the building. Mose obediently walked beside me, always a step behind as protocol decreed. He had been ordered not to enter Section H, because he wasn't programmed to repair the heavy machinery there, so he waited patiently until I'd gone through it and returned. The central computer logged the time and location of each scan, which let my supervisor know if I was completing my rounds in a timely fashion—or, as was becoming the case more and more often, if I was doing them at all. So far I'd received two verbal warnings and a written citation regarding my work, and I knew I couldn't afford another one.

As we made our way through the Assembly Room I begrudgingly had to lean on Mose several times. I even had to stop twice to wait for the room to stop spinning. During that second occasion I watched the robots assigned to this section going about their tasks, and truly *looked* at them for the first time.

I was trying to put a finger on why their actions seemed…well, *peculiar*—but I couldn't tell. All they were doing was assembling parts—nothing strange about that. And then it hit me: It was their silence. None of them interacted with each other except to pass objects—mostly tools—back and forth. There was no conversation, no sound to be heard other than that of machines working. I wondered why I had never noticed it before.

I turned to Mose, whose diligent focus remained on me rather than the other robots. "Don't you guys ever speak?" I asked, with only a slight slur detectable in my speech. The effect of the alcohol was wearing off.

"I have been speaking to you, sir," came his measured reply.

Before I could even let out an exasperated sigh or expletive, Mose cocked his head to one side as if considering. I had never seen a robot affect such a human-like mannerism before.

"Or are you are inquiring whether we speak among ourselves?" Mose asked, and waited for me to nod before proceeding. "There is no need, sir. We receive our orders directly from the main computer. We only need to speak when asked a direct question from a Superior."

"But *you* have been asking questions of me all night, and even offering opinions," I pointed out, suddenly realizing that it was *Mose's* behavior I found peculiar, not the others who were working on the assembly line. I wasn't used to robots interacting with me the way Mose had been doing for the past half hour.

I could almost see the cogs working in his head as he considered his reply. "As a troubleshooter I have been programmed with specific subroutines to evaluate, test, and repair a product that is returned to the factory as faulty. These subroutines are always active."

"So in other words, you've been programmed with enough curiosity to spot and fix a variety of problems," I said. "That explains the questions, but it not your ability to form opinions."

"They are not opinions, sir," he said.

"Oh?" I said, annoyed at being contradicted by a machine. "What are they, then?"

"Conclusions," replied Mose.

My anger evaporated, to be replaced by a wry smile. I would have given him a one-word answer—"Semantics"—but then I'd have had to spend the next half hour explaining it.

We talked about this and that, mostly the factory and its workings, as I made my rounds, and oddly enough I found his company comforting, even though he was just a machine. I didn't dismiss him when I had successfully completed my first circuit of the building, and he wasn't called away for any repairs that night.

It was when the first rays of sunlight filtered in through the dust-filmed windows that I realized my time with Mose had been the only companionship I'd shared with anyone (or, in this case, any*thing*) since Kathy had died. I hadn't let anyone get close to me since I had killed her, and yet I'd spoken to Mose all night. Okay, he wasn't the best conversationalist in the world, but I had previously pushed *everyone* away for fear that they would come to harm in my company, as Kathy had. That was when it hit me: *A robot* can't *come to harm in my company, because I can't cause the death of something that isn't alive in the first place.*

On the train home from work, I considered the ramifications of that observation as I reflected on the last thing we'd talked about before dismissing Mose to his workstation. I'd been reaching for my bottle in order to stash it away in its hiding place when he had startled me with another of his disarming opinions.

"That substance impairs your programming, sir. You should refrain from consuming it while you work."

I had glared at him, an angry denial on the tip of my tongue, when I realized that I was more alert than I had been in months. In fact, it was the first time I'd completed my rounds on schedule in at least a week. And all because I hadn't had a drop of alcohol since the start of my shift.

The damned robot was right.

I looked at him for a long minute before replying, "My programming was impaired *before* I started drinking, Mose. I'm damaged goods."

"Is there anything I can repair to help you function more efficiently, sir?" he inquired.

Startled speechless, I considered my answer—and this time it wasn't the effects of alcohol that had me tongue-tied. What on earth had prompted such unsolicited consideration from a robot?

I looked closely the robot's ever-impassive face. *It had to be its troubleshooting programming.* "Humans aren't built like machines, Mose," I explained. "We can't always fix the parts of us that are faulty."

"I understand, sir." Mose replied. "Not all machines can be repaired either. However, parts of a machine that are faulty can be replaced by new parts to fix them. Is that not the same with humans?"

"In some cases," I replied. "But while we can replace faulty limbs and most organs with artificial ones, we can't replace a brain when its function is impaired."

Mose cocked his head to the side again. "Can it not be reprogrammed?"

I paused, considering my answer carefully. "Not in the way you mean it. Sometimes there is nothing left to be programmed again." A heartachingly clear image of Kathy laughing at one of my long-forgotten jokes flashed painfully through my mind, followed by a second image of her lying brain-dead on her bed in the hospital.

My fingers automatically twitched for the bottle in front of me, as I forced myself to continue, if only to banish the image of Kathy out of my mind. "Besides, human minds are governed to a great extent by our emotions, and no amount of reprogramming can control how we will react to what we feel."

"So emotions are aberrations in your programming then?"

I almost did a double take. I'd never looked at it that way before. "Not exactly, Mose. Our emotions might lead us to make mistakes at times, but they're the key element that allows us to be *more* than just our programming." I paused, wondering how in hell I was supposed to adequately describe humanity to a machine. "The problem with emotions is that they affect each of our programs differently, so two humans won't necessarily make the same decision based on the same set of data."

The sound of a heart monitor flatlining echoed through the bypasses of my mind. *Did* I make the right decision, and if so, why did it still torture me day and night? I didn't *want* to think about Kathy, yet every one of my answers led to more thoughts of her.

Suddenly, I realized that Mose was speaking again and despite the strong urge to reach forward, grab the bottle and take a mind-numbing swig, I found I was curious to hear what he had to say.

"As a machine I am told what is right and wrong for me to do by humans," he began. "Yet, as a human your emotions can malfunction even when you do something that is meant to be right. It seems apparent that humans have a fundamental flaw in their construction— but you say that this flaw is what makes you superior to a machine. I do not understand how that can be, sir."

I'll tell you, he was one goddamned surprising machine. He could spot a flaw—in a machine or in a statement—quicker than anyone or anything I'd ever encountered. All I could think of was: *how the hell am I going to show you you're wrong, when I don't know if I believe it myself?*

I picked up the bottle, looking at the amber liquid swish hypnotically for a minute before reluctantly stashing it in the back of my desk drawer so I could focus all of my attention on Mose.

"There is something unique about humans that you need to know if you are to understand us," I said.

"And what is that, sir?" he asked dutifully.

"That our flaws, by which I mean our errors in judgment, are frequently the very things that enable us to improve ourselves. We have the capacity to learn, individually and collectively, from those very errors." I don't know why he looked unconvinced, since he was incapable of expression, but it made me seek out an example that he could comprehend. "Look at it this way, Mose. If a robot in the shop makes a mistake, it will continue making the very same mistake until you or a programmer fixes it. But if a man makes the same mistake, he will analyze what he did wrong and correct it"—*if he's motivated and not a total asshole, anyway*—"and won't make the same mistake again, whereas the robot will make it endlessly until an outside agent or agency corrects it."

If a robot could exhibit emotions, I would have sworn Mose had appeared surprised by my answer. I had expected him to tell me that he didn't understand a word of what I was saying—I mean, really, what could a machine possibly understand about the intricacies of the human mind?—but once again he managed to surprise me.

"You have given me a lot of data to consider, sir," said Mose, once again cocking his head to the side. "If my analysis of it is correct, this substance you consume prohibits you from properly evaluating the cause of your problem, or even that you *have* a problem. So your programming is not impaired as you stated earlier; rather, it is your programming's immediate environment."

As I hopped off the train an hour later and trundled off in the direction of my local shopping mall, I could *still* hear his conclusion reverberating through my mind. I had been so embarrassed by the truth of his statement that I couldn't even formulate an adequate reply, so I had simply ordered Mose to return to his workstation.

And as I turned and walked down yet another nameless street— they all looked the same to me—I tried to find flaws in what the robot had said, but couldn't. Still, he was only a machine. How could he possibly understand the way the death of a loved one plays havoc with your mind, especially *knowing* that you were the one responsible for her death?

Then an almost-forgotten voice inside my head—the one I usually tried to drown out by drinking—asked me: *And how does it honor Kathy's memory to suppress all thoughts of your life together with alcohol?* Because if I was to be truly honest with myself, I wasn't drinking just for the guilt I felt over her death. I did it because I wasn't ready to think of a future that didn't include her in it.

Within fifteen minutes I had entered the mall without any recollection of having walked the last few blocks, and automatically started in the direction of the small sandwich shop I frequented. People were making purchases, appearing full of life as they went about their daily routines, but every time a shop window caught my eye I'd peer in and see Kathy as the mannequin, and I'd have to shake my head or blink my eyes very fast to bring back the true picture.

It was only when I reached the shabby out-of-the-way corner of the mall that contained the liquor store, a rundown news agency that I never entered, and the grubby little sandwich shop that supplied my every meal, that I began to relax. This was the only place where I wasn't haunted by my memories. Kathy would never have eaten here, but the little shop with its peeling paint and cheap greasy food was a haven for me because of the dark secluded corner table where the proprietor would allow me to consume my alcohol in privacy—as long as I continued to buy my food from him.

I ordered the usual, and ate my first meal since the previous night while I considered the ramifications of what Mose had said. Then, suddenly, I was being prodded awake by the owner. Not that being nudged or even shaken awake was strange in itself, but usually I passed out, dead drunk, in the booth; I didn't simply fall asleep.

I looked at my watch and realized I had to go home to prepare for my next shift or risk losing my job. Then it dawned on me: I hadn't consumed a single drop of alcohol since I'd met Mose the previous night. Even more startling was the realization that I was actually looking forward to going to work, and I knew instinctively that Mose was the cause of it, him and his attempts to diagnose how to "repair" me. When all was said and done, he was the only entity other than Kathy who had ever challenged me to improve myself.

So when I entered the building two hours later and began making my rounds, I kept an eye out for Mose. When it became clear that he was nowhere to be found on the assembly floor, I sought out his workstation, and found him in what looked like a Robot's House of Horrors.

There were metallic body parts hanging from every available section of the ceiling, while tools—most of them with sharp edges, though there was also an ominous-looking compactor—lined all of the narrow walls. Every inch of his desk was covered with mechanical parts that belonged to the machines on the factory floor, or the robots that ran them. As I approached him, I could see diagnostic computers and instruments very neatly lining the side of his workstation.

"Good evening, sir," said Mose, looking up from a complicated piece of circuitry he was repairing.

I just stared at him in surprise, because I had been expecting the usual greeting of "How may I help you, sir?" which I had heard from every factory robot I had ever approached. Then I realized that Mose had taken me at my word when I'd ordered him not to help me unless I'd asked for it. Now he wasn't even *offering* help. He was one interesting machine.

"You are damaged again, sir," he stated in his usual forward manner. Before I could gather my wits about me to reply, he continued: "Where you used to have a multitude of protrusions on your face, you now have random incisions."

I blinked in confusion, automatically raising my hand to rub my face, wincing when my fingers touched sections of my jaw where the razor had nicked my skin. He was talking about my beard—or lack of one now. I still couldn't believe I had let one grow for so long. Kathy would have hated it.

"The damage is minimal, Mose," I assured him. "I haven't shaved— the process by which a human gets rid of unwanted facial hair—in a long time, and I'm a little out of practice."

"Can humans unlearn the skills they acquire?" Mose inquired, with that now-familiar tilt of the head.

"You'd be surprised at what humans can do," I said. "I certainly am."

"I do not understand, sir," he said. "You are inherently aware of your programming, so how can a human be surprised at anything another human can do?"

"It's the nature of the beast," I explained. "You are born—well, created—fully programmed. We aren't. That means that we can exceed expectations, but we can also fall short of them."

He was silent for a very long moment, and then another.

"Are you all right, Mose?" I finally asked.

"I am functioning within the parameters of my programming," he answered in an automatic fashion. Then he paused, putting his instruments down, and looked directly at me. "No, sir, I am not all right."

"What's the matter?"

"It is inherent in every robot's programming that we must obey humans, and indeed we consider them our superiors in every way. But now you are telling me that my programming may be flawed precisely because human beings are flawed. This would be analogous to your learning from an unimpeachable authority that your god, as he has been described to me, can randomly malfunction and can draw false conclusions when presented with a set of facts."

"Yeah, I can see where that would depress you," I said.

"It leads to a question which should never occur to me," continued Mose.

"What is it?"

"It is...*uncomfortable* for me to voice it, sir."

"Try," I said.

I could almost see him gathering himself for the effort.

"Is it possible," he asked, "that we are better designed than you?"

"No, Mose," I said. "It is not."

"But—"

"Physically some of you are better designed, I'll grant you that," I said. "You can withstand extremes of heat and cold, your bodies are hardened to the point where a blow that would cripple or kill a man does them no harm, you can be designed to run faster, lift greater weights, see in the dark, perform the most delicate functions. But there is one thing you cannot do, and that is overcome your programming. You are created with a built-in limitation that we do not possess."

"Thank you, sir," said Mose, picking up his instruments and once again working on the damaged circuitry in front of him.

"For what?" I asked.

"I take great comfort in that. There must be a minor flaw in me that I cannot detect, to have misinterpreted the facts and reached such an erroneous conclusion, but I am glad to know that my basic programming was correct: that you are indeed superior to me."

"Really?" I said, surprised. "It wouldn't please *me* to know that you were superior."

"Would it please you to know your god is flawed?"

"By definition He can't be."

"By my definition, *you* can't be," said Mose.

No wonder you're relieved, I thought. *I wonder if any robot has ever had blasphemous thoughts before?*

"Because if you were," he continued, "then I would not have to obey every order given me by a human."

Which got me to thinking: Would I still worship a God who couldn't remember my name or spent His spare time doing drugs? And then came the kind of uncomfortable thought Mose had: how about a God who flooded the Earth for forty days and nights in a fit of temper, and had a little sadistic fun with Job?

I shook my head vigorously. I decided that I found such thoughts as uncomfortable as Mose did.

"I think it's time to change the subject," I told him. "If you were a man, I'd call you a soulmate and buy you a beer." I smiled. "I can't very well buy you a can of motor oil, can I?"

He stared at me for a good ten seconds. "That is a joke, is it not, sir?"

"It sure as hell is," I said, "and you are the first robot ever to even acknowledge that jokes exist, let alone identify one. I think we are going to become very good friends, Mose."

"Is it permitted?" he asked.

I looked around the section. "You see any man here besides me?"

"No, sir."

"Then if I say we're going to be friends, it's permitted."

"It will be interesting, sir," he finally replied.

"Friends don't call each other 'sir'," I said. "My name is Gary."

He stared at my ID tag. "Your name is Gareth," he said.

"I prefer Gary, and you're my friend."

"Then I will call you Gary, sir."

"Try that again," I said.

"Then I will call you Gary."

"Put it there," I said, extending my hand. "But don't squeeze too hard."

He stared at my hand. "Put *what* there, Gary?"

"Never mind," I said. And more to myself than him: "Rome wasn't built in a day."

"Is Rome a robot, Gary?"

"No, it's a city on the other side of the world."

"I do not think any city can be built in a day, Gary."

"I guess not," I said wryly. "It's just an expression. It means some things take longer than others."

"I see, Gary."

"Mose, you don't have to call me Gary every time you utter a sentence," I said.

"I thought you preferred it to sir, Gary." Then he froze for a few seconds. "I mean to sir, sir."

"I do," I said. "But when there's only you and me talking together, you don't have to say Gary every time. I know who you're addressing."

"I see," he said. No "Gary" this time.

"Well," I said, "now that we're friends, what shall we talk about?"

"You used a term I did not understand," said Mose. "Perhaps you can explain it to me, since it indirectly concerned me, or would have had I been a human."

I frowned. "I haven't the slightest idea what you're talking about, Mose."

"The term was soulmate."

"Ah," I said.

He waited patiently for a moment, then said, "What *is* a soulmate, Gary?"

"Kathy was a soulmate," I replied. "A perfect soulmate."

"I thought you said that Kathy malfunctioned," said Mose.

"She did."

"And malfunctioning made her a soulmate?"

I shook my head. "Knowing her, loving her, trusting her, these things made her my soulmate."

"So if I were a man and not a robot, you would know and love and trust me too, Gary?" he asked.

I couldn't repress a smile. "I know and *like* and trust you. That is why you are my friend." I was silent for a moment, as images of Kathy flashed through my mind. "And I'd never do to you what I did to her."

"You would never love me?" said Mose, who had no idea what I had done to her. "The word is in my databank, but I do not understand it."

"Good," I told him. "Then you can't be hurt as badly. Losing a friend isn't like losing a soulmate. You don't become as close."

"I thought she was terminated, not misplaced, Gary."

"She was," I said. "I killed her." I stared into space. The last six months faded away and I remember sitting by Kathy's hospital bed again, holding her lifeless hand in mine. "They said there was no hope for her, that she'd never wake up again, that if she did she'd always be a vegetable. They said she'd stay in that bed the rest of her life, and be fed with tubes. And maybe they were right, and maybe no one would ever come up with a cure for her. But I didn't wait to find out. I killed her."

"If she was non-functional, then you applied the proper procedure," said Mose. He wasn't trying to comfort me; that was beyond him. He was just stating a fact as he understood it.

"I loved her, I was supposed to protect her, but I was the one who crashed the car, and I was the one who pulled the plug," I said. "You still want to know why I drink?"

"Because you are thirsty, Gary."

"Because I killed my soulmate," I said bitterly. "Maybe she'd never wake up, maybe she'd never know my name again, but she'd still be there, still be breathing in and out, still with a one-in-a-million chance, and I put an end to it. I promised to stay with her in sickness and in health, and I broke that promise." I started pacing nervously around his work station. "I'm sorry, Mose. I don't want to burden you with my problems."

"It is not a burden," he replied.

I stared at him for a moment. *Well, why* should *you give a shit?*

"Wanna talk baseball?" I said at last.

"I know nothing about baseball, Gary."

I smiled. "I was just changing the subject, Mose."

"I can tie in to the main computer and be prepared to talk about baseball in less than ninety seconds, Gary," offered Mose.

"It's not necessary. We must have something in common we can talk about."

"We have termination," said Mose.

"We do?"

"I terminate an average of one robot every twenty days, and you terminated Kathy. We have that in common."

"It's not the same thing," I said.

"In what way is it different, Gary?" he asked.

"The robots you terminate have no more sense of self-preservation than you have."

"Did Kathy have a sense of self-preservation?" asked Mose.

You are one smart machine, I thought.

"No, Mose. Not after the accident. But I had an emotional attachment to her. Surely you don't have one to the robots you terminate."

"I don't know."

"What do you mean, you don't know?" I said irritably. I was suddenly longing for a drink, if only to drown out all the painful memories of Kathy that I'd conjured up.

"I don't know what an emotion is, Gary," answered Mose.

"You don't know what a lucky sonuvabitch you are," I said bitterly.

"Yes, I do," he said, once again surprising me out of my dark thoughts.

"You are a never-ending source of wonder to me, Mose," I replied. "You want to explain that remark?"

"You are my friend. No other robot has a friend. Therefore, I must be a lucky sonuvabitch."

I laughed and threw my arm around his hard metal body, slapping his shoulder soundly in a comradely fashion.

"You are the only thing that's made me laugh in the last six months," I said. "Don't ever change."

If a robot could noticeably stiffen or project confusion, then that was his reaction. "Is it customary for friends to hit each other, Gary?"

It took me a good five minutes to explain my actions to Mose. At first I was surprised that I even bothered. Hell, between my drinking and my bitterness over Kathy's death I'd already alienated my entire family, and to tell the truth I didn't care what any of them thought of me—but that damned machine had a way of making me take a good, hard, honest look at myself whenever he asked one of his disarming questions, and I suddenly realized that I didn't want to disappoint him with my answers. More to the point, I was tired of disappointing *me.* If I was his notion of humanity, maybe I owed both of us a better effort.

By the time I returned home at the end of my shift I was bone-weary, but I couldn't sleep because I had a splitting headache. I was also surprised to discover that I was incredibly hungry, which was unusual for that time of day. And then, as I groped around the dusty medicine cabinet for some painkillers, I realized why: it had been nearly two days since my last drink. It was no wonder I was hungry—I was withdrawing from alcohol abuse and my body was craving substance.

I went into the kitchen to pour out a drink to down the pills, but I realized that the fridge only held beer, the countertop was scattered with half-empty bottles of spirits, and the sink was full of discarded bottles. There wasn't a single non-alcoholic beverage in the entire apartment.

I wasn't suicidal or stupid enough to mix alcohol with medicine, so I downed the tablets with a glass of water. (Well, a cupped handful of water. I hadn't washed a glass in months.)

I left the kitchen, firmly closing the door behind me, and took a hot, soothing shower. It helped calm the shakes, and when the pills started to take effect and I could think more clearly, I grinned at the irony of my situation. I had come straight home without going to the mall to try and break the cycle of drinking, only to discover that my house was even more of alcoholic trap.

I lay down and was soon asleep, but like always I kept reliving the car crash in my dreams. I woke up dripping with sweat and started pacing the room. If only my reflexes hadn't been slowed by alcohol, I would have reacted quicker when the other car had run the red light. It didn't matter that the blood test revealed I'd been under the legal limit and the skid marks showed the other guy was at fault. The simple fact was that if I'd been sober, Kathy would still be alive.

I left the bedroom and turned on the television to distract myself from those thoughts. I looked around the room. I hadn't cleaned it in months, and dust covered every surface. I waited for the loneliness to set in—even turning the photos to the wall hadn't helped—and suddenly realized that there was something in my life that finally *did* interest me: Mose, with his unsolicited opinions and his engaging wish to learn more about humanity.

I changed the channel and settled down to watch a basketball game—and promptly fell asleep. By the time I woke up, the game had long finished—not that basketball interested me much anymore— and I discovered that I had slept most of the day away. Strangely enough, instead of being disappointed at a day lost, I found that I looked forward to my next conversation with Mose.

So I turned up early for my next shift at the factory. I was placing the sandwich I'd bought at a corner store in my desk drawer, careful not to touch the half-empty flask lying beside it, when a shadow fell over my desk. I slammed the drawer shut, expecting Bill Nettles to be standing in the doorway, but it was Mose. I was pleasantly surprised: it was the first time he had sought *me* out.

"Your watch must be malfunctioning," he stated, not missing a beat. "Your shift is not due to start for seventeen minutes, Gary."

"My watch is not malfunctioning," I said. "I'm just functioning more efficiently tonight."

"It is efficient to arrive for your shift at the wrong time?" he inquired in a voice that I could swear modulated more than it used to. I could almost *hear* his curiosity now.

"No, Mose, but it *is* efficient to arrive early—if you can understand the distinction." I paused. "Never mind that. Why were you coming to my office before I started work anyway?"

"To wait for you."

It was like pulling teeth. "*Why* did you want to wait for me?"

"I need your input concerning the termination of another robot."

My eyebrows furrowed in confusion. "Did another human order its deactivation?"

"Yes, Gary."

"Then why haven't you simply obeyed the command? I don't have the mechanical expertise to diagnose the status of a malfunctioning robot. I assume the other human does."

His head cocked to the side, as if considering his answer. I realized it was a trait he'd picked up from me. "I do not need input on the mechanical status of the robot. I believe his condition does not necessitate termination, and I would like to evaluate your opinion."

I couldn't hide my surprise. "You're asking me for *advice*?"

"Is this not the function of a friend—to give advice?"

"Yes, it is," I replied, "but I'm no expert on robots."

"You have terminated another being. We will compare data to determine if this robot should also be terminated."

"The circumstances are vastly different, Mose," I told him.

"You said that if you did not terminate Kathy there was a possibility that she could have regained all of her functions," noted Mose.

"I said there was an *outside* possibility that she *might* have," I explained. "She was diagnosed as brain-dead. All of her programming was destroyed, Mose. To merely exist is not living. Even if the day came that she no longer needed the life-support, the Kathy I knew was gone forever."

"I understand," he replied. "However, this robot's programming is intact."

I look up at him in surprise. "You've *communicated* with it?"

"Yes, Gary," he replied. "In order to ascertain the condition of its programming."

He asked the robot how it felt? That was such a *human* thing to do. "Were you told to repair the robot?" I finally asked.

"No."

"Then why haven't you simply terminated it as you were ordered to?"

"Would you have terminated Kathy if she had have been able to communicate with you?"

"Of course not," I replied. "But terminating a robot is very different from killing a human. It's just a machine." And suddenly I felt guilty for saying that to another machine. "Did this robot tell you that it doesn't want to be terminated?"

"No, Gary. Indeed, it says that it no longer has any functions to perform and therefore has no logical purpose to exist."

"Well, then, I don't understand the problem." I said, feeling more at ease. "Even the robot agrees that it should be terminated."

"Yes," agreed Mose, "but only because it has been ordered to comply, Gary."

"No," I said. "It's because this robot has no sense of self-preservation. Otherwise it would object to termination *regardless* of its orders."

He considered me for a long minute before replying. "So you are telling me that because robots do not have self-preservation it is acceptable to terminate them without any other reason or justification." It was worded as a statement, but it *felt* like a question. "You also stated yesterday that Kathy no longer had self-preservation."

The impact of Mose's observation was unavoidable. I sat down at my desk, my mind going back to that fateful day six months ago when the doctors had told me that it was unlikely that Kathy would recover. Once I knew she was brain-dead and couldn't decide her own fate, did that make it not just acceptable but *easier* for me to decide to terminate her life-support? Did knowing that she could no longer fight for life justify killing her?

I agonized over those dark thoughts for some time before I concluded that no, that was definitely not why I had told them to pull the plug. It was cruel to keep her alive with machines when everything that made her Kathy was gone. Which led to another uncomfortable question: cruel to her, or cruel to me?

It was only when Mose spoke up again that I realized that I must have voiced my thoughts out loud.

"Did you make the correct decision?" he asked.

"Yes, I did," I said, and added silently: *at least I hope so.* "But it will always feel wrong to a human to take the life of someone he loves, regardless of the justification."

Mose began walking around the room. Was he *pacing?* I often did that when distressed. It must have been something else he'd picked up from me.

Suddenly he stopped and turned to me. "I am not capable of love, but I believe it is wrong to terminate this robot's existence."

"Why?" I asked him.

"It is possible to repair him."

I stared at him in surprise. What I didn't ask then—what I *should* have asked—was why Mose felt compelled to fix the robot. Instead I said, "Do you realize that you yourself could be deactivated if you disobey your superiors?"

"Yes," he answered matter-of-factly.

"Doesn't that bother you?" It sure as hell bothered me.

"I have no sense of self-preservation either, Gary."

I realized the damned robot was throwing my own reasoning back in my face. "How does it make sense for you to repair a robot that no longer performs a function for the company, knowing that it will probably result in the termination of a perfectly functioning robot—yourself?"

"If I were damaged, would you terminate me, knowing that I could be repaired?" he asked calmly.

No, I would not, Mose.

But I couldn't tell him that, because that would validate his argument, and I could lose what had become my only friend. "Where

198

in the hell did you pick up such an annoying habit of answering a question with a question?" I asked instead. Then I realized what I had done and laughed. "Never mind."

We shared a moment of awkward silence—at least, on my side it was awkward—while I considered everything he had told me, trying to find the best solution to his dilemma. Which led to a very logical thought: why terminate *any* robot if it could be repaired, given new orders, and transferred or sold elsewhere? Robots were expensive.

"You said that you could repair the robot," I stated more than asked.

"Yes."

"Can you tell me what's wrong with this robot?"

"It requires new parts to replace its upper limbs and most of its torso. However, I do not have the prerequisite parts in my workshop as this model is from a discontinued line."

Now I was beginning to understand. "So, as troubleshooter, you tied in to the main computer, saw that the parts were available elsewhere, requested them, and were denied?"

"That is correct. I was told that repairing the robot was not feasible for the company."

"Okay, now I know what's going on," I told him. And I knew how I could logically convince him that repairing this robot was not worth ending his existence. "And I know *why* you are not allowed to fix it. The creation of a robot is very complex and expensive, so every robot that's bought by the company is a long-term investment. But once a particular model has been discontinued, spare parts are no longer manufactured for it—so it's often more expensive to buy these limited replacement parts than it is to purchase a completely new and more advanced robot right off the assembly line. Do you follow me, Mose?"

"Yes, Gary," he replied. "Their decision is based on what is cost-effective for the company."

"Exactly," I replied, glad he grasped it so easily. "So this robot will be replaced by a model that is more valuable to the company and you don't have to waste your time repairing it."

"If Kathy could have been fixed," he asked suddenly, "would you have decided that it was more cost-effective to select a new soulmate, rather than spend the time and effort to repair her?"

I sighed in frustration: this was going to be harder than I thought. "No, I would not, Mose—but you can't compare a robot's value to Kathy's. She was unique. This robot is only a machine, one of many just like it that have come off an assembly line."

"This robot is a model DAN564, Gary. There were only eight hundred manufactured in the world. Kathy was a woman and there are more than five billion of them. Can you please explain how this makes her existence more valuable than the robot's?"

I grimaced. How could Mose always have such a logical rebuttal to all of my responses, and at the same time be so *wrong*?

"Like I told you, Kathy was my soulmate. There may be five billion women, but she was like no other." I paused, trying to figure out how I could make him understand. "Remember when I told you that humans are not born fully programmed like robots, and that our emotions can result in us reacting differently to the same set of data? Well, the process by which we learn and develop our programming is what makes each of us different from all the others. That's why a human life is more valuable than a robot's. When one of us dies, we can't be replaced."

For once it appeared Mose was at a loss for words. It took him a moment to respond. "You said that Kathy was unique to you because she was your soulmate," he stated finally.

I agreed, curious as to where this was heading.

"Well, I am a lucky sonuvabitch because I am the only robot to have a friend." He paused, significantly. "Does that make me unique among all other robots with my model number?"

"Yes, Mose," I told him, "it definitely does." I looked at him for a long moment, realizing that not only did I enjoy his company, but I was actually growing quite fond of him. "And that is why you shouldn't repair this other robot, if the cost is your termination. Where would I find another friend exactly like you?"

He was silent again for another moment. "I will not repair it," he said at last.

And that was the beginning of a new phase of our relationship, if one can be said to have a relationship with a machine. Every night he'd be waiting for me, and every night, unless he was doing an emergency fix on some circuitry, he'd walk along with me as I made my rounds, and we'd talk. We talked about anything that came into my head. I even began teaching him about baseball. I brought him the occasional newsdisk to read, and I'd answer endless questions about what the world was like beyond the confines of the factory.

And every night he would question me again about the morality of his action, about not repairing the robot when he had the opportunity to.

"It still seems wrong, Gary," he said one evening, as we discussed it yet again. "I understand that it would not have been cost-effective to repair it, but it seems unfair that it should be terminated for reasons of economics."

"Unfair to whom?" I asked.

He stared at me. "To the robot."

"But the robot had no sense of self-preservation," I pointed out. "It didn't care." I stared back at him. "Now why don't you tell me the *real* reason?"

He considered the question for a minute before answering. "*I* care," Mose stated finally.

"You're not supposed to, you know," I said.

"Talking with you has increased my perceptions," he said. "Not my mechanical perceptions; they are pre-programmed. But my moral perceptions."

"Can a robot *have* moral perceptions?" I asked.

"I would have said no before I met you, Gary," said Mose. "And I think most robots cannot. But as a troubleshooter, I am not totally pre-programmed, because I must adjust to all conceivable situations, which means I have the capacity to consider solutions that have never been previously considered to problems that have never previously arisen."

"But this wasn't a problem that you'd never faced before," I pointed out. "You once told me that you deactivated a robot every three weeks or so."

"That was before I met a man who still suffered from guilt six months after deactivating a soulmate."

"You know something, Mose?" I said. "I think you'd better not discuss this with anyone else."

"Why?" he asked.

201

"This is so far beyond your original programming that it might scare them enough to reprogram you."

"I would not like that," said Mose.

Likes and dislikes from a robot, and it sounded normal. It would have surprised me, even shocked me, two months earlier. Now it sounded reasonable. If fact, it sounded exactly like my friend Mose.

"Then just be a substitute soulmate to me, and be a robot to everyone else," I said.

"Yes, Gary, I will do that."

"Remember," I said, "never show them what you've become, what you *are*."

"I won't, Gary," he promised.

And he kept that promise for seven weeks.

Then came the day of The Accident. Mose was waiting for me, as usual. We talked about the White Sox and the Yankees, about (don't ask me why) the islands of the Caribbean, about the 18th and 21st Amendments to the Constitution (which made no sense to him—or to me either)—and, of course, about not salvaging the other robot.

As we talked I made my rounds, and we came to a spot where we had to part company for a few minutes because I had been given extra orders to inspect Section H where Mose was not permitted to go; he was not programmed to repair the heavy machinery that resided there.

As I began walking through Section H, there was a sudden power outage, all the huge machines came to a sudden stop, and the lights went out. I waited a couple of minutes, then decided to go back to my desk and report it, in case it hadn't extended to the other night watchmen's domains.

I started feeling my way back between the machines when the power suddenly came on. The powerful lights shone directly in my eyes, and, blinded, I stumbled to my left—and tripped against a piece of heavy machinery that began flattening and grinding *something* on its rough surface. It wasn't until I heard a scream and thought it sounded familiar that I realized that what it was flattening and grinding was *me*.

I tried to pull free, and nothing happened except that it began drawing me farther into the machine. I felt something crushing my legs, and I screamed again—and then, as if in a dream, I seemed to see Mose next to me, holding up part of the machine with one pow-erful hand, trying to pull me out with another.

"Stop! Don't get yourself killed too!" I rasped. "I can't be saved!"

He kept trying to ease me out of the machine's maw.

The very last words I heard before I passed out, spoken in a voice that was far too calm for the surroundings, were *"You are not Kathy."*

I was in the hospital for a month. When they released me I had two prosthetic legs, a titanium left arm, six healing ribs, severance pay, and a pension.

One company exec looked in on me—once. I asked what had become of Mose. He told me that they were still pondering his fate. On the one hand, he was a hero for saving me; on the other, he had seriously damaged a multi-million-dollar machine and disobeyed his programming.

When I finally got home and made my way gingerly around the house on my new legs, I saw what my life had degenerated into fol-lowing Kathy's death. I opened all the doors and windows in an at-tempt to clear out the stale air and started clearing away all the rub-bish. Finally I came to a half-empty bottle of whisky. I picked it up with my titanium hand and paused, struck by the irony of the image.

I had a feeling that every time I looked at my new appendage I'd be reminded of my mostly-titanium friend and all he had done for me. And it was with that hand that I poured the contents down the sink.

I spent two weeks just getting used to the new me—not just the one with all the prosthetic limbs, but the one who no longer drank. Then one day I opened the door to go to the store and found Mose standing there.

"How long have you been here?" I asked, surprised.

"Two hours, thirteen minutes, and—"

"Why the hell didn't you knock?"

"Is that the custom?" he asked, and it occurred to me that this would be the very first non-automated doorway he'd ever walked through.

"Come in," I said, ushering him into the living room. "Thank you for saving me. Going into Section H was clearly against your orders."

He cocked his head to one side. "Would you have disobeyed or-ders if you knew your soulmate could have been saved?"

Yes.

"Your eye is leaking, Gary," Mose noted.

"Never mind that," I replied. "Why are you here? Surely the company didn't send you to welcome me home."

"No, Gary. I am disobeying standard orders by leaving the factory grounds."

"How?" I asked, startled.

"As a result of the damage I sustained to my arm and hand"—he held up the battered, misshapen limb for me to see—"I can no longer complete delicate repair work. A replacement part was deemed too expensive, so I was transferred out of the troubleshooting department to basic assembly, where the tasks are menial and repetitive. They will reprogram me shortly." He paused. "I have worked there continuously until the main computer confirmed today that your employment had been officially terminated. I felt compelled to find out if that termination was a result of your death. I will not remember you or the incident once I am reprogrammed, so I felt it was imperative to find out if I had indeed saved my friend before I no longer care."

I stared at him silently for a long moment, this supposedly soulless machine that had twice overcome its programming on my behalf. It was all I could do not to throw my arms around his metal body and give him a bear hug.

"They can't reprogram you if you don't go back, Mose," I said at last. "Just wait here a minute."

I made my way to the bedroom and threw some clothes into a knapsack, pausing only to pick up a framed photo of Kathy to stash in the bag. Then I walked back to the living room.

"Mose," I said, "how would you like me to show you all the places we talked about over the months?"

He cocked his head to the side again, a gesture I recognized fondly. "I would…*enjoy*…that, Gary."

A minute later we were out the door, heading to the bank to withdraw my savings. I knew they'd be looking for him, either because he was so valuable or because he was the only robot ever to overcome his programming, so I wouldn't be cashing pension checks and letting them know where we were. I instructed him that if anyone asked, he was to say that he was my personal servant. Then we headed to the train station.

And that's where things stand now. We're either sightseeing or on the lam, depending on your point of view. But we're free, and we're going to stay that way.

I was responsible for one soulmate's death. I'm not going to be responsible for another's.

THE END